DEATH AS A FINE ART

DEATH AS A FINE ART

Gwendolyn Southin

TouchWood
Editions

TouchWood Editions
touchwoodeditions.com

LIBRARY AND ARCHIVES CANADA CATALOGUING IN PUBLICATION
Southin, Gwendolyn
Death as a fine art / Gwendolyn Southin.

(A Margaret Spencer Mystery)
Also issued in electronic format.
ISBN 978-1-927129-42-5

I. Title. II. Series: Southin, Gwendolyn. Margaret
Spencer mystery.

PS8587.O978D34 2012   C813'.6   C2012-902552-6

Editor: Linda L. Richards
Proofreader: Lenore Hietkamp
Cover design: Tobyn Manthorpe

| Canadian Heritage | Patrimoine canadien | | Canada Council for the Arts | Conseil des Arts du Canada | | BRITISH COLUMBIA ARTS COUNCIL |

We gratefully acknowledge the financial support for our publishing activities from the Government of Canada through the Canada Book Fund, Canada Council for the Arts, and the province of British Columbia through the British Columbia Arts Council and the Book Publishing Tax Credit.

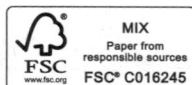

MIX
Paper from
responsible sources
FSC
www.fsc.org   FSC® C016245

1 2 3 4 5   16 15 14 13 12

PRINTED IN CANADA

Dedicated to the memory of my daughter, Wendy, and my husband and life companion, Vic.

PROLOGUE
Saturday, January 27, 1962

Jonathan Standish stood back from the sculpture that had given his gallery its name: *The Silver Unicorn*. The piece was definitely his best work and, as he had intended from the start, it set the standard for all the work he accepted to sell on commission in the gallery.

Even though it was getting late he wandered through the softly lit room, touching first this piece and then that one. He lingered the longest on his favourite porcelain pieces—the little girl playing with her dog, the woman laughing as she held onto her hat in the wind . . . The Two Js. What a difference they had made to his life!

He sighed. Time to go home. He made sure the alarm was set and the doors firmly locked, then flipped the lights and walked back the length of the gallery to slip inside his office for his thick winter coat and hat. There was a separate alarm system for the rear of the building, and he would set that before exiting by the back door. His car was parked just outside in the yard.

The sound of a key scraping in the back door stopped him in mid-reach for his coat. He whirled around.

"My God! You scared the living daylights out of me! What the hell are you doing here at this time of night?"

"We need to talk."

"I am not going to change my mind."

"Sit down at your desk, Jonathan, and let us talk."

"I'm through talking with you."

"Then perhaps this will persuade you. Sit down, Jonathan."

"Are you mad? Stop waving that ridiculous gun at me."

"Sit down. I mean it."

Jonathan sat, and felt the muzzle of the gun pressing against his head just above his right ear. "Let's talk rationally about this." Although his heart was racing, he tried to keep a semblance of calm in his voice. "You'll be charged with murder."

"But I'm not committing murder. You are committing suicide. You are so worried about business, and then there's the affair that's eating at you and the effect it will have on your loving wife . . . it's just too much for you to bear. Your suicide note is quite explicit."

He tried to struggle to his feet but the muzzle of the gun pushed even harder against the side of his head. He shuddered and subsided back into his seat. "There will be no suicide note. If you kill me, it will be murder!"

"Don't be ridiculous, Jonathan. You have already written it. And it is quite clear that you *did* write it. You see, the fingerprints on the paper and on the typewriter keys are yours, nobody else's." His tormentor gave a course laugh. "In fact, it will be the perfect murder—but the verdict will be a definite suicide—so sad!"

"What do you want from me? Money? Tell me!" There was a shrill note in his voice as he tried once again to get to his feet, but Jonathan's world and all his hopes for the future were suddenly shattered by a single shot.

CHAPTER ONE
Monday, April 9, 1962

The sky was an azure blue, the wind warm, flowers abundant. Earlier that morning, as Maggie walked down the narrow garden path leading to her back alley garage, she had revelled in the warm air and the wonderful smell of the late spring flowers, and most of all the lilac bushes—the scent of the purple lilac so heady she had immediately been transported back to her childhood growing up in Maidstone, Kent. The county of Kent, nestled in the southeast corner of England, really lived up to its name: The Garden of England. In fact, it was a perfect April day in the city of Vancouver, but Margaret Spencer—Maggie to everyone who knew her well—was wishing she was anywhere but inside a courthouse in downtown Vancouver.

It was the final day in the trial of two people Southby and Spencer, Private Investigators had helped bring to justice—and it was mainly Maggie's testimony concerning her kidnapping and attempted murder that had clinched the prosecutor's case. But Maggie didn't want to listen to the summaries. Instead, she and her partner, Nat Southby, left the court as soon as she finished giving her testimony.

"I think you need a good cup of tea," Nat said, tucking her arm into his. He had become very protective since her near-death experience on their last case, and although she hated to admit it, she was still feeling a little fragile. "And there happens to be a restaurant just down the street," he continued.

Fifteen minutes later, taking a sip from her tea, Maggie said, "I don't know about you, but I'm ready for a real break from investigating crimes."

Nat thought for a while before answering. "Why don't you come with me to Victoria this Thursday? You can mooch around the shops and museums while I have my final meeting with Jake Houston." The previous January Southby and Spencer, Private Investigators had been hired by the Ministry of Forests to look into some clear-cutting scams, and Jake Houston had been Nat's contact during the investigation. "We could have the whole weekend over there and return on Monday."

"What a wonderful idea," Maggie exclaimed. "But what about leaving the agency?"

"We don't have any big contracts on at the moment," Nat answered. "And Henny can handle the office on her own for a few days. You know how she loves to be the boss."

"And I can get my next door neighbour, Carol, to look after Emily and Oscar."

"I think you worry more about your darned cat and dog than you do about me," Nat teased.

"You know that isn't true, Nat," she answered, leaning across the table to take his hand in hers.

NAT HAD BEEN right: Victoria was a good idea and Maggie loved it.

"Do you know, Nat," she said after she had unpacked her bags the following Thursday afternoon, "Victoria is more English than England." She laughed. "Just look at this room!" They had decided to stay in Oak Bay just outside Victoria at a private guesthouse—aptly named Windsor Rose Cottage—instead of an ordinary hotel.

Nat had been stationed in the south of England during the Second World War, so he understood exactly what she meant. They had been given the Pink Room, and the walls were papered in small pink roses while the bedspread, the two easy chairs, and the drapes were covered in matching cretonne. Even the pictures on the walls depicted English gardens.

"There's plenty of room for your clothes in here," Maggie said as she carefully hung her silk dress in the small closet.

"Naw! Haven't got much. I'll keep them in my bag on the floor. Nice bed," he added, throwing himself onto it. "Which side do you want?"

IN THE MORNING, breakfast was set in a glassed-in extension to the dining room. "It's almost like sitting out in the garden," Maggie whispered as she flipped her white linen napkin onto her lap.

"But without all those pink roses," he whispered back. "Just look at those birds," he continued. The garden was full of them—hummingbirds at the two feeders, robins bathing in the concrete birdbath, and various other species pecking away at wooden birdfeeders hanging from the branches of two huge maple trees.

"Wouldn't Emily just love this garden?"

"But the birds wouldn't like Emily," Nat stated. They both looked up as two women approached their table.

"Mind if we join you?"

"Of course not," Maggie said, smiling. Nat immediately jumped to his feet and pulled chairs out for them.

"I'm Jane Weatherby and this is my sister, Alice Standish," the older of the two women announced as she sat down. Alice smiled shyly as she sat in the chair opposite Maggie, then adjusted the pink and turquoise chiffon scarf that had slipped off her shoulders.

"Nat Southby." Nat leaned across the table to shake hands. "And this is Maggie."

Maggie was intrigued by the two sisters. Jane Weatherby, her grey hair twisted into a neat bun, was tall, angular, and dressed in tweeds and sensible walking shoes. Alice, her unruly chestnut hair cascading over her shoulders, wore a beige linen tunic over a floral-patterned dress. As far as Maggie could see, she was at least a good head and shoulders shorter than her sister. And, Maggie estimated, at least ten years younger.

Jane picked up the menu and passed it to her sister. "Go easy on the cream. You know how it upsets you," she said sternly.

As Alice studied the menu, the slight blush to her peaches and cream complexion showed her annoyance. Adjusting the scarf once again, she placed the menu on the table, brushed a strand of hair away from her blue eyes, and then turned to Nat. "Have you been staying here long?" she asked.

"We got in last night," he replied. "And you?"

"A couple of days ago," she answered.

The four of them chatted over the huge English-style breakfast. They were at the toast and marmalade stage when Jane leaned toward Nat and asked, "And what do you do for a living, Mr. Southby?"

"Nat," he answered. "I'm a private investigator."

"How exciting. Don't tell me you investigate real murders?"

Nat laughed. "Yes, even those at times."

"And what about you, dear? What do you do when he's out investigating foul crimes?" Alice asked.

"I help him," Maggie answered. "We're partners."

"Do you mean you're an investigator, too?" Jane asked in a

shocked tone. "That's a very unusual job for a woman."

"And are you taking a few days' rest like us?" Maggie asked, refusing to be drawn into a discussion of her unusual job—yet again.

Jane nodded. "I've recently retired from teaching history at a private college here in Victoria."

"And you . . . ?" Maggie asked, turning toward the other woman.

"My husband and I own—or I should say we owned—an art gallery on South Granville, but . . ." she faltered. "He died suddenly a couple of months ago."

"Oh, I'm so sorry," Maggie said quickly.

"That's why we're taking this little vacation," Jane cut in, leaning over to pat her sister's hand. "Before I move in to help—not that I know too much about art . . . but I'm a quick learner."

"But Sheldon is doing his best," Alice cut in.

"His best to take over, you mean," Jane answered brusquely, then stopped when she saw her sister's stricken face. "I'm sorry. I'm sure he's doing an admirable job. Now where shall we go this morning?"

Nat glanced at his watch and hastily threw his napkin down on the table. "I know where I'm going!" he exclaimed. "Meet you in front of the Empress at four, Maggie, okay?" He bent and kissed her.

"I'll get a taxi into town," she called after him.

"Can we give you a lift?" Jane asked after Nat had departed. "We're going into the city around nine-thirty if that would be any help."

"Thank you, I accept. Would you mind dropping me off at the Empress Hotel?"

She spent a wonderful morning shopping, browsing, and having lunch in a restaurant that overlooked the harbour. In the afternoon she had afternoon tea at the Empress Hotel—an absolute must for anyone visiting Victoria—finally meeting up with Nat for dinner and the return trip to the guesthouse.

"Jake Houston was very pleased with the investigation we did," he said as he drove into the driveway of the guesthouse. "He said that he's spread the word to other government departments and there could be more work for the agency if we're interested."

"That's good to know," she answered. "Things are a bit slow so we may have to take him up on that."

Saturday and Sunday they toured Victoria's waterfront, visited the famous Butchart Gardens, discovered the scenic Sooke area, and enjoyed the breathtaking views from the Malahat Pass. And each morning they breakfasted with the two sisters who seemed to delight in helping them plan their route for the day, although Maggie noticed that the sisters never allowed the conversation to return to the subject of the art gallery.

When Monday morning rolled around, Maggie, although sorry the short vacation was over, felt ready to get back to work. Jane and Alice were also leaving that morning.

"A friend of Jane's has taken over her apartment," Alice informed them as they made their goodbyes in the small parking lot. "And we've loaded up both of our cars with the stuff she can't do without."

"What's the name of your gallery?" Nat asked as he slung his and Maggie's luggage into the back of his old Chevy.

"The Silver Unicorn."

"What a lovely name," Maggie exclaimed.

"Named after one of my husband's favourite pieces," Alice told them, her eyes misting over. "As well as being a talented painter, Jonathan did wonderful work with hand and wheel pottery."

"Of course," Maggie said suddenly. "Jonathan Standish. I'm a great admirer of his work."

"Well then, you probably know that the gallery is on South Granville. We'd love to have you call in sometime."

"We will," Maggie answered. "And here's one of our business cards. That's my home address and phone number on the back. I'd love to hear from you, too."

Alice looked at the card. "Margaret Spencer!" she said surprised. "Then you're not . . ." She looked embarrassed.

Maggie smiled. "No. Nat and I aren't married."

"Oh. Ah," the other woman said, ducking to hide her blush.

Maggie ducked her head as well, but to hide her amusement. It was true: her relationship with Nat was complicated, but it was possible there was something about that both of them liked. And it had nothing to do with shame.

CHAPTER TWO

Within a couple of weeks Maggie and Nat's short Victoria vacation seemed like a pleasant dream, but Maggie often thought about the two sisters and wondered how they were getting on. To Nat she remarked that Alice would probably find her older sister a bit too bossy to live with for long, and Nat wondered if Sheldon, whoever he was, would find his match in the formidable Jane.

"We must make an effort to visit the gallery, Nat," Maggie said. "Perhaps this weekend?" But that idea slipped away when Midge, the younger of Maggie's two daughters, called Friday night to ask her mother to go shopping with her for a wedding gown. Maggie was thrilled to be asked, and she decided to look for her own mother-of-the-bride dress at the same time. After all, the wedding was only a couple of months away.

Their Saturday morning shopping spree was a great success, and after they had picked out the perfect wedding dress for Midge, they found the perfect dress for Maggie in the same boutique.

It seemed to be a weekend of surprises as that evening, just as Maggie was settling down to her favourite TV program, Barbara, her elder daughter, called to ask if Maggie had picked out a dress for the great affair. "Why couldn't Midge have waited to get married until after I've had the baby?" she moaned to her mother. "I'm going to look like a blimp in a maternity dress."

"You'll look just lovely, dear," Maggie assured her, deciding not to tell Barbara about the shopping spree. "And just imagine how cute Oliver will look as the ring bearer."

"That's another thing, mother. Why does she need to have a ring bearer? I only had two bridesmaids."

"It's Midge's day," Maggie rebuked her daughter quietly. "Now, what have you been up to lately? Does Oliver still love his train set?" Once on the subject of her family, Barbara was ready to chat for hours. And she did.

AT THE OFFICE on Monday morning Henny, the agency's girl Friday, wanted to know all the details of the upcoming wedding. When Maggie had satisfied her, she smiled broadly.

"Midge make a lovely bride, ja!" she said in her Dutch-accented English. "She is very pretty." She rolled a fresh piece of paper into her typewriter. "I sometimes think it be nice to haf a girl. But my two boys they keep me . . . hopping! That a good word for my boys, ja?" She laughed as she opened the buff folder beside her typewriter. "Oh, I forget. You have phone call from a . . ." She picked up a slip of paper . . . "Miss Weather?"

"Miss Weather?" Maggie frowned. "Did she say what it was about?"

"No. Said she met you in Victoria. Here is number."

"You mean Miss Weatherby. I'll call her right away."

"No, no. She said not to call her back. She call you." Henny looked up as the outer door opened. "Ah, Mr. Nat. I have coffee for you right away."

"Apparently Jane Weatherby called this morning," Maggie said as she turned to walk into her office. "I wonder what she wants?"

"Better call and find out," he answered as he followed her.

"Henny says she doesn't want me to call. She will get back to us later."

"It's probably just an invite to the gallery," Nat answered, settling into the chair in front of Maggie's desk.

"How did the job for Jones, Jenkins and Smyth go?"

"It really paid off," he answered, "and they want us to do some snooping on another client of theirs. I'm meeting Jenkins for lunch to get all the details."

"You don't need me on that one, do you?" Maggie asked. "I'm just finishing up on that child custody case. He's still insisting she isn't a fit mother if she has a boyfriend on the side. I feel sorry for those two little kids."

"Don't let it get to you, Maggie. Keep on the outside." Maggie nodded as he left the room, knowing full well that was a tough order as she still thought as a mother first.

IT WAS LATE in the afternoon when Jane Weatherby called again. "I need to talk to you," she said. "Is it possible to meet you for coffee somewhere?"

Maggie glanced at her watch. "I'm leaving for home shortly. Where are you?"

Jane gave a nervous laugh. "Actually, I'm just across the street from you. The phone box in front of the drugstore."

"Then I suggest that you come on up. We're on the third floor. Suite 301."

The other woman arrived with what seemed to Maggie to be surpising speed.

"I'm sorry I called you so late in the day," Jane said as she entered the office. "I expect you want to get home."

"That's not a problem," Maggie said as she took Jane's coat to hang it up. "I've often thought about you and your sister since our meeting in Victoria. How is Alice doing?"

"That's the reason I'm here," Jane answered as she followed Maggie into her office.

"Can I get you anything?" Maggie asked before she sat down behind her desk. "Coffee?"

"No, nothing, thanks." She fiddled with her handbag. "You'll probably think I'm worrying over nothing."

Maggie waited.

"I've known all along that something was wrong. I thought that the week's vacation on the Island would help Alice, but there's something deeper going on that I can't get her to talk about."

Maggie leaned forward. "How did her husband die?"

"Shot himself in the head. But for the life of me I can't see why he did it as they seemed perfectly happy ... as a couple, I mean. And," she continued, "the gallery was doing very well."

"Did he leave a note?"

"Yes. I didn't see it, but Alice was heartbroken when she told me about it. He said that he couldn't go on living a lie as he had met someone else."

"But that's not a reason to kill oneself," Maggie said. She sat thinking for a moment. "Was the note handwritten?"

"No. He used the typewriter in their office. That was where he was found—slumped over the machine."

"Was the note still in the typewriter?"

"No. On the desk." She gave a little laugh. "Held down by a paperweight that Alice had given him—crystal with the words 'love you forever' etched on it. Rather ironic, don't you think?"

"And that's the reason you doubt it was suicide?" Maggie asked. Jane nodded. "Exactly!"

"Were the police happy with the suicide verdict?"

"I suppose so as nothing else was done. But I'm sure that Alice has a hard time accepting it. She insists they were perfectly happy and were planning a second honeymoon trip to Mexico."

"And you say the business is doing well? You mentioned someone called Sheldon when we were on the Island ..."

"Ah, yes. Sheldon White. He was Jonathan's assistant." She paused and then continued, "You've heard of Uriah Heap?"

Maggie nodded. "The creepy clerk in Charles Dickens' *David Copperfield?*"

"Need I say more?"

Maggie laughed. "I can't believe any real person could be that creepy."

"Well, I'm probably exaggerating as I can't stand the man."

"I don't know too much about art galleries. Where does the art sold at the Silver Unicorn come from?"

"Well, Jonathan's oils and sculptures and porcelain figurines were and still are the main attractions, and Alice sells quite a lot of her own stuff—mostly watercolours. The rest is work that is sold on commission—there are some wonderful artists in this city."

"So what do you want Nat and me to do?"

"Look into Jonathan's death, I suppose." She opened her purse and held out a couple of tickets. "Here are two invitations to a wine and cheese party this Friday evening. Alice is launching a new artist, Caitlin Harrow—she's quite good, actually—and you could get the feel of the place."

Jane stood up. "Perhaps I'm being paranoid, but I know Alice can't accept Jonathan's death as a suicide, and there's something strange going on there . . ." Her voice trailed off, then she said, "I guess I'm too protective."

"Alice is a few years younger than you?" Maggie asked, trying to pose her question diplomatically.

"Twelve years. She's just fifty-three. We're half-sisters. My mother remarried after my dad died," she explained. "Hence the difference in our ages."

Maggie quickly flicked her desk calendar to Friday. "Well, it happens that I'm free on Friday evening, and I'm sure Nat has nothing on. We'll see you there."

CHAPTER THREE

The gallery was packed, the noise level high, and Maggie and Nat had trouble even getting near the table where the glasses of wine were being dispensed.

"There you are!" Jane Weatherby, head and shoulders taller than anyone else, bore down on them carrying two glasses of wine. "So glad you made it," she boomed over the babble. "Come and talk to Alice," she added, handing them each a glass.

They followed in her wake to where her sister and a tousle-haired man were gesturing madly at a painting. As they got closer, Nat realized that it could be a twin of a painting he'd seen in a client's office a few years earlier—and he hadn't been able to make heads or tails of that one, either. Alice was dressed in a long pale-green dress and flowered silk shawl. She passed the tousle-haired man on to a young woman standing nearby and floated toward them, her face lighting up when she saw who it was.

"How lovely to see you." She held out her slim hands and then looked enquiringly at her sister standing behind them.

"I sent them an invitation," Jane said. "I didn't think they would come on their own."

"This must be one of your husband's pieces," Maggie said, walking toward a nearby black-draped pedestal. The sculpture on it was a unicorn standing on its two hind legs. It was about two feet high and finished in a remarkable glaze that looked like polished silver.

"His most famous sculpture. We named the gallery after it. It's not for sale, of course. But my favourite pieces are the porcelain figurines over there." She pointed to a tall glass stand. "Come and see." They were indeed beautiful and the model for all of them seemed to have been the same woman.

"I see what you mean," Maggie breathed. "Especially this one," she added, indicating a twelve-inch statuette of a young woman trying to hold a large hat on her head. Jonathan Standish had managed to capture a look of sheer joy as the girl fought the wind for that hat. "Who was the model?"

"I've no idea. I think Jonathan just used his imagination."

"But she looks so real." Maggie ran her fingers over the beautiful face. But Alice didn't answer and looked so sad that Maggie quickly changed the subject. "Who is this Caitlin Harrow that you're feting this evening?"

"Come and I'll introduce you to her and her watercolours."

A few canapés and glasses of wine later, Maggie caught Nat's eye across the room. He was beginning to get fidgety—she was surprised that he had lasted as long as he had.

"When can we slip away?" he whispered when she reached his side.

"We'll make our way over to Alice," she replied, taking the glass out of his hands before he spilt the last of his wine on the blue carpet. "I'd like to know which one of these arty young men is Sheldon."

"The one Jane likened to Uriah Heap? The only Dickens character I remember is Scrooge."

Maggie laughed. "Now that might be him over there." She tilted her head to where a sandy-haired man was standing next to Alice. "And I can see what Jane means," she added as she watched him limply shake hands with one of the departing guests. "Come on, let's get in line."

"You're not leaving?" Alice asked when they said their good-byes. "We were hoping you two would join us for a little supper at the restaurant across the street."

Nat glanced at his watch. "It's getting late."

"We'll be through here in ten minutes," Jane urged. "And Alice and I want to discuss something with you."

Nat raised his eyebrows at Maggie and she nodded in reply. "Okay. But can we help you clear up?" she asked.

"I haven't met you, have I?" Sheldon asked, holding out his long, tapered fingers. "Sheldon White. And there's no need for you to help as I'll do it after you've all gone for your meal." He turned to Alice. "You know I'm always here for you, my dear Mrs. Standish."

Jane gave a derisive snort. "And there's no need for you to stay, either, Sheldon," she said curtly to the man. "The caterers brought the stuff in and they'll take it out. Alice and I are quite capable of locking the place up."

"Of course . . . I only want to help." Maggie caught the look of pure loathing that he shot at Jane.

"Then I suggest you collect those dirty glasses and take them over to the caterers while Alice and I say goodbye to the last of her guests."

"You were a bit hard on Sheldon, Jane," Alice remarked as he left to collect the glasses. "He was only trying to help."

"When are you going to see through the little sneak?" Jane answered. "Oh, come on, let's get over to the restaurant."

"YOU SAID YOU wanted to talk to us," Maggie said after they had ordered.

"It's about Jonathan's death," Alice answered. "Jane has convinced me that we should get you to look into it. But I honestly think it's too late."

"Nonsense!" Jane cut in. "You told me right from the start that Jonathan wasn't the type to take his own life."

"But the police were convinced," Alice answered sadly. "The coroner at the inquest insisted there was no reason to think otherwise." She shrugged. "I'm beginning to think they are right."

"Did you ever find out if he really *was* having an affair?" Nat asked. He leaned back to let the waitress place a plate in front of him, then sighing contentedly, he reached for one of the corned beef sandwiches that nestled beside a pile of fries and a large dill pickle.

"Never," Alice said, and she began chasing a piece of lettuce around her plate with her fork before continuing. "I had no inkling that he was seeing someone else. He . . . he wasn't that kind of man. But," and she looked down at her plate, "I suppose the wife is always the last to know," she added pathetically.

"If you're serious about us making an investigation," Maggie said, "we'll have to ask you a lot of personal questions . . . and we will need to draw up a contract for you to sign."

Alice glanced fleetingly toward her sister. "Do you think we should go ahead, Jane?"

"Of course," her sister answered sharply.

"When is a good time for you to come in?" Maggie asked.

"The gallery is closed on Mondays."

"You free Monday morning?" Maggie turned to ask Nat.

"Nothing until one in the afternoon. Can you make it around ten?"

"We'll be there," Jane said firmly.

CHAPTER FOUR

"Now tell us about your husband." Alice and Jane were in Nat's office. Maggie sat beside him with an open notebook. The two sisters faced them in Nat's comfortable visitors' chairs.

Alice smiled. "Where to begin?"

"How long were you married?" Maggie asked.

"Eight years. I met him when I was recovering after a disastrous marriage. He was kind, considerate—everything my first husband wasn't."

"How did you meet?" Nat asked.

"Hugo, my first husband, died suddenly and left me pretty destitute. I answered an ad for a part-time position in Jonathan's gallery—I'd taken fine arts in college so I was sure I could handle the job—he took me on and the rest is history. We were attracted to each other right from the start," she added.

"That's why that suicide note just doesn't ring true," Jane cut in. "Jonathan adored Alice."

"Was Jonathan married before?" Maggie asked.

Alice nodded. "She died of cancer in 1951." She shuddered. "She was only fifty-four at the time."

"Jane said your husband shot himself," Maggie said. "Where did he get the gun?"

"He bought it for protection after we had a couple of break-ins."

"Anything taken?"

"The alarm scared the thieves off each time."

"Do you still have the suicide note?" Nat asked.

She nodded. "The police returned it to me after the verdict of 'suicide while of unsound mind.'" She gave a derisive laugh as she handed Nat a sheet of paper. "Jonathan was the sanest man I ever knew."

Nat read the typewritten note and then handed it over to Maggie. "I suppose the police dusted it for prints?"

"Yes. Just like the gun. The only prints on it were Jonathan's."

Maggie leaned toward Alice. "Why did your husband hire this man Sheldon White?"

"I was having a terrible time recovering from an appendectomy, and it was a month before Christmas and that's our busiest time. Jonathan insisted that I cut my hours down in the showroom and rest, so he hired Sheldon to help out."

"Is he any good?" Maggie asked.

"He knows his art, I must say that about him. But he does have an unfortunately ingratiating manner toward people. Jane finds him very disturbing."

"But you're recovered now, so why don't you get rid of him?" Maggie asked.

"Because it's hard to find anyone with his knowledge." She glanced quickly at her sister before continuing. "Anyway, do you think there's enough reason to look further into my husband's death?"

"Of course there is!" Jane interjected sharply.

"We'd have to talk to the detectives who were in charge of the case at that time and get a look at the photographs they took of the scene," Nat answered.

"What are your rates?" Jane asked.

"Maggie can give you all that information," he answered. "She'll also get you to sign that contract we mentioned last night. Then we can go ahead."

CHAPTER FIVE

Nat had to go through Inspector Mark Farthing's division of the Vancouver City Police to get permission to talk to the two detectives who had handled the case. Farthing had taken over Nat's job as well as his office when Nat had quit the force a number of years before, and the man still resented Nat's popularity.

"What are you sticking your nose into now, Southby?" Farthing demanded after Nat had been shown to his office. "I've told you repeatedly to keep out of police business."

"But your division wrote this one off as a suicide," Nat answered.

"If my men said it was suicide, then that's what it was."

"Then to satisfy my client, Alice Standish, you can't object to my taking a look at the report and the photographs taken at the scene of her husband's death."

Farthing pursed his lips. "Why can't that woman take our word for it? It was thoroughly investigated at the time."

Nat managed to keep his cool. "The widow still wants me to take a look," he answered. "And if I do come across any more evidence to prove it wasn't suicide, I'll share it with you. Otherwise," he shrugged, "I'll have to get a court order for you to hand them over." Nat waited while Farthing weighed the pros and cons in his mind. It was one thing to deny access to Nat, but it wouldn't look good to deny access to the widow.

"Okay," he said at last. "But you read the reports here at the station."

"And the photographs?"

"Those too." Farthing picked up the phone and barked, "Find out who the detectives were on the Standish suicide. End of January." He looked up at Nat. "My girl will give you the names and then it's up to them if or when they'll see you."

Nat was in luck. Detective Dave Shannon had been a rookie when Nat had been on the force, and he happened to be in the squad room when Nat stuck his head in there after leaving Farthing's office.

"Yeah!" he said to Nat's enquiry. "I remember the case. Man shot himself in the head—very messy!"

"And you were perfectly happy with the verdict of suicide?"

"Well, there was the note and the only prints on the gun belonged to the guy himself." He shrugged. "It was pretty much an open and shut case. Anyway, don't take my word for it. I'll make you a copy of the report on our new Xerox machine." Nat didn't mention the fact that Farthing had stipulated he had to read the report at the station.

"What about the photographs. Can you get me a copy of those, too?"

Shannon gave a quick look around. "Not supposed to. But," he grinned, "seeing it's you, I'll see what I can do."

"Thanks. I'll owe you one."

Fifteen minutes later Nat was sitting staring at the gruesome pictures of Standish's death while he waited for Shannon to make a copy of the report. The first picture showed the back of the man's head slumped over the typewriter, the second was a side shot showing where the bullet had entered and the resultant mess over the desk, walls, and floor. The third was a picture of what was left of Jonathan Standish's face—which wasn't much.

Nat shivered and was glad the prints were in black and white and not glorious Technicolor. The fourth showed the gun on the floor next to Standish's foot where it had supposedly fallen from the man's hand. It certainly looked like suicide, but Nat wanted to speak to the detective and, if possible, see the autopsy reports before going any further.

"Don't tell you much, do they?" Shannon placed a buff envelope next to Nat.

"Thanks. I understand the suicide note was on the desk?"

"Yep! With a paperweight on it."

"What about the autopsy report?"

"There's a copy in there, too."

Nat looked sharply at Shannon. "Do I get the feeling you weren't happy with the suicide verdict?"

"Let's just say that a second look at things wouldn't go amiss. But," he looked around before lowering his voice, "I'd rather my partner doesn't get to hear I made you a copy of the report. And," he added as he scooped up the photos, "I'll see what I can do about these. Pop in tomorrow, okay?"

"What's your reason?"

Shannon shrugged. "Just a gut feeling—but even the autopsy says it appears to be suicide." He paused. "I guess his wife's not happy with that verdict either?"

"No. Anyway, we'll go over everything. Are you okay about answering further questions?"

Shannon pursed his lips. "Only off the record. Galbraith—he's my partner—and Farthing are perfectly happy with the outcome. One less case to worry about—if you get my drift."

Nat nodded, knowing only too well a cop's feeling of relief to get a case solved in record time—because there were always too many cases waiting.

Shannon straightened. "Got to go."

Nat rose from the chair and tucked the buff envelope under his arm. "Thanks again."

"Farthing goes to lunch around 11:45," Shannon said pointedly.

AN HOUR AFTER he'd picked up the photographs at the police station the next day, Nat and Maggie had spread them and the reports over his desk.

"What do you make of the autopsy findings?" Nat asked as he laid down Shannon and Galbraith's report.

"They make a good case for suicide," Maggie answered. "The entry wound was starred and there was soot around the bullet hole, which indicates the gun was held right up against the skin. The bullet was a .45, which accounts for the exit wound and the terrible damage it did to the man's face, and the gun had only his prints on it." She placed the document back on the desk.

"Did you notice anything else on the autopsy report?" Nat persisted.

Maggie nodded. "He had fractured his left leg and right arm at some earlier time. But I can't see that making any difference to the findings."

Nat reached over and picked up the paper. "I saw that, too," he said as he started rereading. Then he sat back in his chair. "I think we'd better have a talk with Alice about that."

"But why? It's not going to make that much difference to the verdict . . ." Then it dawned on her. "His right wrist!" She rolled back her left sleeve. "I slipped on the ice and broke my wrist, see? It must've been at least five years ago—and I still can't bend it very well."

Nat leaned over and picked up the telephone and dialed. "Hello, Jane. Is Alice there?" He waited until Alice came on the line and then said, "I just read the autopsy report. When did Jonathan break his wrist?" He listened to her reply. "The autopsy report states that it was a severe fracture. I see . . . And did it curtail his sculpting or other activities? . . . I'm not sure if it's any help, but we'll get back to you . . . Hold on a minute. Maggie is asking me something . . ."

"Find out how long ago and also the name of the doctor who set the fracture," she called out.

"We were just married—so it must have been a good eight years ago," Alice answered, hearing the question. "We were visiting his older sister in Calgary and he slipped on the icy pavement outside her house. It was set in a hospital in Calgary," she added, "but he had to have it reset by Doctor Osborn at the Vancouver General."

"Thanks, Alice. We'll get back to you." He replaced the receiver and then related his conversation to Maggie. "It was such a bad break that it took ages to heal and he was never able to bend it far."

"What did she say about his painting and potting?"

"She said that he managed quite well, considering. Using the wheel was out, but he preferred hand building, whatever that means, anyway."

"Shaping with one's hands and not on a wheel," Maggie explained, and then she added, "So what's this got to do with his death?"

"The question is, could he bend his right wrist enough to be able to shoot himself in the head at the angle shown in those photos?"

When they met with him the following day, Doctor Osborn agreed with Nat's assessment.

"These are the fractures." In his office, the doctor pointed at the x-ray. "As you can see, he not only fractured the radius and ulna but he had extensive tissue damage to the wrist. Although the break healed well, the tissue damage was another matter and it left him with limited movement in that wrist."

"His wife said he could still sculpt," Maggie said, peering closely at the x-ray.

"That's quite possible, as he still had a lot of movement in his hand and fingers."

"So," Nat asked, "was it possible for him to shoot himself in the head? I mean, he would have to twist his right hand like this." Simulating holding a gun, he raised his right hand to the side of his head. "Here, have a look at these," he added handing over the photographs.

Doctor Osborn took the photographs and sat behind his desk. "In my opinion it would have been absolutely impossible," he concluded. "This looks as if he was shot execution style. And I would have thought that if the man wanted to commit suicide, he would have put the gun in his mouth," he added, handing the photos back to Nat.

"My sentiments exactly," Nat said, slipping them back into the buff envelope. "Thank you for your help. We may have to call on you again."

"To testify, you mean?"

"That's a possibility," Maggie answered.

"SO IT LOOKS as if we have a new murder case," Maggie said as she slid into the passenger seat of Nat's car. "And we will now have to start delving into Jonathan Standish's past."

"But where to start?" Nat answered.

"Alice first and then a long talk with Sheldon White—her little willing helper."

CHAPTER SIX

"You said you and Jonathan had been married for eight years," Maggie said as Alice placed a cup of coffee in front of her. Nat and Maggie were seated opposite the two sisters in Alice's comfortable second-floor apartment overlooking English Bay. Maggie felt that, if she lived in this apartment, she would be sitting at the window all day gazing at the scenery. Sailboats dotted the harbour, cargo boats swung lazily on their anchors, and gulls screeched and plunged to scoop up morsels from the shore.

Alice nodded in reply. "We married a year after I began working for him. I know that looking at me now it's hard to believe, but we were attracted to each other right from the start." She turned away to dab at her eyes. "That was why I couldn't believe he was having an affair. He wasn't like that." She paused for a moment. "I guess I was wrong. But why kill himself?"

"There's every indication that he didn't," Nat said.

"You're saying he *was* murdered?" Jane asked sharply. "Can you be sure?"

"It's the broken wrist," Nat explained. "There was no way he could have bent his wrist to shoot himself at the angle shown in these photographs." He drew them out of the buff envelope and turned to Alice. "Can you face seeing these?" he asked as he spread them out on the coffee table.

Alice nodded but Maggie could see it took a lot of effort for her to bend down and study the pictures as Nat pointed out the position of the body, the bullet hole, and where the gun had fallen on the floor.

"But Jonathan's prints were on the suicide note," Jane exclaimed. "How can that be if he was murdered?"

"I can't explain that one yet," Nat answered, then he turned to Alice "But we do need to look at your husband's office as soon as possible and interview your assistant, Sheldon White."

"The gallery is open tomorrow," Alice answered. "Sheldon usually gets in around ten."

"But Jonathan's been dead for nearly three months," Jane cut in, "and Sheldon's been using the office since then."

"Has he rearranged it?" Maggie asked.

"No. Naturally we had to thoroughly clean everywhere." Alice shuddered. "We threw away the area rug and bought a new leather chair."

"And the typewriter?" Nat asked.

"I couldn't stand looking at it so I put it up in the attic. I use my own portable in the office."

"Any objection to us going there this afternoon?" Nat asked.

Alice shook her head. "Do you want me along, too?"

"Yes. We need you to show us around."

Thirty minutes later Nat, Maggie, and Jane were following Alice out of the brilliant sunshine and into the foyer of the darkened gallery. They waited while Alice opened a cabinet just inside the door and pulled the switch to deactivate the burglar alarm.

"I don't want to open the shutters," she explained, flipping on light switches. "The office is at the back," she added as she led the way, "but wait here for a minute. The back part of the premises is on a separate alarm system." She opened a small cabinet in the back hallway and pulled a switch. "That door leads to a small studio that Jonathan and I used for painting."

"Wait a sec," Maggie said as she opened the studio door. There was no need to switch on the light here as several skylights illuminated the room. A couple of easels, several stools and a table cluttered with paints and brushes and other painterly paraphernalia were the only furnishings. Canvases were stacked against every wall.

Jane, peering into the room over Maggie's shoulder, pointed to the easels, and said, "You should get back to your painting again, Alice. It would do you the world of good."

"Perhaps you're right," Alice answered, "but I don't seem to have the heart for it."

Before Jane could continue her advice to her sister, Maggie asked, "Where did your husband create his ceramic pieces?"

"In the big studio on Quebec Street. He shared it with six other ceramic artists."

"And where does that door lead?" Nat asked, pointing to a door at the end of the short hallway.

"It's a small workroom where we uncrate paintings and prepare new displays," Alice explained.

As Alice put out her hand to open the door to the office, Maggie stopped her again. "Don't go in yet. Close your eyes and think back to when Jonathan worked in there." Maggie waited a few moments before reaching past Alice to open the door. "Now, open your eyes and tell me if everything is still in the same place."

Alice opened her eyes and took several steps into the room and gazed around her. "Everything seems the same," she said, turning to Maggie and Nat. "Except that he isn't here." Again she raised a handkerchief to her eyes, and Jane pushed gently past Maggie to put her arms around her sister.

The room was only half as wide as the showroom. Nat, followed closely behind Maggie as she walked past a large leather-topped desk and swivel chair, then stood beside her as they peered through the dusty panes of an eight-foot-window. The scene before them was a dreary backyard with weedy grass and several sorry-looking rhododendrons. Aside from the desk, there was a metal filing cabinet, a bookshelf, and a credenza with a crystal ice bucket and several bottles of liquor. Against the wall was a steep, narrow wooden staircase leading up to a trapdoor in the ceiling.

"What's up there?" Nat asked.

"Odds and ends. You know, the usual stuff that accumulates when you've occupied a building as long as this," Alice said.

"How long has the gallery been here?" Nat asked.

"Jonathan owned it for at least twenty years before I met him," Alice answered.

"And that door?" Nat asked, pointing to a door beside the window that looked into the backyard. "Is it used often?"

"Not since Jonathan died. He parked his car out there and always left through that door."

"Nothing's been moved in here?" Maggie asked, looking around the office.

"Only the typewriter, and as I told you, I couldn't bear looking at it so I put it up in the attic." She paused for a moment. "And I also told you that I replaced the chair and rug."

"Your assistant Sheldon White uses the desk?" Nat said as he lowered himself into the swivel chair and looked at the neat piles of papers and files.

"He did up to a month ago," Jane said, "but I've insisted that Alice take over the business herself."

"How did Sheldon take that?" Maggie asked.

"Not well. He keeps insisting he promised Jonathan that he would take care of me and the business."

"Taking care of himself, if you ask me," Jane said bitterly.

"How's the gallery doing?" Nat asked.

"I thought we should be doing better, but Sheldon insists it's because of the time of the year. Things should pick up once the tourists start arriving."

"Let's take a peek in the attic now," Nat suggested.

The attic was huge, covering the entire gallery and office space below, though not the studio. Rays of late afternoon sunlight filtered through a dusty uncurtained window to show boxes full of books, shelving jammed with more books, and several discarded chairs spilling papers onto the floor. There were several canvases, a couple of broken easels, and a Remington typewriter. Nat guessed it had been Jonathan's. He reached down through the trapdoor and helped Maggie up.

Walking over to the window, she peered down onto the backyard before gazing around the loft. Both were neglected and sad.

"Nobody has been up here since he died," Alice said forlornly as she pulled herself through the opening to stand beside Nat. Then her gaze fell on the typewriter. "Except when I brought that up."

"Do you mind if I take it with me?" Nat asked.

"No. But whatever for?"

"Do you know if the police did a comparison test on it?"

Alice looked puzzled for a moment. "Oh! You mean to compare the type with the suicide letter. I honestly don't remember."

"We should clean this whole place up," Jane said, poking her head through the opening. "In fact, I'll start on it tomorrow," she said firmly. "You won't recognize the place once I've finished with it."

"Would you hold off on the cleaning for a few days?" Maggie asked. "I think Nat and I should really go over the attic thoroughly."

"Oh, of course," Jane answered. "It's waited this long . . ."

"You said that Sheldon will be in tomorrow morning," Nat said once they were all back on the main floor again and trouping through the office toward the gallery.

"At ten. He's always very punctual."

As they approached the door to the street, Maggie turned to Alice. "Did your husband have any children from his first marriage?"

"A son, Aaron. He's an evangelist minister in one of those born-again churches. I'm afraid his choice of career didn't sit well with his father."

"Where's the church?" Nat asked.

"Near Mission, out in the Fraser Valley. He's married to a very quiet girl, Irma, and they have two young daughters, Iris and Pansy. But Aaron came to the funeral by himself." She looked pensive. "I arranged for him to meet Jonathan's lawyer the next morning, and then he took off and I haven't heard from him since—he doesn't exactly approve of me."

"Did he benefit from your husband's estate?" Maggie asked.

Alice nodded. "But he didn't get much because Jonathan left the gallery to me."

"And the apartment?" Maggie asked.

"No, I own that." She paused. "I really thought there would be more money but I guess business wasn't doing as well as I thought."

"How much did Aaron get?"

"Only five thousand." She gave a rueful smile. "I got the impression that he thought he should have got everything."

"Five thousand isn't very much," Nat commented.

"And I don't suppose he makes much being a pastor," Maggie added.

"No. It's in a very sparse rural area and I don't think his church has many followers."

"That must make it quite a struggle to bring up two kids," Maggie said quietly.

Alice nodded. "I did offer to help them but Aaron refused. He said he has a part-time job at one of the dairy farms close by."

"But you couldn't have helped him much if your husband only left you the gallery," Maggie said.

"My sister hasn't had much luck with husbands," Jane said tersely. "Neither of them left her any money."

"The gallery has been fairly successful and it's worth quite a bit," Alice answered defensively.

"But if it has been successful for close on thirty years," Jane insisted, "where's the money gone? All I can say is that he must've been a very poor manager not to have had some assets."

"I'd love to take another peek at those figurines," Maggie interceded quickly. "The details are so beautiful—it's hard to believe anyone could make something so delicate."

"I'D ALSO LIKE to know where Jonathan Standish's money went," Maggie said later as Nat drove away from Alice's apartment.

"Didn't Alice look after the books?" Nat asked.

"Yes. Perhaps a little cooking, do you think?"

"Nah! I can't see gentle Alice being a crook. Probably just some bad investments. I would think running an art gallery could be quite risky at times."

"You're probably right," Maggie answered pensively.

CHAPTER SEVEN

It was another lovely day, and when Maggie and Nat arrived at the gallery a little after ten, the shutters were open and in the daylight the place looked completely different.

"Sheldon is waiting for you in the office," Alice greeted them before turning back to an anxious-looking bearded young man who was showing her a medium-sized painting.

"Another one of those weird pictures," Nat muttered under his breath.

"Shush, he'll hear you," Maggie whispered back as she opened the door into the office.

Sheldon White stood up from behind the desk and offered his hand to Maggie.

"You were the one who found Jonathan Standish," Nat said after they had both shaken hands with him.

Sheldon nodded. "Please sit down." He waved toward the two visitors' chairs in front of the desk and sat down behind it. "It was terrible. I couldn't believe he would do such a thing."

"How long had you known him?" Maggie asked.

He closed pale blue eyes for a moment before answering. "Six months. But I became his right-hand man, so to speak."

"And was there any indication that something was worrying him?" Nat asked.

"Well, he was worrying about his wife—she had a very serious operation, you know."

"She told us," Maggie said. "An appendectomy."

"So I was only *too* happy to take over so that she could recuperate. And contrary to what Miss Weatherby—Mrs. Standish's sister—thinks, Jonathan was very appreciative."

"Are you an artist, Mr. White?" Nat asked.

"I dabble in my own small way." Then he added, with a smile, "Jonathan thought I had real potential."

"Please tell us about the time just before Mr. Standish's death," Nat said. "Did he have any visitors, any mail, telephone calls or anything that might have upset him?"

Sheldon ran his long tapered fingers through his sparse sandy hair. "Now that you come to mention it, he was very upset after receiving a couple of phone calls." He sat back in his chair and folded his hands on the desk. "I don't know who it was as he always asked me to leave the office, but he was very short-tempered after each call—which was *so* unlike the dear man."

"Let's go back to the day of his death."

"I'll never forget it. It was a Sunday evening—you understand we're not open on Sundays. Anyway, Mrs. Standish called me and said that Jonathan wasn't answering the telephone and she was worried about him."

"Why didn't she go to the studio herself?"

"Jonathan had taken the car. So I was only too happy to oblige."

"And?" Maggie prompted.

"The front door was unlocked—which was very unusual as Jonathan was always very strict about that. And there he was—dead!"

"Did you call Mrs. Standish?"

"No. When I saw all that blood and . . ." he gave a dramatic shudder, "I came over very faint and I sort of staggered out into the gallery. It took a few minutes for me to pull myself together. Then I called the police."

"So who *did* call Mrs. Standish?" Maggie insisted.

"Oh! I let the police do that. But why are you asking me all these questions? He did commit suicide, didn't he?"

"No," Nat answered sharply. "He was murdered!"

"Murdered!" Sheldon's face blanched. "But who would kill that lovely man?"

Maggie quickly rose from her chair. "Are you okay?" Sheldon looked so ill that she was afraid he was going to have another fainting spell.

"I'm fine . . . it's just . . . just too awful to contemplate." Sheldon visibly pulled himself together. "Jonathan was so well liked by absolutely everybody."

"If you can think of anything else that would help us," Nat said, getting to his feet, "we'll be upstairs in the studio."

"Can I be of help? I know where everything is up there."

"We'll call if we need you."

"SO WHERE DO we start?" Maggie asked as they contemplated the attic. "Perhaps we should tackle the bookcase first."

"Good idea. Let's drag that table over to it and we can pile the books up as we go. I'll begin with the top shelf and work my way down."

It was a dusty, messy process, and it was obvious that most of these books hadn't been touched in years. Maggie, methodical as always, scooped up a piece of paint rag so she could give each book a quick swipe before leafing through it. They soon discovered that most of the books covered various types of art—sculpture, drawing, painting, ceramic sculpture, and woodwork—and although they riffled through each one before placing it on the table, apart from a few rough sketches, nothing of interest fell out of them. It wasn't until they reached the bottom shelf that Maggie found, wedged between two books, a yellow Kodak folder containing several photographs and their negatives.

"Nat, look what I . . ."

"Found anything interesting?" She turned to see the top half of Sheldon in the open trapdoor. "I haven't been up here since Jonathan's death," he continued, his pale blue eyes sweeping the room as he prepared to come the rest of the way up the steep staircase. "Do you need any help?"

Maggie quickly pushed the packet back between the books. "No, we can manage, thank you. We'll be down shortly."

"I second that," Nat said grimly as he descended the library ladder. "We need a break before we choke to death on all this dust."

"There's some dusters in that old chest," Sheldon answered, pointing. "Here, I'll get them for you." Before either Nat or Maggie could protest, the man had pulled himself up into the attic. "Here, why don't I dust the shelves for you and then you can hand the books back up to me?"

"We can manage perfectly well, thank you," Maggie said coldly.

But nothing fazed the man. "No, no. I'm here to help any way I can." Open-mouthed, they watched him grab up a cloth, climb the library ladder, and begin to vigorously clean the top shelf. "Okay! You can pass the first batch up." Dutifully, they handed up the books.

"We'll tackle the bottom shelf after we've had that break," Maggie said firmly.

Reluctantly, Sheldon climbed down. "Oh, you shouldn't bother with those." He indicated the huge volumes on the lower shelf. "They're too heavy for you to haul out, and they're only reference books—you know—the life and times of the great masters. I can easily go through them for you."

"Actually," Nat said firmly, "we're all going back downstairs for a much needed drink of some sort." He waved a hand toward the trapdoor. "After you, Sheldon."

Maggie made sure she was the last to leave, but before following, she slipped the packet of photographs into her jacket pocket.

"Oh, there you are, Sheldon," Alice said as she entered the office from the gallery. "I was looking for you to take over in the gallery."

"Just giving a hand upstairs," he answered.

"Next time tell me when you're going to disappear," she said sharply. "Please go in and relieve my sister." After Sheldon had gone, she turned to Maggie and Nat. "How are you making out?"

"Okay until your assistant decided to help us," Maggie replied wryly.

"I can see what Jane means—he never gives up," Nat cut in. "Is there a chance of a glass of water—it's so dusty up there."

"Of course. I'll put on the kettle for tea."

"So what were you going to show me?" Nat said as soon as Alice had left the room.

"These." She pulled out the packet of photographs. "I haven't had time to have a good look at them, but . . ."

"Family photos," Nat said, spreading them on the table.

"But what family?" Maggie answered. There were six photos in all. The first one was of a pretty, dark-haired woman in her thirties, holding a girl around eight years old on her lap. The second showed the same little girl building a snowman with a black and white puppy sitting beside her. In the third she was serving tea to a couple of dolls and a teddy bear with the same little dog in attendance. The other three were of the woman alone: tending pink roses in a flower garden, laughing into the camera on what was obviously a windy day, and in the last one, blowing kisses to whoever was holding the camera. On the back were simple notations: "Judith and Jenny." "Judith and roses." "Judith and hat." "Jenny with Tippet and snowman." "Jenny serving tea." They were all dated June 1960.

"What have you got there?"

"Some photographs," Maggie answered as Alice put a tea tray down on the desk. "Do you know these people?"

Alice studied each one carefully. It was several minutes before she shook her head. "No. No, I've no idea who they are. Where did you find them?"

"Stuffed between some books. Mind if we take them?"

"If you think it will help. Find anything else?"

Maggie shook her head as she picked up a mug of tea and drank thirstily. "So much dust up there. I sure needed this." She took another gulp of tea. "Another hour and we should be through."

As Sheldon had said, the bottom shelf contained reference books featuring coloured plates of many of the old masters as well as more modern ones showing art of the twentieth century. But unlike the books on the other shelves, they were bereft of dust, and there were several bookmarks stuck in them—especially those with illustrations of the more modern paintings. A few minutes later, as they sorted through the mass of papers piled on the chairs, Nat found a number of pencil sketches of Jonathan's sculptures, including some of the beautiful figurines on the glass shelves in the gallery.

"Where are the photographs we found this morning?" Maggie asked as she removed several of the sketches and carefully flattened them onto the table.

"Downstairs in my jacket pocket. Why?"

"Slip down and get them, would you?" A few minutes later Maggie laid the snaps down on the sketches. "I thought I was right. Look!"

"Well I'm damned! These sketches were all made from the photographs."

"I think we'll keep this to ourselves for the moment," Maggie answered. "But we'd better take a closer look at those figurines on our way out."

"FINISHED UPSTAIRS?" JANE asked as they descended the stairs. She was sitting behind the desk writing in an account book.

Maggie nodded. "Yes. Now I need to go home and have a good soak to get rid of the dust." She laughed. "But before we go, do you know if Jonathan had a Rolodex or an address book?"

"Yes, I think he kept an address book." She opened the side drawer on the desk and began searching through its contents. "It's here somewhere. Ah! Here it is. Anybody in particular?" she asked as she opened the thin, hard-covered book.

"No. We need to look up some of his business contacts. Do you think Alice would mind if we took it with us? We'll get it back to you tomorrow."

"She's slipped out for a while, but I'm sure she wouldn't mind."

"Do you recognize these people?" Maggie asked on a sudden impulse, placing the photograph of the woman and child in front of Jane.

"No. Can't say I do," she answered picking the snapshots up. "But you can see they're mother and daughter. Who are they?" She turned the photograph over. "Judith and Jenny! Where did you find it?"

"Upstairs on one of the bookshelves."

"I guess Jonathan could have used them as models. Oh my, yes—they do look exactly like that figurine of the mother and child in the studio, don't they? Just the way they're posed . . ." Jane was silent for a moment. "You know, there was a bouquet of roses at the funeral from 'the two Js.' I remember I asked Alice who they were, but she had no idea."

"There were a lot of flowers at the funeral?" Maggie asked.

"Oh yes, there were so many flowers from all sorts of people.

So many people loved his art, you know." She was silent for a moment, and as she handed the photo back, she asked, "Do you think they could be the ones leaving roses on Jonathan's grave?"

"On his grave?"

Jane nodded. "Yes. There were fresh roses on two of the occasions that Alice and I visited his grave. Alice said they must have come from one of Jonathan's secret admirers." She laughed. "And perhaps that's all these two are—just admirers. After all, they must've posed quite a number of times for him." She picked up her pen again. "Must get back to these books."

As they got into the car, Nat said under his breath, "We need to find you, Judith and Jenny. Where are you?"

CHAPTER EIGHT

Maggie glanced happily around her as she walked Oscar through the small park on Fifth Avenue in Kitsilano. She had never regretted moving into her small house on the same street, but on beautiful late spring days like this one, she knew she had been very lucky to find it. While Oscar happily sniffed and then peed on his usual landmarks, her mind wandered to her own family. Midge and Jason's wedding was going to be held on June 16th and although Midge had wanted a very small wedding and reception, Harry, Maggie's estranged husband, had insisted that the couple get married in Vancouver's Christ Church Cathedral, followed by a reception at the Hotel Vancouver. The thought of meeting up with old friends, neighbours, and business acquaintances who would be sure to attend the wedding ceremony, if not the reception, sent cold shivers through her. *I must remember it's Midge's special day.* Then she smiled as she thought about her very pregnant elder daughter, Barbara, and how angry she was that Midge wouldn't put off the wedding until after her second child was born. *Anyway, Harry will be in his element, giving away his youngest and showing off his four-year-old grandson.* She glanced down at her watch.

"Oh blast! I'm going to be late. Come on, Oscar."

NAT WAS WAITING for her when she arrived at their office on Broadway. "I've managed to get hold of the Standish family lawyer," he said, beckoning her into his office. "He's been out of town."

"That explains why he never called back," she answered. "What did you say his name was?"

"I *didn't* say." He paused, enjoying the moment. "Does the name Humphrey Crumbie ring a bell?" he asked, grinning.

"Oh no!"

"Yup! Humphrey Crumbie of Snodgrass, Crumbie and Spencer," Nat said enunciating each syllable.

"Harry's firm."

"We have an appointment for two this afternoon."

"You don't need me." She headed for her own office.

He followed her. "Yes, I do," he answered firmly. "You have to face up to things like this happening—it's part of the job. Anyway," he added with a wicked grin, "this could be fun. Is he as stuffy as Harry?"

THE LAW OFFICES hadn't changed since Maggie's last visit. Luckily, Humphrey Crumbie had his own suite of rooms so she didn't have to face Harry's bitchy secretary, Miss Fitch-Smythe. But she remembered as they entered Crumbie's reception area that Amelia Randall, his watchdog, was just as snooty and bitchy.

"Yes. Can I help you?" After looking Nat up and down, her gaze took in Maggie without a sign of recognition.

"Southby and Spencer to see Mr. Crumbie," Nat answered.

"The detective persons." She looked down at her appointment book. "He's with a client. Take a seat."

"MARGARET, MY DEAR!" Humphrey Crumbie was now in his seventies. Short, bespectacled and wearing a grey herringbone three-piece suit—the buttons on the vest seriously straining in their effort to hold everything together—he walked over and took Maggie's hands in his and gently raised them to his lips. "My dear, what a wonderful surprise. And this is . . . .?"

"My business partner, Nat Southby."

"Business partner! I didn't realize . . ."

"Southby and Spencer, Private Investigators," Maggie answered. She dug into her purse and handed him one of her business cards.

"Harry did mention that you were in some kind of business, but . . ." His voice faltered. "Anyway, come into my office, my dear, and tell me what I can do for you."

"Did Alice Standish call you?" Nat asked after they were seated.

"Alice? Oh yes . . . of course." Looking even more confused, he turned to Maggie. "That was so sad, Jonathan . . . ahem . . . killing himself like that."

"That's why we're here," Nat cut in. "We are certain he didn't kill himself."

"You don't mean he was murdered! Oh, my!" Crumbie sat looking down at his pudgy pink fingers before reaching for a cigar, then raising his eyebrows at Nat, he indicated the box. Nat gave a quick glance at Maggie before reaching for one. "But who would do such a thing?" Crumbie asked as he carefully cut the end of his cigar with a silver knife. "Though I can see that would make a difference." He leaned over and handed the knife to Nat.

"A difference to what?" Maggie asked, looking daggers at Nat as he lovingly cut the end of his fat Cuban.

"Why, the insurance, of course." He gave a tremulous laugh. "Please forgive me, Margaret, but it is so unusual for *you* to be asking *me* the questions." He leaned back and drew on his cigar. "Now, back to the insurance. Alice couldn't claim because of the

suicide clause, but if it can be proved that he was murdered—
then that is a different kettle of fish, as it were."

"Yes, it would be," Nat said. "Alice says you talked to Jonathan's
son, Aaron, after the funeral."

"Yes. Rather a surly type of man. He's some kind of preacher.
Wasn't too happy that his stepmother got to keep the gallery."

"So we heard. You handled all of Jonathan Standish's affairs?"
Maggie asked.

"He's been with us for years just like his father before him.
Why do you ask?"

"Do the names Judith and Jenny mean anything to you?"

"Judith and Jenny?" He paused before continuing. "No.
Should they?"

Maggie wondered if she had imagined hearing the slight hesitation before he answered. "We found some photographs with
those names on the back," she continued.

"Probably models. Jonathan used a lot of different models for
his work over the years."

"We thought about that, too," Nat said as he withdrew the
photographs from the manila envelope and placed them in front
of Crumbie. "These two were definitely used for the figurines we
saw in the gallery."

"Well, there you are then." He gave the snaps a cursory glance
before handing them back to Nat.

"We tend to think there was more than just a painter/model
relationship."

"I very much doubt it. I hope you haven't asked Alice about this."

"We showed the photographs to her but she didn't recognize
either of them."

"Jonathan's death is still fairly recent, so I wouldn't push that
aspect if I were you." He glanced at the ornate clock ticking on the
mantelpiece. "Was there anything else?"

"No. We were really only interested in the woman and child."

"Sorry I can't help you there." He got to his feet and leaned over to shake Nat's hand. "Please tell Alice to get in touch about the insurance." Then walking around the desk, he put his hands on Maggie's shoulders. "Margaret, thank you so much for sending the wedding invitation. Emma and I will be delighted to attend. You and Harry must be so excited that she's bringing a doctor into the family."

"Yes, Jason is a very nice boy. And it was so good seeing you again, Humphrey." Maggie walked toward the door that Nat was holding open, but she turned back as Crumbie spoke again.

"Margaret, could I speak to you in private for a moment? You don't mind waiting in reception?" he asked Nat.

A look of annoyance flashed across Nat's face and he raised his eyebrows at Maggie.

"It's okay, Nat. I'll only be a minute." She waited until Nat had closed the door and then turned to face Crumbie. "What is it, Humphrey?"

"My dear, you and Harry really must kiss and make up and get over that little squabble that's keeping you apart. The dear boy has never been the same since you two parted."

"I'm sorry, Humphrey, but I can't go back," she answered gently. "I love my independence, my own small house, and most of all, my job with Nat Southby."

"But look what you had, my dear! Most women would give their eye teeth for the home you had with Harry."

She laughed shortly. "I guess I'm not *most women*."

"Well, I've done my best to persuade you." He gave a deep sigh and shook his grey head. "I don't know what the world is coming to." He put out his hand as she turned toward the door again. "There is one other thing, Margaret . . . don't dig too deeply into this Judith woman. You will only hurt your client."

"Then you do know of them!"

"Forget them and get your ... uh ... partner to concentrate on proving Jonathan didn't commit suicide so that Alice can claim that insurance. It's a considerable amount."

"SO WHAT WAS so important that he had to speak to you alone?" Nat said as they walked toward the elevator.

"He wants me to kiss and make up with Harry."

"Kiss and make up! I hope you told him to mind his own damn business."

"I did in a gentle way. I'm very fond of Humphrey and Emma Crumbie and I didn't want to upset him. But I'm sure he *does* know who Judith and Jenny are."

"But he said he hadn't heard of them."

"As I was leaving, he warned me about digging too deeply as it could be harmful to Alice. But he refused to say more and we're no nearer to finding them."

"I wonder if Alice knows about the insurance money?" Nat mused.

"Humphrey said it was a considerable amount so she should be pleased if we can prove that Jonathan didn't kill himself."

"She should be ecstatic," he answered wryly. "And Crumbie admitted to you that he knew about Judith and Jenny. I wonder what he knows? And," he continued as he opened the outer door for Maggie, "more importantly, how do we find out?"

Maggie glanced at her watch. "It's still early. Why don't we take a trip to the cemetery and have a look at Jonathan Standish's grave?"

"I don't think he's going to hop out of the grave and answer our questions."

"Humour me," she said and tucked her arm into his as they walked toward the car.

THEY FOUND THE grave quite easily. It was in a quiet corner of the cemetery with a carved white marble headstone. A layer of white pebbles had been spread between the matching curbs. The inscription read: *Jonathan Standish. June 18, 1900–February 5, 1962. A true artist, a gentleman, and very much missed.* Below this was a quote by Michelangelo: *I saw the angel in the marble and I carved until I set her free.* At the foot of the headstone was a brass vase filled with fresh pink roses.

"Alice or the elusive Judith?"

"You guess is as good as mine." Maggie knelt and reverently touched the flowers. "There's no name on them." The lawnmower's abrasive sound cutting into the tranquility made her get to her feet and glance around. "I wonder if he would know?" Her footsteps crunching on the gravel path, she walked briskly over to a man in green overalls walking behind a power lawnmower.

Nat, standing by the graveside, watched the workman turn off the noisy engine to listen to Maggie who, as usual, was using her hands as she talked. After a few minutes the man bent and pulled the cord to restart the mower and Maggie turned to walk back.

"Any luck?" he asked as she drew near. Maggie's answering nod and smile answered his question.

"He says it's a young woman and she comes most Sunday evenings. He talked to her once and she told him the flowers are from her own garden."

"I don't suppose she told him where the garden is?"

"No. But he did mention there's often a young girl with her."

"Most Sundays." Nat mused as they walked toward the entrance. "It's funny that Alice hasn't noticed the fresh flowers on the grave."

"Perhaps she doesn't visit the cemetery very often."

"SHE WENT THERE a lot at first," Jane answered when Maggie phoned later that afternoon. "But she said that Jonathan's not there so what's the point? Why do you ask?"

"We were there today and it's such a tranquil spot."

"Yes, it is. But it certainly wasn't tranquil here! Sheldon didn't turn up for work, and we had the first real spate of tourists for the season."

"Is he sick?"

"No idea. I called his home several times, but there's no reply. And Alice says that this is very unlike Sheldon. He's always so busy making himself indispensable."

"We'll be leaving the office shortly. Would you like us to call around there and see if he's okay? Where does he live?"

"Somewhere in Strathcona. Hold on a moment . . ." There was a long pause and then, "Here it is—1271 William Street. But there's no need for you to go. I'm sure he'll turn up."

"I agree with Jane," Nat said when Maggie had hung up the phone. "That guy's a bad penny and he's bound to turn up."

"I suppose. But he's such an oddball. I'd like to see where he lives."

"You promised me a fish and chip supper at Woodwards," Nat teased. "Are you wriggling out of the deal?"

"We'll have that first and then go and find Sheldon."

CHAPTER NINE

It was after eight before Maggie and Nat found the old house on William Street. It was badly in need of a paint and repair job—even the front porch listed to one side—and it looked deserted.

"No lights," Maggie said with a shiver.

"Perhaps he likes sitting in the dark. Come on." But after repeated knocking there was still no answer. "Let's try the back."

"You go first," Maggie said nervously. "It's your idea." She couldn't see anything attractive about the house—a large square box sitting on a double lot, walls covered in grey, weather-beaten shingles, sash windows on either side of the front door, and three more on the second floor—a dismal place. The light was fading fast, but as they rounded the corner of the house, they could see an unkempt backyard overgrown with blackberry vines, thistles, and dandelions.

"Nat!" she whispered, tapping him on the shoulder. "Look over there. It's some kind of barn."

"Looks fairly new," he answered. The tall, wooden build-ing loomed ahead in the dusk. "Can't be a garage," he continued. "There's no street access and there's only one small door."

"And why such large windows and all those skylights?"

They had stopped beside the back door of the house, and Nat lifted his fist and banged hard on it. "Now that's odd—it's open."

Poking his head inside, he yelled, "Sheldon! Anyone home?" He waited, then yelled again, "Sheldon!"

"He's obviously not here, Nat," Maggie said, tugging at his jacket. "Let's go."

"I'll just have a quick look inside."

"No. That's trespassing." She stopped for a moment. "What's that terrible smell?"

"Garbage?" he said hopefully.

"Please, let's get out of here." She was remembering other houses they had entered uninvited in the past, only to find dead bodies.

But Nat had pushed the door open wider and entered a mudroom that contained a wringer washer, a laundry tub, and shelves laden with cans and jars of food. A wooden clothes dryer hanging from the ceiling was draped with shirts, pyjamas, underwear, and socks, and Nat pushed through them to open an adjoining door. He flicked on a light that revealed a surprisingly clean kitchen. "Come on, Maggie," he called back to her.

"I don't like this, Nat," she said when she had joined him. "Call again, and then let's go home."

"Sheldon," he yelled again. Turning to Maggie he said, "Why don't you have a quick look around down here while I go upstairs and make sure he isn't ill or something." Not waiting for her reply, he strode through the dark hallway and disappeared up a flight of carpeted stairs.

Maggie watched him ascend and, turning back into the kitchen, opened the door into the adjoining sparsely furnished dining room. Her face wrinkled with distaste when she saw the plate of congealed eggs, shrivelled bacon, and a half-eaten slice of toast. In front of the plate, propped against a bottle of ketchup, was a large open book. The facing page showed a reproduction of a painting of a snowy farm scene that seemed faintly familiar to

Maggie. A wooden chair had been pushed back from the table and lay on its side. "Seems he left in a hurry—so what scared him?" she asked the empty room.

Closing the door, she walked back through the kitchen and into the hall and stood at the foot of the stairs. "You okay, Nat?" But all she could hear were creaking floorboards as he went from room to room. *Can't wait to get out of this spooky place.* She turned the white and blue porcelain doorknob to the last room on the ground floor and gasped when a musty smell rushed out to meet her. Taking a deep breath, she fumbled on the wall until she found a switch, but the light from the dusty chandelier did little to enhance the Victorian parlor. Red velvet drapes covered the window, and a patina of dust covered the solid oak furniture, the bric-a-brac displayed on a wicker stand, and even the overstuffed sofa and armchairs. But she found herself drawn to a large oil painting set over the marble mantelpiece. It was of a prim-looking elderly woman, not even a hint of a smile on her sharp features, wearing a white lace mobcap—and her beady black eyes followed Maggie's every move. Maggie turned quickly and rushed out of the room, pulling the door firmly shut behind her.

"I'm going outside," she called to Nat. "I need some air." She didn't wait for his reply but continued out through the kitchen and mudroom into the backyard. But even the fresh air seemed tainted.

The moon had risen and was casting long shadows over the backyard and the tall wooden structure at the end of the garden. Taking her flashlight from her purse, Maggie walked slowly down the cement path that led to the entrance of the building, but it took her several minutes to figure out how to deal with the heavy wrought-iron hasp that fastened the door before she could fling it open.

The smell! That tell-tale smell. Holding one hand over her mouth and nose, she used her flashlight to locate a light switch.

When the light flooded the room, her first thought was that she was looking at red paint. But as she got a little closer, she could see it was blood that had spurted from the gaping slit in the man's throat. His body, artistically arranged with blood-soaked filmy draperies, was lying on a chaise-lounge that had been set on a dais in the middle of the room. And what made the scene especially bizarre were the dozen or so easels that had been placed in a circle around the dais, as if waiting for the painting lesson to begin.

"Oh, blast! Why do I always find them?" Backing away from the tableau and still holding her hand over her mouth, she stumbled out of the building. He had obviously been dead for a good many hours, and even though Maggie and Nat had seen several dead bodies in their investigations, she still found the smell of death hard to take.

"Where have you been?" Nat called from the back door of the house. "I've been calling you."

"In there," she answered and pointed with a shaky hand.

"What's in there?"

"He's . . . he's dead."

"Who's dead?"

"Sheldon. Go and see for yourself."

Nat stuck his head into the studio but withdrew it within seconds. "Bloody hell!" Firmly shutting the studio door, Nat walked to where Maggie was standing and gently pulled her into his arms and held her close. "Come on, let's get to a telephone."

"At least we know what the building is used for," she laughed shakily. "Apart from the dead body, I'd say it's a very fancy art studio."

THEY WAITED IN front of the house for the first patrol car to turn up.

"You the one called in about a dead man?" the portly officer asked as he climbed out of the car. He was followed by a baby-faced younger cop.

Nat nodded. "Around the back." He led the way.

"Holy cow!" the senior officer exclaimed from the doorway of the studio a few minutes later. "You haven't touched anything?"

Nat shook his head. "Not a thing."

"Call into the station and tell them it's a homicide," the officer said to his green-around-the-gills partner. He turned back to Nat. "I'll talk to you back in the kitchen with your wife."

Maggie was standing outside the back door inhaling deep breaths when the officer passed her on his way to the kitchen.

"You know the man?" he asked, beckoning her inside.

"We think he's Sheldon White, an employee of one of our clients," Nat answered, handing over one of his cards.

"Private investigator! So what were you investigating?"

"The man hadn't turned up for work."

"And you were hired to find him?" the officer asked incredulously.

"No," Maggie answered. "He's part of a major investigation. When he didn't turn up for work, we naturally came to look for him."

"And you are . . . ?"

"Margaret Spencer. The other name on that card."

"So what are you and this . . . ahem . . . lady investigating?" he asked Nat with a smirk.

"Murder," Maggie answered curtly.

"Murder!"

Maggie couldn't help smiling at the look on the man's face. It was quite obvious he had expected something much milder—maybe a wandering husband or wife.

"Would you care to fill me in?"

"No," Nat answered. "We'll wait for the officers who deal with homicide."

"Stay put," the very disgruntled cop ordered.

APART FROM A few preliminary questions, it was a good hour before the officer who was dealing with the homicide came back into the house to talk with them. "I've spoken to headquarters," Sergeant Angelus explained. "They seem to know of you, and Inspector Farthing wants the pair of you in his office nine sharp in the morning. *Capiche?* The inspector said you make a habit of stumbling over dead bodies, Mrs. Spencer. Is that right?" Not waiting for an answer, he turned and went back to the scene of the murder.

"BUT WHY WOULD anyone want to kill Sheldon?" Alice Standish cried. "I know he wasn't a likeable kind of person, but to kill him . . . ?"

Maggie and Nat had driven directly to her apartment on English Bay to break the news to the two sisters. Jane had immediately mixed a stiff Scotch and soda for all of them.

"I can't very well say cheers," she said, "but we all can do with a drink." After taking a gulp, she leaned toward Nat. "Do you think there's a link between the two deaths?"

"The police will definitely have to take another look into Jonathan's death now," Maggie said before taking an appreciative sip of her drink.

"I guess we'll have to brace ourselves for a visit from them," Jane said.

"Maggie and I have been told to report to Inspector Farthing tomorrow morning," Nat said. "We'll know much more after that."

"Are you sure there was no dispute between your husband and Sheldon? Perhaps money problems?" Maggie persisted.

"Jonathan was always a little concerned about money," Alice answered. "An art gallery doesn't generate that much income, especially in the off-season between Christmas and Easter. He'd told me that he was even thinking of extending his art classes to twice a week."

"Art classes?"

Alice nodded. "Drawing, painting, but mostly clay sculpture."

"Where did he give these classes?" Maggie asked.

"Some of them were night school classes sponsored by the school board but he also gave some private lessons."

"You paint," Nat said. "Do you do any ceramic stuff?"

"I'm really not good enough," she answered with a short laugh. "And there certainly wasn't room for me in the 'holiest of the holies.'" Seeing their confused look, she explained, "The studio on Quebec Street." Maggie was about to ask where exactly on Quebec Street, when Alice added, "But Sheldon did some teaching."

"Sheldon?"

"You know, that studio in his backyard?" Alice answered.

"Of course," Maggie said. "All those easels."

"He didn't wait long after my husband's death before he started persuading Jonathan's pupils to take lessons with him." She sighed. "Though I suppose I can't really blame him."

"Was Sheldon that good?" Nat asked.

"Jonathan was a great teacher and Sheldon an astute learner," Jane answered sourly. "He could copy practically anything."

"Copy?"

"Not one single original idea in his whole head," Jane said.

"I tried to keep him out of Jonathan's studio," Alice added. "Several sketches have gone missing."

"So there could be a connection with Sheldon's death," Nat said slowly. "I take it you've been to Sheldon's place?"

Alice nodded. "He wanted Jonathan's advice on the lighting. We couldn't help but be impressed with the size of the place."

"He just wanted to gloat," Jane said scathingly.

"Well, it didn't do him much good," Maggie said with a shiver, remembering the way the body had been arranged on the chaise-longue—it had been so bizarre.

longue (long chair)

"Perhaps Sheldon would still be alive, Jane, if you had accepted Jonathan's death as a suicide," Alice said sadly, "and just let it go . . ."

"Don't be ridiculous," Jane answered sharply. "I'm sure Sheldon had it coming to him! He was probably mixed up in something really nasty—he could even be the one responsible for Jonathan's death." She turned to Nat. "When can we expect the police?"

"Probably tomorrow."

THE NEXT MORNING, Tuesday, Farthing greeted Maggie and Nat with the complaint, "You two have been meddling in police business again!"

"Come off it, Inspector," Nat answered. "We didn't know the man had been murdered. Just our bad luck that we found him."

"How do you do it?" Farthing fumed, glaring at Maggie. "Just one body after another!" He leaned back into his leather chair—it was much better than the one Nat had been provided with when he had occupied the same office. "So what were you doing there?"

"We are investigating the so-called Jonathan Standish suicide. If you remember, I did come to you and ask permission to speak to your detectives."

"And I remember that I told you we were perfectly in agreement with the verdict of suicide. That still doesn't answer my question—why were you at Sheldon White's house last night?"

"He works, or I should say, worked at the Silver Unicorn Gallery."

"That's the gallery Jonathan Standish owned and where he committed suicide?"

"Was murdered," Nat corrected. "Sheldon had agreed to stay on to work for the present owner, Alice Standish. She was worried because he hadn't turned up at the gallery for a couple of days and wasn't answering his phone. She asked us to go to his house and make sure he was okay."

"And was he?"

"What do you mean, was he?" Nat asked, puzzled. "You know we found his body. Hey! You don't think *we* cut his throat, do you?"

"How well did you know this Sheldon White?"

"We spoke to him a couple of times at the gallery."

"And you, Mrs. Spencer?"

"Slightly. The same as Nat. Why?"

"And you were the one who discovered the body," Farthing continued, looking at Maggie. "How close did you get to it?"

"I didn't get close," Maggie answered, "but I could see he was covered in blood, that his throat had been cut, and by the terrible smell I knew he'd been dead for at least a day or so."

"And you, Mr. Southby?"

"I didn't want to contaminate the scene so I didn't go past the doorway."

"Why are you asking these questions?" Maggie asked. "You already know we went to Sheldon White's house and found his body in the studio."

"So, if asked, you could identify the victim as Sheldon White?"

"I suppose so," Maggie answered slowly, wondering what Farthing was getting at.

Farthing gave one of his rare grins. "That's great, considering that the corpse is not Sheldon White."

"What!" Maggie and Nat cried simultaneously.

"White's aunt went to identify the body this morning," he said, by now laughing so hard that he could barely get the rest of the sentence out, "and she stated categorically that the body is *not* that of her nephew."

"Then who is it?" Maggie asked, and then had to wait while Farthing stopped laughing.

"Your guess is as good as mine," Farthing answered, wiping the tears from his eyes. "Sorry about that, but it's so great to have one over on you two for once." He stood up from behind his desk. "So, get yourselves over to the morgue right away and see if you can identify the body, and after that, get back to your divorces and chasing errant husbands, and let us do our job."

"FARTHING SURE ENJOYED his little moment, didn't he?" Maggie said, sliding into the passenger seat of Nat's Chevy. "Let's get this morgue visit over with," and Nat obviously agreed because he stepped on the gas so quickly, Maggie was flung back against the seat. It seemed like they reached their destination in no time flat and found themselves looking down onto the white, waxen face. A sheet had been pulled up to hide the terrible gashed throat, so that the face they saw looked quite peaceful—but neither of them had seen the man before.

"I was so sure it was Sheldon," Maggie murmured. "I know I should have gone right up to the body when I discovered it, but the smell and the blood made me panic."

"I'm just as much to blame," Nat answered, putting his arm around her shoulder and pulling her close to him. "I didn't go inside the studio, I just took your word that it was Sheldon."

"Can you think of anyone who could identify the body?" the police officer on duty asked them after he had escorted them out to the reception area.

"The only person I can think of is Alice Standish," Nat answered. "It's a long shot, but there's a possibility that he might have visited the gallery."

"We'll get her to come in if you could give us her address and phone number."

"Would you mind if we went to see her first?" Maggie asked. "She's already had a bit of a shock thinking that the body was her employee. Then we could bring her back to the morgue if you like."

"AND YOU'RE ABSOLUTELY sure it's not Sheldon?" Alice asked when they entered into her apartment and broke the news to her. "Then why was the body in his studio and where has he disappeared to?"

"We looked at the body in the morgue ourselves," Nat answered. "The victim has dark brown hair and hazel eyes. Sheldon's hair is sandy and, if I remember correctly, he has pale blue eyes."

"So why did you think it was Sheldon in the first place?" Jane asked sharply.

"The body was in Sheldon's studio and Sheldon himself was nowhere to be found," Nat answered.

"The body was covered in blood," Maggie added slowly. "We got out of the place as quickly as we could and I'm afraid we just assumed it was Sheldon."

"And there was no sign of that little sneak in the house?" Jane mused as she placed coffee in front of each of them.

Maggie shook her head. "He must have been scared out of his wits because he left a half-eaten meal on the table and his chair had been tipped over on its side as if he'd rushed out of the room."

"Scared shitless," Jane said, and gave a little laugh. "I told you he had no guts," she added to her sister. "Here, have a biscuit."

"I don't want a biscuit," Alice replied angrily. "You can be so heartless, Jane."

"But it's not Sheldon who's been killed." She turned away from her sister and added under her breath. "More's the pity."

"But it could have been," Alice replied, turning to Nat. "So how do we go about finding the poor man?"

"Stop worrying about Sheldon," Jane said. "You know he'll turn up. Now let's go and have a look at that man in the morgue."

A half hour later found Maggie and Nat waiting in reception while the two sisters viewed the body.

"I hope they don't take too long," Maggie said, glancing at her watch. "I promised Midge I'd pick up the bridesmaids' dresses for her. I can't believe the wedding is only a month off!"

"So you keep telling me," Nat answered with a grin. He stood up as the door opened.

"I didn't recognize him," Jane said as she rejoined them in the reception area, "but I haven't been working with Alice long enough to know all her clientele."

"What about you, Alice?" Maggie asked.

"As I told this nice officer, I'm sure I've seen him before somewhere. Let me think for a bit." She sat on one of the hard benches then looked back up at the cop standing beside her. "I'm sure I've seen him in our gallery a couple of times, but it was when my husband was alive. I think he wanted Jonathan to sell some paintings for him and I vaguely remember Jonathan and the man discussing technique and oil versus acrylics."

"Did Jonathan sell any paintings for him?" Nat asked.

"I'm sorry. I can't remember."

"He hasn't been back to the shop since your husband died?" the police officer asked.

"The shop? Oh, you mean the gallery. No. I'm sure I would have remembered. Perhaps Sheldon would know . . . Oh, dear. And poor Sheldon is missing." Alice began searching in her handbag for a handkerchief.

"What about you, Mrs. Weatherby?" the officer asked, turning to Jane.

"*Miss* Weatherby," Jane corrected, pulling a handkerchief out of her pocket and handing it to her sister. "No. I'm sure I've never set eyes on the man before."

"Perhaps you could look through your husband's records," the police officer said as they prepared to leave. "You might find something to jog your memory."

"You mean try to put a name to the face? I'll try," Alice answered, "but I don't think it will do much good." She turned to Maggie and Nat and asked, "Are you coming back to my apartment?"

"I'm sorry," Maggie replied, glancing at her watch, "I have an errand to run for my daughter."

"You have a daughter?"

"Two. And the youngest, Midge, is getting married in a month's time. Her father and I want her wedding to be everything she's ever dreamed of."

"But I thought you were divorced," Jane said.

"Separated. But we're working together to make Midge's big day perfect."

"DO YOU THINK this murder has anything to do with Jonathan Standish?" Maggie asked as she and Nat drove back to the office.

"Sheldon worked in the art gallery and the owner gets killed, and now some unknown man gets his in Sheldon's studio. That seems like just too much of a coincidence."

"Let's go over everything tomorrow," she said tiredly. "I really mustn't be late for the dressmaker."

"Don't overdo everything, Maggie," he said as they pulled up at the office. "You have a whole month before the wedding."

"Nat. You don't realize how much there is to do. I'll see you in the morning."

Nat was very pensive as he watched her get into her own car and drive away.

CHAPTER TEN

"Why did I oversleep, today of all days?" Maggie muttered as she placed a piece of bread on each of the two metal side flaps of the toaster and then pushed them shut—she had to keep an eye on the contraption because she was sure it had a mind of its own and would burn the bread if she glanced away for even a moment. She checked the kitchen clock. Almost 1:00 PM. *At least I'm dressed and ready to go for when Midge arrives.*

She was just swallowing the last of the only slightly burnt toast that enclosed her breakfast/lunch sandwich when the doorbell rang.

"You look a bit bushed," Midge commented, watching her mother rinsing her cup under the faucet.

"So would you be if you'd had a week like I've just been through." Maggie shrugged on her coat and opened the front door.

"What, another juicy murder? How do you and Nat find them?"

Maggie laughed. "Oh, that part is easy. The hard part is being interrogated by our friend Inspector Farthing, and then having to look at the dead man in the morgue."

"Not my idea of fun."

"No." Maggie shuddered. "This last murder has been really horrible. I'll tell you about it sometime. Now," she said as she climbed into Midge's car, "give me the latest on the number of guests."

"It's been so hard cutting it down," Midge answered, slipping the car into gear. "But it's already up to a hundred."

"Is your father happy with that figure?"

Midge nodded. "He said to try and keep it to under a hundred if possible. But there is something I am worried about, and it's a bit awkward. What do I do about Nat?"

"Inviting him, you mean? Midge, he doesn't expect you to invite him to the reception. He wouldn't spoil your special day for anything. But he will be at the church."

"I'm glad. I just didn't want to hurt his feelings by not inviting him. Oh, look," she said as they drew up outside the Hotel Vancouver, "there's Dad."

"You're looking tired, Margaret," were the first words Harry said after giving his daughter a hug. "I was beginning to think you weren't coming," he added, peering at his gold pocket watch.

"Oh, Daddy, don't be such an old grouch. We're only five minutes late." Taking his arm in hers she led him through the hotel's entrance. "Come on, let's go and order a scrumptious and very expensive wedding breakfast for my big day. You did mention a five-tiered cake?"

"I certainly did not," he said, but he chuckled. "I'm not made of money, you know."

She certainly knows how to wind her father around her little finger, Maggie thought as she followed them.

After everything had been discussed, down to the serving plates and the colour of the table napkins, the three of them sat in the restaurant for a much needed afternoon tea.

"I hear you bumped into Humphrey a few days ago," Harry said as he extended his cup and saucer to Maggie for a refill.

"Yes, he told me that he and his wife are looking forward to the wedding," Maggie answered, wondering what else Humphrey had told Harry.

"He didn't say where he'd seen you." He paused and looked expectantly at Maggie, but when she didn't volunteer any more information, he added, "But Miss Smythe said you came to his office."

"How did dear Miss Fitch-Smythe hear that?" she asked sweetly. "I didn't see her."

"Well . . ." he raised his napkin and coughed into it. "Well, I gather Humphrey's secretary mentioned it to her." He had the grace to look uncomfortable.

"It was on a private matter," she remarked, then turning to Midge, she asked, "More tea?"

"She said you had that man with you," he pushed on. "What kind of business could you have with Humphrey?"

"If you mean my partner, Nat, yes he was with me. And the business we were on was—and is—strictly private." She turned back to Midge. "Is there anything else that needs discussing about the wedding?"

Midge, who had been following the exchange between her parents with dismay, shook her head. "No. Everything seems to be going smoothly. I did tell you that when we return from our honeymoon in Yellowstone, we'll be moving into a larger apartment, didn't I?"

"Yes, dear. Yours is really barely big enough for you and Snowball. And that reminds me, who's looking after her while you're away?" Snowball was the pure white Sealyham that a grateful client had given to Maggie the previous year. But Emily and Oscar were enough for her to cope with, and Midge, having had a part in that adventure, loved the little dog.

"We're taking her with us."

"Why in heaven's name would you take that animal with you?" Harry demanded. "There are some perfectly good kennels around."

"But she would hate that," Midge answered. And folding her napkin, she stood up. "You ready, Mum? I'm meeting Jason after I've dropped you off at your house."

Harry, every bit the gentleman, insisted on escorting the two women to the parking lot. After giving his daughter a hug, he looked uncomfortably at Maggie before giving her a peck on the cheek. "You do look tired, Margaret," he said, helping her into the passenger seat. "Do try and rest up for the wedding."

"He's still very fond of you, Mum," Midge said as they drove out of the lot.

"I know," Maggie answered. "And I'm still fond of him, too, in the way that people who've lived together for twenty-five years become fond of one another, but there is no way I could go back to that stifling life."

MAGGIE WAITED UNTIL Midge's car had turned the corner before opening her own front door. Oscar bounced around her legs, encouraging her to reach down and pet him. Emily, sitting in her favourite place on the window sill, jumped down, stretched languidly, and then wound herself between Maggie's legs. "Now is this love?" she asked the two animals, "or is it just cupboard love and you want your supper?"

After letting both animals briefly into the backyard, she coaxed them back again by tapping on their food dishes, then sank into her armchair, kicked off her shoes and gave a huge sigh of relief. "Phew! What a day. But there's nothing to think about until Monday—no wedding, no office, no Harry, and even no Nat"—he was entertaining his brother from out of town for the weekend—"and definitely, no murders!" And Monday was Victoria Day so she would have two whole days to herself.

IT WAS NEARLY seven on Sunday evening when Maggie remembered that she and Nat had intended to go to the cemetery in hopes of seeing the young woman and child who left the flowers on Jonathan's grave. There was no point in getting in touch with her partner now because he would be busy with his brother, and in any case, it was probably already too late to see the young woman. She dithered for a moment then decided she might as well go.

But the fresh flowers on the grave were the only indication that the mother and child had been there. She had missed them again.

CHAPTER ELEVEN

"Do you think we should mention the flowers to her?" Maggie asked. Maggie, Nat, and Henny were sitting in Nat's office having their usual first day of the work week meeting of minds.

"Blast! I'd completely forgotten that we were going to the cemetery Sunday night," Nat said.

"I remembered, but I was too late. That's why I wondered if we should confront Alice about them."

"Maybe we should wait a bit," he answered. "Have either of you seen the paper this morning?" He handed it across the desk to Maggie.

She read the story aloud:

> Gory murder on William Street. The police have confirmed that the body of an unidentified young man was discovered at 1271 William Street on Friday evening. The owner of the property, Sheldon White, was not available for comment. The authorities are asking for help from anyone who might have seen or heard anything that would help their inquiries.

"And you saw this body with its throat all cut?" Henny asked, giving an exaggerated shudder.

They all turned as they heard the outer door opening. Henny was half out of her chair when Sergeant George Sawasky called, "Anyone home?"

"You sit in my chair," Henny said, going to meet him, all smiles. "I will get you coffee, and I brought in new cookies today."

"That's lovely, Henny." Then turning to Maggie and Nat, he said by way of greeting, "I see you are treading on our inspector's toes again."

"I suppose he told you that he tried to make us look like a couple of fools?" Nat answered grimly.

"Yes. He did seem a little on the gleeful side when he called me yesterday. Thanks, Henny," he added, as she placed the mug of coffee and two of her famous mangled cookies in front of him. "But last time we spoke, you were trying to change a suicide verdict into a murder. Something to do with an art gallery and a couple of old ladies."

"And we were right," Maggie answered. "Farthing was too ready to accept Jonathan Standish's death as suicide, and we've more or less proved that it was murder."

"But Standish died at least three months ago. So where does this cutthroat murder fit in?"

Between them, they brought George up to date on Sheldon White, his attitude at the gallery and their surprise on seeing the elaborate studio in his backyard.

"And this Sheldon guy has disappeared?"

Maggie nodded. "He wasn't in the house, and by the look of it, he hadn't been there for at least a couple of days."

"And the murder must have taken place around the same time he disappeared," Nat added.

"So he could be the killer?" George said.

"I wouldn't have thought he'd have the guts to cut someone's throat," Maggie answered. "But," she shrugged, "who knows what he would do if he was provoked?"

"I think you go and see his aunt," Henny said from the doorway. "She would know what he is really like."

"You've got a point, Henny," Nat replied. "Trouble is, we don't know her name or where she lives. And naturally Farthing won't give that bit of info to us."

George, in the act of stuffing the last bit of Henny's overbaked cookies into his mouth, suddenly realized that the entire staff of Southby and Spencer, Private Investigators was looking at him. "No," he said quickly, standing up. "Farthing would kill me if I pass anything on to you people."

"Come on, George. He'll never know," Maggie wheedled. "Just a quick phone call . . ."

"Do you think he'll do it?" Maggie asked after George had made a quick exit.

"Mr. George will get address for us," Henny said confidently. "He is a good friend."

"Well, just in case he doesn't," Maggie said as she walked toward her own office, "I'll give Alice a call and see if she knows." But it was Jane who answered the telephone at the gallery.

"Alice had a sudden whim to go to Jonathan's grave. Can't see what good that will do, but she insisted on going alone. Can I help?"

"Did Sheldon ever mention the name of his aunt? You know, the one who went to the morgue to identify his body?"

"Not to me. But then, we weren't exactly on friendly terms. I'll ask Alice when she comes back."

But George was the first to come through with the information. Henny took the call from him and then relayed the message to Maggie.

"Mr. George said that her name is Harriet Montrose and she lives in retirement apartments called Hollies . . . or something like that."

"Did he say where this place is?" Maggie was used to coaxing information out of Henny by degrees.

"Kensington Avenue. I have written her telephone number down, but Mr. George said she is very deaf lady."

Maggie glanced at her appointment book. "Would you check with Nat and see if he wants to go with me—say around three."

"Mr. Nat say he's tied up with lots of paper," Henny reported back. "He say it would be better if you go and talk with old lady on your own."

"You tell Mr. Nat that he's a coward," Maggie answered, laughing and reaching for the phone. "If there's anything he hates more than going to hospitals and nursing homes, it's talking to deaf old ladies."

George was quite right. Harriet Montrose was very deaf, and it took Maggie quite a while to get through to the woman that she would like to call on her that afternoon.

MAGGIE WAS ON the point of leaving for her appointment when Alice Standish called. "Jane says you called earlier to ask about Sheldon's aunt. He did mention her a couple of times, but I'm sorry, I can't remember her name."

"It's okay," Maggie answered. "We've found her. Her name is Harriet Montrose."

"That's good," Alice replied. "But I need to talk to you about something else. It's about Jonathan's grave."

"Yes?"

"Somebody is still leaving roses on it."

"Still?"

"Somebody had left roses on his grave just after he was buried, and Jane said it was probably an admirer. But I've been thinking about his suicide note . . . he said he was having an affair. Do you think it could be this same person?" She made the word "person" sound like something unclean.

"Perhaps it was one of the models who posed for him," Maggie said warily.

"Perhaps. But I knew most of his regular models, and the caretaker at the cemetery said this person leaves the flowers on a weekly basis." She paused for a moment. "He said it's a young woman with a little girl." Maggie heard the catch in Alice's throat.

"Do you remember I showed you a photograph of a young woman and child?" Maggie asked. "It was when Nat and I were going through your husband's books."

"Yes. Do you think that's the woman who's putting the flowers there?"

"It could be."

"Can you find out who she is?" she asked. "Jane still insists it's just some love-sick admirer . . ."

"But you don't think so," Maggie replied.

"Well, that doesn't make sense when he's been dead for over three months, does it?"

"We'll try and find out who she is, okay? But there is something that Nat and I want you to do in the meantime."

"Anything that will help."

"Could you make a list of Jonathan's relatives, friends, business acquaintances, students . . . anyone who knew him when he was alive?"

"That will be quite a list."

Maggie was silent for a moment, then she said gently, "Alice, Jonathan could have known the person who killed him."

CHAPTER TWELVE

The Hollies on Kensington Avenue wasn't hard to find. Holly bushes, covered in dust from the road, had been planted on either side of the entrance of the grey-stone building. The large building must have been quite elegant at one time, Maggie thought as she climbed the three steps to the scarred double door, but years of neglect had faded the name that had been etched into the lintel, and the holly berries and leaves that had entwined the name had mostly broken away.

Reading the faded hand-written list inside the main entrance, Maggie saw that Mrs. Harriet Montrose lived on the second floor. She opted for the stairs rather than the ancient elevator, then walked along the dingy corridor until she came to number 202. It took repeated knocks before the door was finally opened a crack. The face that appeared had rouged cheeks, thick magenta lipstick, and smudged mascara, and a heavy-handed pancake application had filled in the lines and cracks.

"You that woman who called?"

"Maggie Spencer. It's about your nephew."

"Speak up. Why do people always mumble?"

"Yes," Maggie yelled. "Can I come in?"

"No need to shout. I'm not deaf." The door opened wider. "You'd better come in."

Maggie was suddenly hit with stale air, the mousy smell of old furniture and the insidious odor of mothballs. She was sure the grimy sash windows hadn't been cleaned for years.

"What do you want?" Harriet Montrose asked. Wearing a blond wig that was slightly off-kilter, she nodded to one of the two armchairs placed in front of the window. "You can sit there." Sheldon's aunt was at least five foot ten inches tall with large breasts straining a hand-knitted, hot-pink sweater. A floral print skirt came midway to her calves, and white cotton socks and a pair of running shoes completed her ensemble.

Maggie tried not to stare. "It's about your nephew," Maggie repeated.

"Who?" Harriet Montrose cupped her ear and leaned forward.

"Sheldon. Your nephew," Maggie repeated in a louder voice.

"What's that useless jerk done now?"

"He's missing."

"He's listening? What's he listening to?"

"I said he was *missing*."

"Missing. That's no loss. Told my sister Dolores, God rest her soul, she'd rue the day she had him."

"Have you any idea where he could have gone?" Maggie's throat was beginning to feel the strain of yelling.

"Won't come here."

"Would you call me if he does?" Maggie handed over one of her cards.

"He won't come here," Harriet Montrose repeated. "Can't stand him. Slimy. That's what he is, slimy." She stood up. "I was on the stage, you know?" She walked over to the mantelpiece and took down a faded sepia photograph in a silver frame. "That's me." She shoved the picture into Maggie's hands. "Second one on the left."

Maggie looked at the line of simpering girls in filmy dresses and showgirl hats. "Actress?"

"Mattress. What's a mattress to do with it?"

"You were an *actress*," Maggie repeated, enunciating each word.

"Vaudeville. We played in Blackpool, Brighton. You know, all the seaside places. I was a beauty in my day." Taking the photograph from Maggie's hands, she replaced it on the mantel. "Anything else you want?"

"Was your sister on the stage, too?"

"My sister's age? What about it?"

"Was she on the *stage*?"

"Dolores? Good God, no. It was beneath her."

"What made you come to Canada?"

"Love." Harriet gave a chuckle. "I met a handsome Canadian sailor." She reached for another photograph. "That's my Bert. Passed over twenty years ago."

"And Dolores?" Maggie yelled, thinking her throat would never be the same.

"Came over with me, didn't she? Anything else you need to know?" She waited for Maggie to stand up and then led her to the door. "Was it him that killed that man?"

"We don't know."

"Wouldn't put it past him," she said, placing Maggie's card on the small telephone table before opening the door. "Mark my words, he'll turn up." She was starting to close the door on Maggie when she said suddenly, "You could try that old shack his father had on Galiano." But before Maggie could ask where on Galiano, Harriet had firmly closed the door.

Maggie was standing beside her car taking several deep breaths of clean fresh air when she heard her name being called. Looking up, she saw Harriet Montrose, her blond wig now covering one eye, leaning out of the window.

"Ask at the general store when you get off the ferry." The window slammed shut.

"Nat, you don't know what you missed by not coming with me," she said as she put the car into gear. She giggled all the way back to the office.

"YOU FOUND OLD lady then?" Henny asked as she wound her latest scarf creation—knitted in green, purple, and yellow—around her neck.

"Yes, I found her," Maggie answered, then added, "Henny, you really don't need that scarf today. It's beautiful outside."

"I sneeze two times today. And my moeder always say better be safe than sorry."

After Henny had left, Maggie gave a gentle tap on Nat's door before opening it. But she had to wait to get his full attention for quite a few minutes while she listened to his one-sided telephone conversation. Finally, he replaced the instrument on its cradle, finished scribbling on a yellow pad, and looked up.

"Who was that?" she asked.

"Alice with her list." He handed it over to her. "Hopefully we'll be able to weed some of the names out."

"I see what you mean. She's even included all the trades people as well as the mailman. But these could be interesting." She walked around Nat's desk, and laying the list in front of him, she pointed. "These six."

"Yes," Nat said. "Alice says they were joint partners in leasing that art studio on Quebec Street that she mentioned the other day. Jonathan plus four men and two women."

Maggie stared at the names. "I don't recognize any of them, do you?"

"No. But I know absolutely nothing about art. Alice said that the seven of them—now, of course, six—split the cost of the studio and hiring the models when they were doing figure modelling—whatever that is. She also said that some were professional models but most were just people they knew. Can you believe this?" Nat continued. "They apparently go out onto the street and if they see someone with an interesting face or other attributes, they ask them to sit for them. Alice said that most times people agree."

"Perhaps that's how he met the young woman and her little girl."

"Quite possibly."

"So where is this studio?"

"It's the old Dunhill's Bakery on Quebec Street. According to Alice, they've been working there for years—sharing ideas, critiquing each other's work." He pointed to the names farther down the list. "These are business associates and these are personal friends."

"Quite a lot, though," Maggie said thoughtfully.

"So how did you get on with Sheldon's aunt?"

By the time she got through describing her visit to the eccentric Harriet, she had Nat laughing so hard that he was wiping tears from his face. "Galiano, eh?"

"It may be worth a visit."

"We'll give him another couple of days."

"I wonder if the police have finished with Sheldon's house and studio," Maggie said, picking up the list.

"You're not thinking of us going over there, I hope?"

Maggie smiled and turned to go out the door. "Wouldn't hurt. Perhaps he *has* turned up."

"You mean this evening?"

"Of course."

THE HOUSE ON William Street looked just the same as it had on their previous visit—no lights, everything shuttered and still. Nat gave a few thumps on the back door, but there was no answer, and when he tried the handle, he realized that it was now locked. Turning away from the house, they walked toward the studio. The rope the police must have fastened across the front of the building now flapped in the slight breeze that had sprung up. A large padlock was now fastened to the wrought-iron hasp.

They moved together to the large side window to peer in. There was enough daylight to see that the dais was gone and the easels had been pushed back against the walls.

"I suppose the police put the padlock on," Maggie observed. "But who locked the house up?" She walked back toward the house with Nat following close behind.

"The lock's probably a push-button from the inside. All the cops had to do was push the knob in and then pull the door shut." He stopped speaking and watched Maggie peering into several broken flowerpots that were close to the backdoor. "What are you doing?"

"Ah! Here it is," she said suddenly. She had just turned over the large flat stone on which one of the pots had been sitting. She brandished a brass key. "Our way in."

"Whoa, Maggie. That's trespassing."

"Never stopped you before." A few moments and the door was open. "Just a quick look round," she promised. "You can wait outside if you like."

"I wish you wouldn't, Maggie . . ." But she had vanished inside and he had no alternative but to follow.

She walked straight through the mudroom and kitchen and into the dining room. "I had a hunch," she said over her shoulder.

"What about?"

"There." She pointed to the bare dining room table.

"What about it?" Nat asked, puzzled.

"Everything's been cleaned and put away. And don't tell me the police were kind enough to do that."

"The half-eaten meal, the overturned chair. You're right."

"Let's have a quick look over the rest of the house." And not waiting for her partner-in-crime, she walked through the hall and ran up the stairs.

"Maggie, we must get out of here," Nat insisted as he reluctantly followed. "It will only take one of Sheldon's neighbours to spot our car and call the cops. We'll be in a mess of trouble."

"Just a quick look into Sheldon's bedroom. I'd guess he uses a front one. Well, I was right," she said a few minutes later. "Look." She indicated the open closet doors and the bare hangers. "He's been back, grabbed some clothes and gone."

"Galiano!"

"My thought exactly," Maggie said. "When do we go?"

"Not until we pay a visit to Jonathan's old art buddies."

"I wonder if they still work there?" Maggie began walking back down the stairs. "I'll call Alice first thing tomorrow."

"YES, AS FAR as I know," Alice answered in response to Maggie's enquiry on Wednesday morning, the next day. "Some of them work there every day, but they all make a point of working there on Thursdays so they can exchange ideas." She laughed. "It has to be something very serious for any of them to miss. Would you like me to call Saul Wingate and find out? He was Jonathan's closest friend."

"I'd really appreciate it if you would do that. And would you ask him if he'd mind us coming to ask a few questions tomorrow morning? Tell him we will be as brief as possible."

CHAPTER THIRTEEN

Saul Wingate, a man of medium build with touches of grey in his dark-brown hair, met them in the coffee shop next to the bakery. "Alice said you want to ask a few questions about my dear, dear friend Jonathan." He spoke over his shoulder as he led the way to the defunct bakery next door. Although the faded bakery sign still hung above the shop, the windows were covered with yellowing newspapers taped to the inside of the glass.

As he unlocked the door, he explained, "We each have a key so we can use the place whenever we want. Guys and gals," he called out as he threw open the door, "we've got visitors!"

There was little in the room they entered to suggest it had ever been a bakery. The front counter and shelves were long gone and the artists had even torn out the wall that had separated the shop at the front from the bakery part of the establishment. The place was now a hodgepodge of potting wheels and sturdy wooden tables and work benches, racks and racks of drying pots, rows of metal garbage cans labelled with names like "tenmoku" and "matte crystalline yellow brown," and big tubs labelled "ball clay" and "feldspar" and "tin oxide." Through a window in the rear wall, Maggie could see an open-sided shed where a monster kiln had been set up.

"This is Nat Southby and his assistant, Maggie Spencer," Saul

Wingate announced. "They're looking into Jonathan's death and would like to ask us a few questions."

Several of the artists were working at the wheels, while others were hand building at the tables and benches. Although one or two of them gave a small wave to acknowledge their visitors' presence, there was wariness etched on their faces. Two men who were conferring in front of a large, unfinished abstract sculpture merely looked annoyed at being interrupted and went back to their conversation.

"Thanks for seeing us," Nat said, advancing into the room. "We promise we won't take up too much of your time, but in order to find Jonathan's murderer we need to know more of his background. And I understand you all worked closely with him."

The only response was the continuing whirr of the potting wheels and the low hum of conversation.

"Coffee?" Saul asked. Maggie and Nat shook their heads.

A tall, slim blonde wearing a clay-smudged smock stood back from the enormous lop-sided urn she was hand building. She surveyed it for several moments and then drawled, "If he *was* murdered, why aren't the police asking the questions?"

"Perhaps they don't know about us, Tricia darling," a stocky woman sitting at one of the potter's wheels said sarcastically. "Adele's the name," she added as she threw a fresh lump of reddish-brown clay onto her wheel.

"I don't know why you're trying to prove his death was murder, anyhow. I still think he committed suicide." Tricia reached inside the urn and began pushing outward while enthusiastically smacking the outside of the urn with a flat wooden paddle.

"Oh, come off it," a dark-complexioned man occupying a wheel across the room chimed in. "You'd want to make darned sure it wasn't murder if you had a husband who died under suspicious circumstances. And you'd want to find the bastard who did it."

Adele placed her foot on the flywheel to slow her wheel to a stop. "There was certainly no reason for dear Jonathan to . . . kill . . . kill himself," she said tremulously.

"For God's sake, grow up, Adele. We all know how you felt about him."

Adele's face flushed bright red.

Nat thought it was time to intervene. "Did any of you notice any significant changes in Jonathan? Was he worried? Tense . . . ?"

"He was a dear, dear man." The speaker, a man in his early sixties who had been conferring with a younger man over the unfinished sculpture, placed his coffee cup down on the workbench, crossed the room, and extended his hand toward Nat. "I'm Chris, by the way, Chris Barfield. Why anyone would murder him is totally beyond me." Taking a briar pipe and a can of tobacco out of his pocket, he slowly filled the bowl and tamped it down before lighting it. "But to answer your question, Mr. Southby, I did find him rather distracted, but when I asked, he said it was nothing."

"I didn't know him very well." The speaker was the other man who had been conferring over the unfinished sculpture. He was much younger than the others in the room. "But he gave me a lot of help."

"And you are . . . ?" Nat asked.

"Ian Buckle." He looked belligerently around at the others. "He even sold a couple of my horses in his gallery."

Maggie, hoping that the horses had been ceramic and not the real thing, opened her handbag and took out the photographs. "I have some snaps here and we wondered if you could identify the woman and child in them." She took the photos to each of the artists and waited until they looked them over before asking, "Did Jonathan bring them here to sit for you?"

There was a general shaking of heads, then Saul said slowly, "They do look a tad familiar, but I can't think why."

"I know why," Ian Buckle said suddenly. "Jonathan's figurines. You know, the little girl with the dog and a girl holding her hat in the wind." And then he repeated, "They're Jonathan's figurines."

Adele rose from her wheel and came to look at the snapshots again. "I thought they were figments of Jonathan's vivid imagination, but I think you're right."

"Do any of you know Sheldon White?" Nat asked.

Tricia looked up. "That little creep!"

"Did you know there was a young man found murdered in his studio a few days ago?"

There were nods of assent and then Tricia asked, "Have the police made an identification?"

"Last I heard they were still making enquiries. But Alice thinks she might have seen him in the gallery a couple of times."

"Could be," Saul said. "Jonathan was always being approached by young artists wanting him to exhibit their work. So what has Sheldon to say about the murdered man?"

"Sheldon's gone missing," Maggie answered.

"Typical. Never could see why Jonathan kept him on."

Nat nodded to Maggie then said, "We'll be on our way. I've left a few of our business cards on the table here in case any of you think of something that might help."

Saul walked them out to their car. "Any chance you can get a picture of the man who was murdered? If Alice thinks she's seen him before, there's a good chance that one of us has, too."

"I'll call the cop in charge of the case and see if he's still unidentified," Nat answered. "I'll let you know."

"Here's my address and phone number," Saul said as he handed over a card. "Give my best to Alice and tell her I'll be in to see her soon."

CHAPTER FOURTEEN

"What time is that ferry supposed to leave Tsawwassen?" Nat asked, glancing at his watch.

"Ten o'clock," Maggie said for the fourth time.

"Hope we make it."

"You were the one who wouldn't get up," Maggie chided.

"But it's Saturday," he protested. "You know I like to lie in on Saturdays."

"And if you had read the map properly," Maggie continued, ignoring Nat's protests, "we wouldn't have driven into Ladner and had to find our way back to Tsawwassen. Do sit still, Oscar," she said to the excited dog doing his best to bestow Nat with wet kisses.

"But you're supposed to be the navigator!" Nat retorted, pushing Oscar away. "It's bad enough driving through this bloody rain without having to read a map while I'm doing it."

Maggie thought it prudent not to answer. "Anyway," she said, "according to the sign we just passed, we should be there in ten minutes." It had been many years since Nat had been to Galiano Island and it was a first for Maggie. "I've discovered that there is a ferry boat called the *Motor Princess* that links the islands," she continued, "and it takes just over an hour to get there."

"Anything else I need to know?" Nat asked.

"Well, there is a new causeway where the boats dock."

"Where did you drag up all this information?"

"I telephoned the ferry company yesterday. Anyway, we're here."

"Seems an awful lot of cars."

"I think most of them are going to Vancouver Island. Yes, I'm right," Maggie added excitedly. "See, over there!"

"What?"

"That sign saying Gulf Islands."

THEY WERE HALFWAY to Galiano Island when the rain began petering out and a light wind ruffled the small whitecaps that now glinted in the sun. Maggie, leaning over the ferry's rail, watched fascinated as masses of jellyfish, their transparent bodies pulsing in and out, swam in the clear depths. Then lifting her gaze, she was astounded to see a pod of whales thrusting their huge bodies out of the blue-green sea. When she realized that there were also several porpoises accompanying their boat, she just had to run inside to get Nat, who had insisted on staying in the warmth of the passenger lounge. Of course, these marvellous animals had disappeared by the time he had dragged himself outside, but he did stay with her to watch the approach to the island. She was almost sorry when the announcement came that they would be docking in Montague Harbour in ten minutes.

"Did you know the island is named after the Spanish explorer Dionisio Galiano?" she asked as they went below to climb into Nat's car.

"Not more information," Nat groaned.

"And he sailed these seas in 1792," she continued relentlessly.

"You are beginning to sound like a guide book. Hang on, we've docked."

HARRIET MONTROSE HAD been right. There was a small general store quite close to the ferry terminal.

"Percy White's place?" The girl behind the counter repeated Maggie's question. "I'm not sure where it is. Half a tic and I'll ask my dad."

Dad appeared, wiping his hands on a grimy towel. "Chrissie says you want White's place. Do you know the island?"

"No. It's my first time here."

Pulling a piece of wrapping paper from an overhead roll, he fumbled in his pocket for a stub of pencil. "We're right here, see? Just follow Burrill," he drew a line on the paper, "till it meets Bluff." He peered over the counter to look at Maggie's shoes. "You can walk to it from here."

"Does the house have a number?"

Dad laughed. "Only a few places up that way. You'll know it when you see it."

"I hope you're right," Maggie muttered, walking back to the car where Nat was waiting.

On seeing the muddy, unpaved road ahead of them, they decided to risk taking the car. "Bound to be someplace to turn," Nat rationalized as he bumped over the ruts. "Keep a lookout for the place."

They almost missed the sign saying WHITE'S PLACE, the words roughly painted on a scrap of wood that had been nailed to a gnarled maple tree. They pulled off the road and parked next to a rusty truck that, by the look of it, would never have its deflated tires on a road again. A path led them between a stand of smallish cedars and a log-strewn wasteland. The reason for all the cut logs became evident when they came upon a half-built log cabin.

"It's been a long time since any work's been done on that," Maggie observed, pointing to the pile of logs beside the cabin that were now covered in long grass and blackberry vines.

Nat nodded. "But there's smoke coming out of the chimney of that cottage beyond it." The cottage he referred to was tucked away at the back of the property. "I guess he's home." But although they knocked on the door and peered through the windows, it appeared empty.

"I wonder where he's got to?"

"Maybe he saw us coming and he's hiding," Maggie suggested.

"We'll just have to outwait him then."

"I'm hungry." Maggie glanced at her watch. "Let's go get the hamper I packed this morning."

"Great idea. And I know the perfect place for a picnic."

"Are we taking the car?"

"No. If I've got my bearings right, it can't be far from here. We can walk." Fifteen minutes later, with a happy Oscar running ahead, they emerged onto the bluff that overlooked Active Passage.

"Wow! I can understand you remembering this," Maggie gasped. "It's wonderful. And look, there are two ships passing each other."

"And if I remember rightly, there should be a covered picnic table somewhere around here. Yes. I'm right. Up under that tree, see it?" Taking hold of Maggie's hand, he led her up the gentle slope and placed the basket onto the table. "Where's Oscar gone?" he asked.

"He was with us a few seconds ago." Maggie turned to look down the grassy hill. "There he is. Oscar!" she yelled. "Oscar. Come back here."

But the dog, who was quite sure that everybody loved him, barked joyfully as he ran toward a man who had quickly risen from a huge boulder. Facing the animal rushing toward him, he flapped his arms to shoo him away.

"Call your dog off!" they heard him yell. Then he stopped abruptly. "Go away," he screamed. But now he was screaming at Maggie and Nat and not at the dog.

Maggie grabbed Nat's arm. "Nat! That's Sheldon."

"Sheldon? Are you sure?"

"Of course it's him," Maggie insisted. "Come on, before he gets away." But Sheldon was trying to do just that, running down the slope toward the water with Oscar hard on his heels.

"He can't get far," Nat yelled as he tried to keep up with Maggie, who was running as fast as she could to cut Sheldon off. "That slope's far too steep for him to get down to the water."

"Sheldon!" Maggie yelled again. "Wait! We just want to talk to you."

"Go away," Sheldon yelled back. "Leave me alone." He seemed to suddenly realize that he couldn't go any farther and he turned to face them like an animal at bay. Oscar, having run his quarry down, barked happily, bouncing up and down in front of the man.

"You might as well give up," Nat panted as he arrived to stand beside Maggie.

"How . . . how did you find me?" Sheldon stammered as he backed away from them. "Are the police with you?"

"No. We're on our own."

"But how did you find me?" he repeated. He stopped backing away but remained poised for instant flight.

"Your aunt." Maggie waited until she was close enough to Sheldon, then placed her hand on his arm. "It's okay. Let's take a walk back to the picnic table and you can tell us what happened."

"It was terrible." Sheldon said when at last he sank down onto the bench and buried his face in his hands. "I didn't know what to do."

"Did you know the killer?" Nat asked.

The man lifted a tear-streaked face from his hands. "No. I heard the scream."

"Then what happened?" Maggie asked gently. "Why don't you start from the beginning?"

"I was sitting down to a late supper and was looking through one of my art books while I ate. I give drawing lessons on Thursday evenings," he explained. "I heard a noise in the backyard and thought it must be one of my students turning up early, but I didn't go out to see as I'd left the studio door open for them." He shuddered. "If I'd gone out there, Alex might still be alive . . ." And he began to cry.

"Or both of you could be dead," Nat said. "Carry on."

"It was then I heard the terrible scream. I jumped out of my chair, and I'm ashamed to say it, but I panicked."

"You hid in the house," Maggie said.

He nodded. "In the hall closet. I waited until I thought the coast was clear before I ventured out into the backyard. And then . . . and then . . . I crept up to the studio and saw what had been done to Alex. He was lying on the couch . . . There was blood everywhere."

"You didn't touch anything?" Nat asked.

"No. I didn't even go into the studio. All I could think of was to escape before the maniac came back."

"What about your students?" Maggie asked.

"I only have four on Thursdays and I called and cancelled them."

"Why didn't you call the police?"

"I couldn't."

"For God's sake, Sheldon," Nat shouted. "You should have called them."

"They would have thought I'd killed Alex."

"Did you have any reason to kill him?" Maggie asked.

"No. But that's how the police think. He was in my studio and he was dead."

"And so you ran." Nat couldn't keep the contempt from his voice.

"I was scared the killer would come after me."

"Is there any reason why he would?"

Sheldon didn't answer for a while, and then he said, "Jonathan Standish was killed, wasn't he?"

"You think the two murders are related?" Nat asked.

"We both worked in the art business—even in the same gallery. Don't you think that is just too much of a coincidence?"

Maggie glanced at her watch and stood up. "We want you to come back with us, Sheldon. Let's go back to the cabin and get your things, okay?"

"But . . . but the cops will want to know why I ran. They'll think I killed Alex. I can't go back."

"Yes, you can," Nat said firmly. "We'll be right with you while you explain. When's the next ferry, Maggie?"

"Three-thirty. Let's eat these sandwiches and then go and help Sheldon pack."

"There's no need for you to help me pack. I'll meet you at the dock."

"No. We're staying together. Have a chicken sandwich."

"WILL YOU DROP me off at my house?" a subdued Sheldon White asked later that afternoon as they rolled off the ferry at the Twassassen dock.

"We're taking you back to our office," Nat answered. "But first I'm heading over to that telephone to make a call."

"Not the police!" Sheldon said, panic-stricken.

"No. A friend of ours. He'll know what you should do."

SERGEANT GEORGE SAWASKY had been waiting for them outside the agency. He followed the trio up the stairs and into the main office.

"This is Sheldon White," Maggie said, making the introductions. "We want you to listen to his story."

A half hour later George, who had been taking copious notes, leaned back in Nat's office chair. "And you're positive you don't know why this Alex Donitz was killed?"

"No. He was an artist, a friend. I think the killer thought he was me."

"Why? Have you been threatened in any way?"

Sheldon paused before he answered. "The house and studio have both been broken into."

"You didn't tell us that," Nat said.

"Anything taken?" George said, waving at Nat to be quiet.

"No," Sheldon said. "They just made a terrible mess. Canvases thrown on the floor and paint spilled all over the studio. The house was ransacked, too—closets emptied, pictures taken off the walls. And then there were the phone calls."

"Let's take the phone calls first," George said. "Then we'll deal with the ransacking ..."

"The first one came just after Mr. Standish died. I was in the gallery at the time and this voice asked if I knew what Jonathan had done with the three Krieghoffs. I didn't know what he was talking about, as we only sell local artists' work."

"What's a Krieghoff?" George asked, puzzled.

"He was a famous Canadian painter of the last century," Maggie answered.

"How do you know that?" Nat asked, surprised.

"I quite admire his work—especially his winter scenes," she answered.

"I know very little about art," George said before turning back to White and asking, "Were there other calls?"

"One more, but the person seemed to think I knew where these pictures were. He wouldn't listen when I repeated I didn't know what he was talking about."

"And you're sure you didn't recognize the voice?"

"No. It was kinda gruff." He thought for a moment. "It could've even been a woman ... but deep, if you know what I mean."

"Did you mention these phone calls to Mrs. Standish?"

"Yes." He hesitated for a fraction of a second before he added, "And she was as mystified as I was."

"Do you know if she received any of these phone calls?"

"She didn't mention any to me."

"Go on."

"And then . . . poor Alex was killed. I'm afraid I panicked." He looked from face to face. "So now what happens? Can I go home?"

"That will be up to the detective running this case. We're going down to the police station first." George looked very sternly at Sheldon. "You running away like that hasn't helped this case one bit."

"But I was so scared . . ."

"First things first," George answered. "Get your coat on and we'll get you down to the station so you can give a written statement and then, as I said, it will be up to Sergeant Angelus."

"Did you know that the dead man's name was Alex Donitz?" Maggie asked George.

"We only found that out a few days ago," he answered. "His girlfriend got worried when he didn't turn up for their date and didn't answer his phone." George stood and buttoned up his raincoat. "She eventually let herself into his apartment and could see he hadn't been there for days. We still haven't located any relatives." He turned to Sheldon. "Do you know if he had any relatives?"

"He told me he had come here from Poland on his own and was hoping his brother would join him in a few months. He seemed very serious about his girlfriend, Gloria."

"That's the young lady we spoke to, Gloria Wentworth. She's very cut up about his death. What I can't understand," George continued, "is what he was doing in your studio that night . . ."

"He was part of my Thursday night drawing class." Sheldon looked a bit sheepish. "And . . . well, I rented him space there as well."

"What do you mean—you rented him space there?" George asked.

"There are a lot of artists who can't afford a studio of their own—so I sort of rent space to them. Of course, I charge extra for the use of easels and supplies . . ."

"These artists can come and go as they please?"

Sheldon nodded. "They pay by the hour and sign in and out. You know, the honour system."

"So how many of these artists use your facilities?" Maggie asked.

"I have four regulars—three, now—and I give lessons."

"Nice extra income on top of your job at the gallery," Nat stated.

Sheldon didn't react to the sarcasm in Nat's voice. "Yes. It works out very nicely."

NAT AND MAGGIE waited in silence until they heard the two men's footsteps descending the old wooden stairs and then the outer door banging shut.

"Now what? I don't know about you, but I think that guy's story is just too pat. There's something more going on here." Nat watched Maggie as she gathered her handbag and then reached for the coat she had slung on the back of her chair.

"I don't know about you," she answered, "but I'm going to find the biggest steak and all the trimmings, PDQ. That chicken sandwich was hours ago."

"Great idea. Let's go."

EVEN THOUGH NAT and Maggie each consumed a huge steak that night, the next morning Maggie still managed to get through Nat's version of a full English breakfast. Replete and sitting back in her chair clutching her second cup of coffee, she looked fondly at her partner in love and business.

"I think I'll keep you, Nat Southby," she said.

"You'd have an awful job to get rid of me now." Oscar, his head resting in Nat's lap, gave a contented sigh. "Even your dog likes me."

"Do you think they let Sheldon go home last night?" she asked.

"Well, it was his studio and he did run away. The cops may think they've got a case against him."

"I don't think even slimy Sheldon would have the nerve to commit a murder like that."

"That won't stop the cops trying to pin it on him."

"Are you going to call Saul Wingate?" she asked.

"What about?"

"He asked you to call if you found out the dead man's name, remember?"

"I think I'd rather confront him with it. See how he reacts."

"How's your work schedule for the week?" Maggie asked. "I really think we should pay a visit to Jonathan Standish's son as soon as possible."

"I'm tied up on the Whittaker file for at least another couple of days," he said, "but what's the hurry? Anyhow, I think our first priority is to bring Alice up to date on Sheldon."

Maggie thought for a moment. "Okay, why don't you take a little time out on the Whittaker file and drop in on Alice and bring her up to date and I'll take a run out to Mission and see her stepson."

"You know I don't like you tearing off to places like that on your own. You always seem to run into trouble."

"Oh, Nat, don't be such a worrywart. What trouble could I possible get into going to see a man of the cloth? I'll take Henny with me. She's a great watchdog." She placed her coffee cup in the sink. "And speaking of dogs, let's go and give Oscar a run in the park."

CHAPTER FIFTEEN

Dogwoods, purple lilacs, and yellow laburnum competed with the spring bulbs to greet the beautiful day, and Maggie, driving to work, breathed in the intoxicating scent. She decided that she had chosen the right time for her proposed trip to Mission—she had even packed a picnic basket and brought Oscar along.

"Why you bring that dog in?" Henny asked suspiciously. "You never bring him into office."

"We are going to Mission—and guess what? You are going, too."

"Me? Oh, no, Mrs. Maggie. I am far too busy. I have reports to type and filing and Mr. Nat's coffee to make . . ."

"You can forget all that, Henny. This is business. You know, detective business."

"Ah, detective business!" Henny beamed. She considered herself a better detective than her bosses, anyway. "That's different. When we leave?"

"Give Nat his coffee and then we're off."

BECAUSE OF A stop for their picnic lunch, a couple of "behind-a-bush" stops, and then getting lost a couple of times, it was early afternoon before they found themselves in the vicinity of Aaron

Standish's home. It was actually closer to a small settlement called Deroche than the town of Mission, and Maggie realized that Alice hadn't exaggerated when she said it was very rural.

"He is pastor in church?" Henny asked as they rattled down the dirt road that the owner of the one gas station in Deroche had assured them would lead to the Standish's home. "I do not see how a church would be in a place like this."

"I don't think it's a regular kind of church," Maggie answered as her little car bounced into yet another pothole. "Looks like a turnoff coming up. Let's pray it's Chapel Lane."

Henny laughed. "You are being funny, ja?"

Actually the sign pointing down the road read, HIS HOLINESS GOSPEL CHURCH IN THE WOODS. SEEK AND YE WILL FIND. PASTOR AARON STANDISH.

"Where are woods?" Henny asked. "Just all that yellow broom stuff—and cows!"

"Well, at least cows mean there's a farmhouse close by, and we can always ask where the church is."

There were a few trees in the distance, and as they drove closer, the trees materialized into a stand of poplars and a couple of weeping willows drooping over a small house. Next to it stood a weather-beaten church. A large placard in front of the house stated that it was HIS HOLINESS GOSPEL CHURCH and the scripture for the week was "The sun shall be turned to darkness and the moon to blood, Acts 2:20."

As soon as Maggie pulled into the gravel driveway and opened her door, Oscar, who had decided that he'd been cooped up long enough, gave a joyful bark. Dragging his leash behind him, he bounded out of the car and headed straight for two little girls playing in the yard.

"Oscar, come right back here," Maggie yelled. "It's okay, he won't hurt you," she assured the children who were looking fearfully at the dog. Oscar, who thought everyone loved him, jumped up to lick their faces. Maggie grabbed hold of the dog by the collar and knelt down in front of the girls. "He's just pleased to see you. Behave yourself, Oscar, and let the girls give you a pat."

The door of the cottage opened and a young woman came rushing out. "Are you okay? I thought I heard a dog barking." She stopped short when she saw Maggie and Henny. "If it's anything to do with the church," she said warily, "Aaron's Healing Touch service doesn't start for another half hour." Her auburn hair was scraped back from her face and tied with a shoelace, and she was wearing a shapeless dress that must have come from the same thrift shop as her daughters' dresses. She looked thoroughly worn out.

"Mrs. Irma Standish?" Maggie asked.

The woman nodded warily.

"I'm Maggie Spencer." Maggie handed over one of her cards. "We wanted to talk to you and your husband about his father, Jonathan Standish."

Irma Standish glanced at the card. "You're investigators! Why would you want to talk about someone who committed suicide?"

"But he didn't," Maggie answered. "We are certain he was murdered."

"Murdered!" Then a sly smile played on her lips. "Was it that wife of his? Maybe you'd better come in," she added, turning to Maggie and Henny. The two little girls clung to their mother's skirt as she led the way inside.

"I'll put the dog in the car," Henny said, taking the leash from Maggie.

To Maggie's surprise the kitchen was warm and inviting. A pine table with six matching chairs was centred on an oval braided rug, there was a rocking chair covered in the same red check as the curtains next to a wood-burning cook stove, and the air was filled with the heavenly scent of fresh scones.

"Have a seat."

"What a lovely, cosy room," Maggie exclaimed as she pulled out a chair at the table.

"Courtesy of my parents." Irma Standish walked over to the sink and put the kettle under the faucet. "They may not be happy with my situation, but at least they care. Which is more than I can say about Aaron's family."

"Do your parents live close by?"

"Not now. They moved to White Rock a couple of years back." While she was talking, she had uncovered a plate of hot scones and taken down tea plates from the pine dresser. She placed the scones, butter, and homemade strawberry jam on the table.

"They smell very good," Henny said as she entered the kitchen. "Your girls are lucky to have a mama who cooks. What are their names?"

"This one is Pansy and the little one's called Iris."

Maggie waited until the children had been given their food and a glass of milk and had gone outside before she asked, "Does Aaron have a large congregation?"

Irma looked at her inquiringly.

"I just wondered, as the church seems very remote."

"No. That's why he has to work part-time at Van Dyke's dairy farm." She glanced at an ornate cuckoo clock on the wall. "He should be home soon. If Aaron's father was murdered," she continued, "why haven't the police contacted us? After all, Aaron is Jonathan's only child."

"I think the police hate to admit that they made a mistake," Maggie answered, "especially as it was our agency that proved it was murder and not suicide."

"Daddy, daddy," they heard one of the children call out. "There's a lady with a doggy."

Irma jumped out of her chair and rushed to open the door. "Honey, we have visitors," she called out nervously.

Aaron, topping six feet, husky, brown-haired, tanned, and smelling more like a farmer than a preacher, walked into the kitchen, followed by his daughters. He stared enquiringly at the two women sitting at the table. "And you are . . . ?"

"They're private detectives," Irma burst out. "It's about your father."

"I'm Margaret Spencer and this is my assistant, Henny Vandermeer," Maggie said as she stood up.

"Private detectives. But you're . . . you're *women* . . ."

"Yes, Mr. Standish. I'm a woman and a very good detective, too. My partner, Nat Southby, and I are investigating the death of your father."

"Investigating? But he committed the ultimate sin of taking his own life. I pray for his soul every day."

"No, Mr. Standish, he was murdered. And your stepmother has engaged our agency to look into his death."

"Murdered! But why haven't the police or that woman contacted me directly?"

"You don't get on with your stepmother?"

"Stepmother," he replied scathingly. "She's a conniving Jezebel. The Bible warns the unsuspecting of such women. Did she kill him?"

"I doubt it," Maggie answered. "Why do you dislike her so much?"

"My mother was hardly cold in her grave when he married her."

"When did your mother die?"

"Nine months before he married *that* woman."

"Nine months!" Henny exclaimed.

"And what about my children? His grandchildren?"

"But those little girls weren't born then," Henny said.

"That woman is set for life and living in a luxury apartment," he carried on, taking no notice of Henny's remark, "and . . . and look at us." He stopped suddenly. "But," he added piously, "we bow to the Lord's will."

Maggie opened her handbag and produced the photograph of the woman and child. She handed it to Pastor Aaron. "Do you know these people?"

"No. Should I? Who are they?"

"We don't know. But the woman leaves flowers on your father's grave."

"Another one of his bits on the side! There were plenty of them."

"Aaron," his wife admonished. "How can you say that?" Taking the photo from him, she peered intently at it and then, taking a pair of glasses out of her apron pocket, looked again.

"Why do you think my mother left him so often?"

"You've never mentioned that she had left him, Aaron," Irma replied, handing the photo back to Maggie.

"What are bits on the side, mommy?" Pansy asked.

Irma looked at the girls and said quickly, "Why don't you two go outside or go up to your room and play for a while."

"Don't want to," Iris said stubbornly.

"Do as your mother says," Aaron yelled at the children.

"Aaron, please." Irma shot a look at her husband that spoke volumes and then took each child firmly by the hand and marched them up the stairs.

Maggie waited for a few seconds before she turned back to Aaron. "Care to elaborate on what you were saying?"

"Forget I said anything. It has nothing to do with his death."

"On the contrary," Maggie answered. "It may have everything to do with his murder."

"If you must know," he answered tersely, "my father was a womanizer—a disgraceful womanizer. He deserved everything that happened to him." Red in the face and shaking with emotion, he walked to the foot of the stairs, then turned back to face Maggie and Henny. He lifted his eyes to the ceiling. "Lord, I ask you to forgive me." After another moment, in which his mouth worked in words of silent prayer, he lowered his eyes to gaze at the two women again. "Now I have to prepare myself for His work. Let yourself out."

"I'll leave my card on the table," Maggie said. "It has my telephone number on it. Call if you think of anything you'd like to tell me."

NAT FINISHED HIS Monday morning meeting with one of his old clients—James Whittaker and Associates—had a quick lunch with George then began reviewing a report regarding Jonathan Standish's typewriter. The attached note read:

> Sorry for the delay in getting this to you but have been swamped.
> Best regards, Barry.

Barry, short for Lionel Barrett, was a forensic wizard Nat had worked with in the old days. He reached for the telephone.

"Hi, Alice. It's Nat Southby. Would it be convenient if I came round to see you. Say, in about an hour? . . . Great."

ALICE ANSWERED THE door and led him straight through the living room and onto the balcony that overlooked English Bay. "It's so beautiful today," she said, indicating the chair next to Jane's, "that we decided to have tea out here."

"I almost called the gallery," Nat said as he sat down, "then I remembered you are closed on Mondays."

"Good thing, too," Jane said brusquely, "considering that Sheldon creature went off to God-knows-where. Have you found him?"

"As a matter of fact, yes. Maggie and I located him on Galiano."

"Has he been charged with murdering that young man?" Alice asked. "Though I can't really see him murdering anyone—especially by cutting someone's throat." She shuddered and hastily picked up her teacup and took a hard swallow.

"Too much of a wimp, if you ask me," Jane said. "Want some tea?"

Nat declined. He was not a tea lover. "The police kept him in jail over the weekend. I heard they released him this morning." He paused for a moment to take in the fantastic view before speaking again. "Was Jonathan the only person to use the typewriter in the office?"

"The typewriter?" Alice asked.

"For God's sake, Alice!" Jane cut in. "The one the suicide note was written on."

"I'd forgotten . . . you took it away, didn't you? Jonathan didn't like anyone else to use it."

"But did they?" Nat persisted.

"I have my own portable. Perhaps Sheldon might have used it at some time . . . I really don't know. Why?"

"I got a friend down at the station to take a look at it," Nat explained. "For starters, the suicide note was definitely written on it, and there are only one set of prints on the keys. Jonathan's."

"But that means that Jonathan must have written the note . . . so he did take his own life."

"Not necessarily. The note could have been written before he was murdered and the prints wiped off. Then when your husband used the typewriter again, his were the only prints."

"But the typewriter was in the office all the time."

"Jonathan's murder must have been premeditated," Jane said firmly. "And whoever did it got into the gallery when it was closed."

Nat asked, "Has there ever been any sign of a break-in?"

Alice shook her head. "We would have noticed if there had been. And the alarm would have sounded."

"Then the killer got a key from somewhere and knew how to switch off the alarm. How many keys are there and who has them?"

"Jonathan's, Sheldon's, mine, of course, and a spare," Alice said. "That's four."

"Can you account for all four of them right this minute?"

"Well, I gave Jonathan's key to Jane, mine is on my keychain in my handbag, and I guess Sheldon still has his."

"And where is the fourth?" Nat prodded.

She looked flustered before answering. "At the gallery. Jonathan kept it in his desk in the office. Oh dear, suppose someone's taken it?"

"It seems quite likely," Nat answered. "And how many people know how to switch off the alarm system?"

"Well, I do, and Sheldon, of course. And Jonathan . . . And we've had a number of assistants over the years. Some of them would have known where the switch is located . . ."

Nat started to push himself out of the chair but suddenly sat down again. "Did Jonathan ever talk to you about his first wife? What did she die of?"

"Catherine? Jonathan told me it was lung cancer. Apparently she was a very heavy smoker . . . and I understand it was not a happy marriage."

"Did he say why?"

She looked pensive. "Jonathan was a very attractive man . . . but he was a struggling artist for much of his early career. She couldn't come to terms with his temperament and the lack of money coming in, and she nagged him constantly about getting a regular job like all her friends' husbands."

"And the son?"

"Adored his mother and resented his father."

"Why?"

"Because they were always fighting. Jonathan was on the verge of leaving her several times but then she became so very ill. And finally she died."

"How long did you and Jonathan wait before you married?"

She hesitated. "It was less than a year." She gave a little laugh. "So you can imagine how Aaron felt when I came on the scene so soon after her death. He made it very clear that he disapproved of our relationship."

Nat sat quietly for a moment before asking, "Jonathan ever mention having an affair before his wife's death?"

Alice looked up suddenly. "No. What makes you ask?"

"Just a thought."

She shook her head slowly. "I'm sure he would have told me. But I suppose he could have. After all, he was so unhappy . . ."

Nat pushed himself out of the chair. "I'd better be on my way. Give me a buzz if you find that spare key, okay?"

"I won't sleep a wink until I find out what happened to it," Alice said as she followed him to the door.

"Then we'll go over to the studio right away," Jane said, coming up behind her sister. She turned to Nat. "We'll call you."

THE CALL CAME a half hour after Nat returned to the office. "It's gone!" Alice said. "But who would've taken it?"

"Do you remember the last time you saw it?"

"No. We haven't needed it—so I've no idea at all. Oh, dear."

"Who knew it was there?"

"Only us. Jonathan, Sheldon, and me."

Nat replaced the receiver and sat deep in thought before drawing his yellow pad toward him to make a list of everyone close to Jonathan at the time of his death. First of all, his fellow artists using the studio on Quebec Street—Saul Wingate,

Adele Rousseau, Tricia Forbes, Chris Barfield, Ian Buckle. The dead young man—Alex Donitz. Jonathan's assistant—Sheldon White and, as an afterthought, he included the unknown woman who left pink roses on Jonathan's grave. It was possible that any one of them might have known where Jonathan kept the spare key.

SAUL WINGATE WAS surprised to see Nat at his door. "Come in. What can I do for you?" He led Nat into his spacious penthouse suite. "Have you found that scoundrel, Sheldon?"

Nat was impressed. "Whew!" he said reverently as he walked over the thick silver-grey carpet to look out of the floor-to-ceiling windows. The fantastic view of the North Shore Mountains, dominated by the Lions, took his breath away.

"Never get tired of looking at 'em," Saul said, joining Nat at the window. "What can I get you? Scotch?"

"Make mine a G and T," a sultry voice said behind Nat. "So what brings you into this neck of our woods, Mr. Southby?"

The voice belonged to the blond artist from the shared studio on Quebec Street.

"I don't think we were properly introduced," she said, holding out a slim, tapered hand. "Tricia Forbes. Come," she added, taking Nat firmly by the hand and leading him to an off-white leather couch. "You can tell me all about your latest grisly murder while Saul fixes the drinks."

"Leave the poor man alone." Saul laughed and handed Nat his drink. "Wait a sec while I fix Tricia's gin and then you can bring us up to date."

Nat took an appreciative swig and waited until Saul was seated on an identical sofa on the other side of the square glass coffee table. "The murdered man's name was Alex Donitz," he said. "Ring any bells?"

"'Fraid not," Saul answered. "What about you, Trish?"

She shook her head. "Got a photo of this guy?"

Nat slipped his hand into the inside pocket of his jacket and pulled out a picture of Alex Donitz with his arm around his girlfriend.

"Who's the pretty girl?" Saul asked.

"His fiancée, Gloria Wentworth. It was taken just a few weeks before he was murdered."

"But why was he killed?" Tricia asked. "Mistaken identity?"

Nat nodded. "I think you're probably right there. Alex Donitz was from Poland and had only been in the country a short time. I think he was in the wrong place at the wrong time."

Saul took a sip of his drink and placed the glass on the table. "The studio where he was killed belongs to Sheldon, doesn't it?"

Nat nodded.

"But that would mean that the killer didn't know what Sheldon White looked like," Tricia cut in. "I'll bet it was a contract killing! Hey! This is quite exciting, isn't it?"

Nat, who had seen violent death more times than he wished, couldn't agree less, but he managed to hold his tongue and let the other two talk.

"Of course," Saul said slowly, "there is the possibility that Sheldon and this Alex were into something unsavory."

"But what?" Nat asked encouragingly.

"I don't know . . . something to do with art. Stealing paintings? Forgery? You're the detective."

"Did Jonathan ever mention paintings being stolen from the gallery?" Nat asked.

"Not in so many words, but the dear man was worried sick about something. And if I had been him, I wouldn't have trusted that slimy bastard Sheldon like he did."

"Do you know Sheldon well?"

"I've met him a few times at the gallery, but I don't actually know the man, if you get my meaning, only what Jonathan and Alice have told me."

"Do any of the others in your group know him?"

"Ian's often at the gallery." Seeing Nat's quizzical look, he went on to explain, "Jonathan was able to find a market for his type of work. But I really can't speak for the others."

"And now Sheldon's gone missing," Tricia mused. "Doesn't that make him guilty of something?"

"He's been found," Nat said bluntly. "My partner, Maggie, and I traced him to Galiano on Saturday."

"So what did he have to say for himself?" Saul asked. "Did he tell you why he ran?"

"He was scared out of his wits," Nat answered as he struggled to get up from the deep, soft sofa. "Seems it was a helluva shock to find someone murdered in his own backyard." He gave a final push and managed to stand upright. "You knew Jonathan's first wife, Catherine, didn't you?"

"Yes. Jonathan and I go quite a ways back," Saul answered, getting to his feet. "That woman was never happy." He mused for a moment. "How can I describe her . . . ? She was always looking back and comparing the 'good old days' to the present."

"What about Aaron?"

"The son? His mother spoilt him rotten. He became a pastor in one of those odd born-again churches, you know. But I can't see him living a religious life. In fact," he gave a wry laugh before continuing, "I would've thought he'd end up quite the opposite."

"Can you tell me why?"

"He was a bully and a tattle-tale at school. My twin sons were in the same grade and they hated him. And then we heard he'd become a minister—didn't add up."

"You have twin sons?"

"And very proud of them, too. One's a lawyer and the other's a geologist. Their mother and I split after they went off to university." He paused before adding, "But Beatrice and I are still great friends. Anything else I can help you with?"

"No. You've been a great help. Thanks for the drink. It's been a pleasure to meet you again," he said to Tricia.

"I'll walk you to the door," Saul said.

"No need," Nat replied, "I can see myself out. Oh, just one more thing, Saul . . . do you happen to have a key to the Standish gallery?"

"Key? No. Why would I have a key?"

"Alice can't find the spare that was in Jonathan's desk."

"Well, she didn't give it to me."

"Thanks again." But just as Nat put out his hand to open the door, he was stopped by the sound of a key turning in the lock. The door burst open to reveal a thirtysomething, curly-haired man valiantly struggling with the door key, a briefcase, and a couple of bottles of wine.

"My dear, let me help you." Saul rushed over to relieve the young man of the wine before turning to Nat. "Nat, let me introduce my roommate, Leslie Duncan."

"SO, AS WE expected," Maggie commented later that evening after she and Nat had brought each other up to date, "Saul is attracted to the same sex, and Tricia is willing to take on anyone at all! You'd better watch out."

"Nah. Neither of them are my type," he said. "I like 'em bossy." He laughed and pulled her into his arms.

"I'm not bossy," Maggie retaliated. "I just have to keep you in line, that's all." As she snuggled up to kiss him, she gave a contented sigh and thought how lucky she was.

CHAPTER SIXTEEN

At the office the following day, it didn't take long to get back to business.

"Any idea where we go from here?" Nat asked. Maggie and Henny were sitting in front of his desk with the typewritten reports spread out in front of them.

They sat in silence for a few moments before Henny asked, "Did the police let Sheldon White out of jail?"

"He was to be released yesterday," Nat answered.

"He has missing key." Henny looked smugly at her employers. "You go and see him."

Maggie laughed. "Henny's got a point. And while we're asking him about the key, we should try and have a good look in that studio of his." She gave a shudder. "At least it's been cleaned up."

"What about Gloria Wentworth?" Nat asked.

"Alex Donitz's fiancée? Do you want me to talk to her?"

"You might get more out of her than I would."

"Do we have any idea where she lives?"

"George mentioned that she works in the accounting department of the Bay."

"Great, that's a help." She quickly made a note on her pad. "Anything else we've missed?"

"Don't think so. Do you want to come with me to see Sheldon?"

"No. You go and I'll try and locate Gloria Wentworth. M-m-m," she mused, "I wonder if she still has a key to her boyfriend's apartment."

"Maggie," Nat said in a warning tone, "no trespassing."

"Wouldn't dream of it," she answered, springing up and heading for the door. "I'll see you later."

"Maggie!" But she had made a quick exit.

"I type up notes, Mr. Nat," Henny said hurriedly and quickly followed in Maggie's wake.

"Women!" Nat muttered under his breath as he reached for his telephone.

"IS IT IMPORTANT?" Gloria Wentworth asked when Maggie had located the girl and identified herself. "I'm not allowed to have personal calls."

"What about lunch then?"

The girl hesitated before answering. "We have a cafeteria here. But there isn't much I can tell you."

"What time?" Maggie persisted.

"Twelve-thirty. I'm wearing a blue twin-set and black skirt."

MAGGIE WAS ON the point of leaving for her appointment when George finally returned Nat's call.

"We're busy as hell," he complained, "so I hope you're not asking me to do anything like snooping for you."

"No, no. What's the situation with Sheldon White?"

"He was definitely let out yesterday with the usual warnings to keep himself available and not to leave town."

"Have you finished going over his studio and house?"

"You're not asking me to give out information, are you?"

"Wouldn't dream of it. Just wanted to make sure it was okay for us to go over there and ask him some questions, that's all."

"Nat, you know how Farthing loves you and Maggie, so please watch your step. Anyway, all I can tell you is that the fingerprint guys have finished going over the place."

"Did they find anything interesting?"

There was a pause before George answered reluctantly, "No, other than White's and the dead guy's fingerprints where one would expect to find them."

"What about the house?"

"White's prints and of course yours and Maggie's. So expect a routine call on them."

"Thanks, George. Now that wasn't too bad, was it?"

The answer was George slamming down the receiver.

"HOW LONG HAD you known Alex?" Maggie asked the very young and frightened girl across the table from her.

"I guess about six months. I liked him right away . . . he was so gentle and polite." She dabbed her eyes with a lace-edged handkerchief.

"How did the two of you get together?"

"One of the guys in our office threw a party to celebrate moving into his new apartment, and Alex was living next door so he was invited, too."

"I guess that was a sensible idea," Maggie said, smiling, "knowing how noisy some of these parties can be."

Gloria nodded. "I think Alex appreciated the invitation as he hadn't lived in Vancouver for very long. We got talking and somehow we clicked." She picked up her sandwich and then put it down again. "Why would anyone want to kill him?"

Maggie laid her hand over the girl's. "I don't know, Gloria. Could have been mistaken identity. Can you tell me if he was worried about anything? You know, was he acting different than usual?"

Gloria nodded. "He was different, but not worried. He was

very excited. He said that at last he had met someone who was going to get him well-known.'"

"He was a painter, wasn't he? Watercolours or oils?"

"Oils." Gloria looked down at her plate. "But I have to confess that I know very little about art." She shrugged. "Especially this modern stuff—Alex tried to explain it to me, but I like pictures to show real stuff like flowers and . . . trees . . ."

"His paintings were surreal?"

"Yes, that was the word he used." She gave a humourless laugh. "I really tried to understand, but he said it didn't matter as long as I loved him."

"Gloria, do you still have the key to his apartment?"

The girl nodded. "The lease isn't up for a couple of months. In fact," she said shyly, "I've been staying there for the past few days. I'm sort of thinking of taking over the lease."

"Do you think you could let me see it?"

"I suppose, but there's not much to see." She glanced at her watch. "I have to go now. My supervisor is very strict."

"What time do you get off?"

"Five. Do you mean you want to see it today?"

"Yes. I'll pick you up after work if that's all right."

"Okay," she answered reluctantly.

"WHAT KEY?"

It was early afternoon when Nat stood on Sheldon White's front doorstep facing its very belligerent owner.

Sheldon looked up and down the street before saying, "You'd better come in. The bloody neighbours are already having a field day."

"The spare key to the gallery is missing," Nat explained when they were seated opposite each other at the yellow arborite and chrome kitchen table.

"I've got one of my own."

"Did you lend it to anyone?"

"No. Why would I do that? And you lied to me," he accused.

"Lied to you?"

"You told me they would let me go home. They kept me in a cell—like a . . . a . . . common criminal."

"You're a suspect," Nat answered bluntly.

"Suspect! There's no way I could've killed that man." He shuddered. "He was killed with a knife—I can't stand the sight of blood."

Nat tended to believe him but he answered brutally, "It doesn't take much for someone—even if they can't stand the sight of blood—to kill in a fit of anger."

"Not me, man."

"How long had you known the dead man?"

"Couple of months. I told you he was renting space in my studio."

"Good artist?"

"If you like that kind of painting. He was a surrealist."

"Did it sell?"

"He told me that someone was showing interest. And before you ask me, I don't know who it was. Anything else you want?"

"I'd like to take a look in your studio."

"It's practically empty. All the stuff's been stacked against the wall because I've had to have someone in to clean up." He reached up to a wooden keyboard and selected a large key. "I'll show you."

Just as Sheldon had said, there was nothing to show that a gruesome murder had taken place in the studio. All the easels and the wooden dais, the latter showing dark wet patches, had been folded and placed against the walls along with stacked stools and chairs. The artistic "fainting couch" that had held the bloody corpse had disappeared completely.

"The cops took the couch for evidence," Sheldon explained. He turned and walked out of the studio then waited until Nat had joined him outside. "I think I should have police protection," he announced bluntly. Turning the key in the studio's padlock, he added, "My life is in danger."

"Do you have any enemies?"

"Not as far as I know. But it stands to reason that the man who killed Alex must've thought it was me. Suppose he comes back to finish the job?"

"But you can't see any reason why someone would want you dead?"

"No. But look, I worked for Jonathan Standish and he was murdered, and then Alex gets killed in my studio. They must think I know something." Leading the way back toward the house, he turned to face Nat. "Or someone is jealous because I have all this." He waved his arms to encompass the backyard and the studio.

"I don't think that could be a motive," Nat answered dryly.

"Well, Alex's death has to be connected to Jonathan's murder. They must think I know something."

"Think hard. Do you?"

Sheldon shook his head. "I keep going over those last few days before Jonathan . . ." his voice trailed away.

"And?" Nat encouraged.

"There were several phone calls and he always made sure that he was alone in the office before he would talk to the caller."

"Didn't Alice wonder who was calling?"

"I guess you'd better ask her. I offered to help in any way I could after her husband's death, but she would never confide in me." He gave a bitter laugh. "The only one she talks to is that bitch of a sister, Jane."

Nat started to walk around the side of the house to where he'd parked his car. "Thanks for showing me the studio."

"Wait a minute. Do *you* think I should ask the cops for protection?"

"If you're that worried, talk to them. But if you recall anything that will help us find Jonathan or Alex's murderer—give *me* a call."

MAGGIE FOLLOWED THE girl up the two flights of stairs to the apartment and waited while Gloria fumbled in her handbag for the key to 304. As they entered the small vestibule, stale air, the strong smell of cat, and two tabby felines greeted them.

Gloria bent down and fondled each of the cats before turning to Maggie. "If you wait a sec, I'll open the blinds and get some daylight in here." She disappeared into the gloom, the cats following on her heels mewing plaintively. "I know, I know, you want your supper."

It was a dismal little apartment, and opening the blinds did little to enhance it. Maggie thought that it must have been the girl who had added throw cushions and the multi-coloured crocheted afghan on the worn sofa.

"As you can see," Gloria said apologetically, "it needs some fixing up."

"The cats belong to you?" Maggie asked when Gloria returned to the living room.

"Alex's. Luckily, I like cats. They miss him, though."

"Are these paintings his?" Maggie pointed to three large, brightly coloured pictures hanging on the wall. If they were, she could see why the girl found them hard to understand. They reminded Maggie of some of Picasso's paintings.

Gloria nodded. "They are supposed to be very good. Alex told me he had a buyer for them."

"Did he leave a will?"

"I don't know. I guess all his paintings and the furniture belong to his family now," she said wistfully.

"Has anyone contacted them?"

"The police told me that his older brother would be arriving to make funeral arrangements in a few days." She looked sadly up at one of the paintings depicting half a face and disjointed parts of arms and legs floating among purple and yellow clouds. "It's called *Enchantment*."

"Alex didn't paint *these*, did he?" Maggie pointed at two small paintings lined up on the couch. They were old-fashioned winter scenes.

"I don't think so. I found them tucked away in the small bedroom closet and thought they would look pretty on that wall."

Maggie opened her handbag to extract her glasses. "You found them in a closet?"

"They're so small that I don't suppose they're worth much," the girl replied, "but they're kind of cute, don't you think? There's another one in there, but it's kind of ugly, just some old guy." And she went back into the bedroom and came back with another painting.

"Have you shown them to anyone else?" Maggie asked casually.

"No." Gloria seemed puzzled by the question. "I only found them two days ago."

Maggie straightened up. "Has anybody been around asking about Alex?"

"No one knows I'm here . . . except my parents, of course."

"How do they feel about you living here on your own?"

"They're not happy about it, but I like my independence."

"Let's sit down for a minute," Maggie suggested gently.

"Is something wrong?"

"I think it would be a very good idea if you went back to live with your parents."

"Go back? Why?"

"How old are you?"

"Eighteen. Or I will be in a couple of months. And you don't know what it's like at home—I have to share a bedroom with my sister, my mother is always nagging, and my brother bugs me . . ."

"Gloria, I think you're in great danger staying here on your own."

"But I told you . . . nobody knows I'm here."

"I think these paintings are very valuable and most probably stolen." Maggie paused to add weight to her words. "I think they might be the reason Alex was killed."

"Alex wasn't a thief!" the girl replied indignantly. "He wouldn't have stolen them."

Maggie walked back to the sofa and carefully gathered up the paintings. "Find me a bag or a pillowcase, anything big enough to wrap them up in. And then please hurry and get your things together."

"I don't want to go back home . . . I'll never hear the end of it."

Maggie looked around the room. "Is there a telephone here?"

The girl shook her head. "Alex couldn't afford one. But there's one down in the lobby."

"Okay. While you're packing, I'll dash down and call my partner. Lock the door after me and don't open it for anyone else. I'll give three sharp raps when I come back, okay?"

"But . . ."

Maggie pushed the girl toward the bedroom. "Get going."

"But why? What's so special about those pictures?"

"I'll explain when I come back."

Maggie found the public telephone, naturally in the darkest corner of the lobby, along with a mutilated phonebook hanging by a chain. Written on the grimy wall above the battered instrument were names, phone numbers, messages offering a good time to any caller, and graffiti—in pictures and lurid written detail. Maggie, wondering how anybody would willingly live in such a place, reached for the telephone only to find that the cord had been cut.

HENNY WAS IN the process of covering her typewriter when Nat arrived back at the office.

"Heard from Maggie?" he asked, walking by her to go into his own domain.

"She called an hour ago, Mr. Nat. She went to get that Wentworth girl and they go to the boyfriend's place. She said not to wait for her." She handed him a pile of small yellow slips of paper. "Your messages."

"Did she say what the address was?" he called to Henny as she departed.

"It's on the file somewhere. I haff to go, Mr. Nat. We are taking our boys to the hockey game."

Nat wrote up his notes then made a quick call to George to confirm their usual Friday bowling date. He stood up, stretched, and glanced at his wristwatch. It was close to six.

MAGGIE, TELEPHONE STILL in hand, spun around as the main door of the building slammed open and a tired-looking woman, her wet hair plastered to her face, came in lugging three paper bags of groceries. "That telephone's always on the fritz," she said, hip-shutting the door behind her. "God! It's coming down in buckets out there."

"I don't suppose there's another telephone . . ."

"The superintendent's got one. He'll let you use it . . . for a price." She looked Maggie up and down. "You must be new."

Maggie shook her head. "Just visiting. Where does the super-intendent live?"

"In the basement. Apartment One. You'll have to bang hard as he's deaf as a post and he watches the wrestling on TV this time of night."

Maggie waited until the woman had disappeared up the stairs before descending the concrete steps. It took several thumps on the door before an unkempt man, probably in his sixties, grudgingly opened it.

"What do you want?"

"Can I use your telephone?"

"You're not one of the tenants."

"No. I'm visiting."

"Which apartment?" he asked suspiciously.

"Does it matter? I just want to use the phone."

"Only local and it'll cost you fifty cents. It's over there."

Maggie opened her purse, thrust a couple of quarters into the man's hand, picked up the phone, and dialed. After the fourth ring Maggie realized that Nat and Henny had gone, and she waited on the line for the answering service to cut in.

"Broadway Answering Service."

"Hi Joyce. It's Mrs. Spencer. Would you pass on an urgent message to Mr. Southby to call me at home as soon as possible?"

"Will do. Have a good evening."

"Which apartment did you say you were visiting?" the man asked suspiciously as Maggie walked toward the door.

"I didn't," she replied tersely before shutting the door firmly behind her and making for the concrete stairs that led back up to the lobby. As she put her foot on the first step she head the sound of clattering feet racing down the stairs and then the bang of the front door closing. *Someone's in a hurry!*

Winded after just three flights of stairs? I must be getting old! Maggie leaned against the wall until she had regained her breath before heading down the hall to apartment 304. Reaching out to give the pre-arranged three raps, she saw that the door was ajar. "Gloria," she called, rushing in. "Where are . . . ?"

Gloria was sitting on the floor with her back to the sofa. "I . . . I . . . couldn't stop him," she said. "He was too strong."

"What happened?" Maggie demanded, helping the girl to her feet.

"I heard the raps and I opened the door and he hit me in the mouth . . . and . . . and he took the pictures." She raised a hand to her mouth. "Oh, I'm bleeding . . ."

"Did you recognize him?" Maggie asked, rummaging through her handbag to find a handkerchief. "Here, hold this against your lip."

"He was wearing a toque and he had a scarf around his face."

"Did you notice anything else about him?" She led the girl into the bathroom and began running the cold water.

"No . . . Yes. He smelled like flowers . . . Aftershave, I suppose."

"Okay. Let's see the damage. Do any of your teeth feel loose?" The girl shook her head.

"Now do those cats have some kind of carrier?"

"A carrier?" She shook her head. "Why do you want a carrier for them?"

"Because, my girl, you and those kitties are going back to your mother. Where do you live?"

"My mother doesn't like cats, and I want to stay here."

"Do you want to end up dead like your boyfriend?"

Gloria shook her head. "But . . ."

"Gloria, gather your clothes together," she ordered sternly, "and let's get out of here . . . now!"

It was a struggle to stuff the cats into pillowcases and then get them into the back of the mini, but at long last and with a sigh of relief Maggie pulled away from the apartment block. "Now where to?"

"Sutherland Avenue on the North Shore."

"That's a long way to go."

"Why do you think I wanted to stay in Alex's apartment?"

"SO YOU'VE COME back," Gladys Wentworth greeted her daughter. "Told you, didn't I? And who are you?" she asked Maggie.

"My partner and I are looking into Alex's death, and it's not a good time for Gloria to be alone in his apartment."

"You with the cops, then?"

"Private investigators." Maggie placed the bagged cats down inside the front door.

"What's in those pillowcases?" Gladys Wentworth asked suspiciously.

"They're Alex's cats," Gloria cried. "I couldn't leave them, Mom. I promise I will look after them."

"Any mess and they're out. You understand? Good of you to bring her home," she said to Maggie, and as the woman closed the door, Maggie heard her yelling, "There'll be hell to pay when your father sees those cats!"

"And thank you, too," Maggie mumbled as she ran through the rain and slid into her car. She glanced at her watch. "Ten o'clock! It'll take me most of an hour to get home."

CHAPTER SEVENTEEN

Nat and George were happy. Their team had bowled the pants off their opponents and they had celebrated well at Simon's Bar and Grill next door to the bowling alley.

"When are you and Maggie going to tie the knot?" George asked, shrugging into his overcoat.

"Can't be too soon for me," Nat answered.

"What's holding it up?"

"The stigma of divorce. Maggie won't do anything that might ruin Harry's reputation."

"You'd think he'd want to be free," George said. "Isn't their daughter getting married soon?"

"Next month. I'm hoping Midge's wedding will make Maggie change her mind. Anyway," he said, glancing at the clock, "it's almost my bedtime. Better get going."

IT WAS NINE-THIRTY by the time he arrived back at his apartment, and he debated whether he should call Maggie. She had probably telephoned during the evening and realized that he wasn't home from his bowling date. It was really too late to call her now, and he would be seeing her in the morning anyway.

I'm going to call it a day, he said to himself firmly. He plodded wearily into the bathroom before yanking his clothes off and throwing them toward a chair—they missed. He flopped into bed and blissfully closed his eyes and let himself drift. The jangling telephone brought him to with a start.

"What the hell . . . ?" Grabbing the offending instrument, he yelled, "If this is a wrong number . . ."

"It's Joyce Creswell from your answering service, Mr. Southby. Sorry if I woke you."

"I'm sorry, Joyce. I didn't mean to shout. What is it?"

"I've been trying to reach you all evening."

"I was out. What's wrong?"

"Mrs. Spencer left an urgent message for you to call her. I was just going off duty and I thought I'd try one more time. She did say it was urgent," she repeated apologetically.

"I'll call her right away."

He replaced the receiver and looked at his alarm clock. Quarter after ten. *It's late. Maggie's sure to be asleep. And what could be that urgent?* He snuggled back down into his bed, then sat bolt upright again. "Bloody hell! Better risk being bawled out." He reached for the telephone and let it ring at least a dozen times but there was no answer.

Ten minutes later he was dressed and searching for his keys.

Maggie's house was in complete darkness. Slipping his key in the lock, he slowly opened the door to be greeted by Oscar hurling himself at him. "Down, Oscar. Down. Maggie?" he yelled. "Maggie?" He felt for the hall light. "Where the hell are you, Maggie?"

The dog ran ahead of him, stopped by his empty bowl, and looked up expectantly. Emily, asleep in her basket opened one eye, sat up and then slunk over to her empty dish. "Bloody hell, Oscar. She hasn't been home, has she?" He raced up the stairs and into Maggie's bedroom. The drapes were still open and the bed hadn't been slept in. "Where in God's name are you?" He raced back down the stairs to see both animals sitting hopefully beside their dishes. "Okay. I get the message." After feeding them, he let them have a quick run in the yard then carefully locked the front door. As he climbed back behind the wheel of his car, he thought, *She was going to meet that girl . . . what's her name? . . . Gloria. And the girl was going to take her to Alex Donitz's apartment. But where in hell is the apartment? George could find out but it's far too late to call him.* Then suddenly he recalled Henny's last words as she left the office: the address was in the files.

The whole building was dark, and as he flooded the agency's offices with light, he hoped the cop on the beat didn't come to check what he was up to. Thank God for Henny's up-to-date filing system. Hauling the Standish file out of the cabinet, he quickly scanned the contents. "Ah! Here it is. Alex Donitz, 1505-East 3rd Avenue, Apartment 304." He ran down the stairs, rammed the car into gear, and sped toward the east end of the city.

MAGGIE WAS EXHAUSTED by the time she turned into the alley that led to the back of her house, and after carefully locking the garage doors, she walked up the pathway and opened the back door. "I'm home, Oscar. Where are you, Emily? Did you think I'd forgotten you? You poor things, you must be starved."

Oscar rushed to meet her, but Emily only opened one eye to acknowledge her presence before going back to sleep again. Then Maggie saw the cat and dog food on the table and remnants of food still in Emily's dish. "Nat must have been here and he must wonder wherever I've got to." She picked up the phone and dialed. But there was no answer. *Now what do I do?*

EXCEPT FOR A dingy, wire-caged light over the door, the apartment building was in complete darkness, and of course the doors were locked. Nat scanned the names on the residents board until he found Donitz and leaned on the bell. No answer. *Of course, she could have gone someplace with the girl. But where? Something must've happened. I've got to get inside.* He pressed the superintendent's bell.

The man was not happy. "What do you want? Go away or I'll call the cops."

"I am the cops," Nat lied. Two minutes later a bleary-eyed man in striped pyjamas peered out of the door.

"I thought you said you were the cops?"

"Plain clothes." Nat flashed his PI card.

"Where's the rest of you guys?"

"Coming. I need to get into 304. Go get the pass-key."

"Wait a minute. There ain't anyone in that apartment. The guy's dead. Murdered."

"Get the key," Nat answered menacingly.

THE APARTMENT WAS empty and there was no sign of Maggie or the girl, Gloria.

"Told you the place was empty." The superintendent looked suspiciously at Nat. "You sure you're the cops?"

"Have you let anyone into this apartment tonight?"

"Only the girl that comes in to feed those cats, and she's got a key."

"What cats?" Nat asked.

The man looked around the apartment. "Where's those blasted cats, anyway?" He stalked back into the bedroom and peered under the bed. "Maybe they escaped," he said hopefully. "I told her she's got to shift them by the end of the week."

"For God's sake, man. Forget the bloody cats." Nat had closely followed on the superintendent's heels. He now yanked open the closet door and pushed the few clothes hanging there to one side. "Have you seen any strangers in the building?"

"No . . . wait a minute. There was this woman wanting to use the phone. Said she was visiting."

"What time was that?"

"Lemme see . . . I was watching Gorgeous George pummeling the bejesus out of Pretty Boy. 'Bout six."

"What did she look like?"

"I dunno. Middle-aged, nice figure. Wearing a black raincoat. Wasn't very friendly, though. Can't remember anything else . . . Oh! She called someone . . . and told her to pass a message on to Nat."

"I thought you had the TV on."

"Turned it down, didn't I? You finished in here?"

"Yes," he said, walking back into the living room. A moment later he knelt and picked up a key that was lying under the edge of the couch.

"Here! What you got there? You can't take nuffin' out of the place."

"Evidence," Nat answered walking toward the door and trying the key in the lock—it didn't fit. "I'll sign for it, if you like," he said, dropping it into his pocket. "I also need to use your phone."

"This time of the night . . ." The look on Nat's face shut him up. "Make it quick then."

"Nat," Maggie's voice sounded relieved. "Where are you? I've been calling your place for the past half hour."

"I'm coming right over, just stay put."

"You owe me fifty cents," the superintendent said, holding out his hand. "For the phone call."

"I WAS WORRIED sick," Nat said a half hour later, releasing Maggie from his tight embrace. "Especially when that brute of a superintendent said you'd used his phone to call me." He paused. "What did happen to those two cats?" He looked around the kitchen. "You didn't bring them here, did you?" he added suspiciously.

Maggie laughed. "I may be stupid when it comes to animals, but not that stupid. Get your wet coat off while I make you a hot chocolate and I will tell you all."

MAGGIE SPIKED NAT'S chocolate liberally with brandy, and he drank it appreciatively. "And these paintings . . . you think they're really valuable?"

Maggie nodded. "If they're genuine."

"And you think they are."

Maggie nodded.

"I know absolutely nothing about art. Who is this Cornelius what's-his-name, anyway?"

"Cornelius Krieghoff. A Dutch painter who lived in Montreal in the nineteenth century. My aunt had several framed prints of his works on her walls—don't you remember seeing them when we were there last Christmas?"

"Not really . . . Oh, do you mean those old-fashioned snowy farmhouse scenes above the fireplace?"

Maggie nodded. "But those were just prints. I'm sure these three are originals."

"Wait a minute," Nat said suddenly. "Those phone calls Sheldon was talking about—they were about some Krieghoff paintings. Do you remember?"

"Of course," Maggie said slowly, "but they could have been very good fakes."

"But they . . . whoever they are . . . wouldn't kill for fakes. It's a pity that girl didn't give you a better description of the man who attacked her."

Maggie picked up the mugs and placed them in the sink. "I'm bushed. Are you staying or going back to your own place?"

"I can't face going out in that rain again," Nat said then added, "and your bed looked very inviting when I was up there earlier." It wasn't until he had snuggled down into the warm bed and was slipping into a comforting sleep that he remembered the key in his coat pocket. *It will have to wait 'til the morning.* He closed his eyes.

IT WAS UNDERSTANDABLE that they were very late getting to the office the following morning and Henny was waiting for them.

"You forget you have a meeting at nine this morning, Mr. Nat?"

"Oh, blast. Would you call Mr. Clive and tell him I'm running a little late?"

"He is important client," she answered primly as she lifted the telephone receiver.

Maggie tried to hide a smile before slipping into her office and before Henny could rebuke her on her tardiness as well.

CHAPTER EIGHTEEN

It was Saturday morning and Nat and Maggie were just about to sit down to a leisurely late breakfast of scrambled eggs and toast when the telephone gave its insistent ring.

"Drat, who can that be this time of the morning?" she said as she reached for the phone.

"Sorry to call you on a Saturday. It's Irma . . . Irma Standish. You did say to call if I remembered anything . . . and Aaron has gone to get the church ready for a meeting with the elders, so . . ."

"That's quite okay, Irma," Maggie replied, handing her plate back to Nat to put in the oven to keep it warm. "What can I do for you?"

"It's about that photo—you know? The one with the woman and little girl. They came here."

"To your place? Why didn't Aaron mention that when I was there?"

"Because he doesn't know. I didn't tell him."

"Perhaps you'd better explain."

"That woman . . . she said that Aaron should know that her little girl was his sister—or half-sister, to be precise."

"And you didn't tell your husband?"

"No. I thought she was making it all up, and knowing how Aaron felt about his father's . . . infidelities . . . I didn't want him to get angry. He can get very … very angry, and sometimes I worry about my girls."

"So why are you telling me about this now?"

"Maybe she was telling the truth, and suppose she comes back?"

"Did she give you an address or a phone number?"

"Yes, a telephone number. But she said not to let anyone have it except Aaron."

"Did she say why?"

"She said that Jonathan was murdered and she was scared for herself and her daughter. I didn't want to believe her, but after your visit …"

"Did she give you her full name?"

"No. Just the number where I could reach her."

"I think you'd better give it to me."

"But suppose she really is in danger? It could be my fault if anything bad happened."

"That's exactly why you need to let me have it. She didn't tell you where she lived, I suppose?" Maggie asked hopefully.

"No, but it's definitely in Vancouver … Aaron and I lived on Prince Albert when we were first married and it was the same phone exchange. Do you think I *should* tell Aaron?"

"Wait until we've looked into it."

"Thank you," she breathed. "God knows how he's going to take the news that he has a sister only a couple of years older than his own daughters. And," she added, "by one of his father's … women."

"I GATHER FROM your conversation that Irma has met the elusive Judith." Nat said as he reached into the oven to reclaim her breakfast. "This will be all dried out now."

"No. It's just great." She forked a mouthful of eggs into her mouth before she continued. "Irma didn't tell her husband about the visit."

"M-m-m. That's asking for trouble."

"At least she's given me Judith's phone number. Irma doesn't know either her surname or address—but I'm pretty sure that she must live close to the cemetery. How do we find out?" she mused.

"Call the number."

Maggie hesitated before reaching for the phone. "What do I say?"

Nat shrugged. "Ask if we can see her?"

Three rings went by before a child's voice said all in one breath, "Oak-Tree-Clinic-we-are-closed-on-Saturdays."

Before Maggie had a chance to speak, she heard a woman's voice ask, "Who is it, Jenny?"

"I told them we're closed."

"I am so sorry. What can I do for you?"

"I think I must have the wrong number," Maggie answered. "The child did say Oak Tree Clinic?"

"That's right."

"Am I speaking to Judith?"

There was a pause and the woman answered warily, "Yes."

Maggie digested this bit of information and then she asked, "My name is Margaret Spencer. Would it be at all possible for me and my partner to visit you?"

"I'm a children's doctor—a pediatrician. I don't treat adults."

"No. This is another matter. I believe you knew Jonathan Standish."

There were a few moments of silence. "What is this about?"

"My partner and I are detectives and we've been hired to find Jonathan Standish's murderer."

"Is this some kind of sick joke?"

"No. We will explain when we see you."

"How did you get my number?" the woman asked in a panicky voice.

"Please, we really need to talk."

It seemed an age before she replied. "I'll give you half an hour—say about midday. But I'll need credentials from you."

Maggie copied down the address before replacing the receiver. "Well, that's a surprise. She's a doctor."

"You mean this Judith we've been trying to find?"

"That's right. She's a pediatrician. She lives on 41st Avenue and has reluctantly agreed to see us around noon. My car or yours?"

"Mine. It's out front."

They were just putting on their coats when the telephone rang again. "Oh, leave it," Nat said, plunging his hand in his pocket for his car keys.

"I'd better answer it." Maggie turned to walk back into the kitchen. But this time it was Harry.

"Margaret," he began, "we must get together this weekend to go over the guest list. I don't think you know how close it is to the wedding."

"There is no reason to go over the list, Harry. I've sent all the invitations out. Your Miss Fitch-Smythe sent me your list and Midge and Jason gave me theirs ages ago."

"Well . . . there's the seating in the church and the reception— we've got to discuss that . . . and the cars have to be ordered . . . I think it would be proper if you left from here . . . after all, you will want to be with Midge to help her dress . . . and then there's the bridesmaids . . . and my mother."

That's all I need, Honoria Spencer! "How about I come over tomorrow, Harry? Then we'll go over everything together." She realized she was placating him, but she wanted this wedding to go smoothly for Midge's sake. But the look on Nat's face as he listened to the one-sided conversation spoke volumes.

"That was Harry," she said unnecessarily.

He nodded. "I found this on the floor of that apartment," he handed her the door key. "I was so anxious to see you the other night that I completely forgot all about it."

"Gloria had a key to the place. She must've dropped it." Maggie shrugged into her coat.

"It didn't fit. I tried it myself."

"Do you think the man who attacked Gloria could've dropped it?"

"It's quite possible. We just have to find the door that fits the key."

Maggie laughed as she led the way out of the house. "Like looking for the proverbial needle in a haystack."

CHAPTER NINETEEN

It was a perfect spring day. Ideal for walking through the beautiful grounds of Mountain View Cemetery. Oscar, as if he knew he had to behave, walked decorously on his lead between Maggie and Nat, even doing his best to ignore the pesky squirrels that darted invitingly over the gravesites.

Nat came to a sudden halt in front of a very large tombstone. "Have a look at this," he said.

Maggie joined him and read the inscription. "Who was Robert McBeath?"

"A very young police officer killed in the line of duty in 1921—a bit before my time on the force, but I've read about him."

"It says here he was awarded the Victoria Cross for bravery—just twenty-three years old—so young," she added before turning away.

A few minutes later they were standing before Jonathan Standish's grave. "It's evident that Judith hasn't been here today," Nat commented, nodding toward the withered remains of pink roses on the grave. "So let's go and meet her."

AFTER LOCKING OSCAR in the car, they walked up the narrow cement path between neat privet hedges that led to a blue door and a brass plaque bearing the words, OAK TREE CHILDREN'S CLINIC. Maggie reached for the doorbell.

The door was opened by a girl around ten years old who was trying her best to hold onto the collar of an eager black and white spaniel. "Mommy's not open on Saturdays and she's a children's doctor, not for grown-ups."

"We aren't patients," Maggie answered, laughing. "We're here to speak to her on business."

"You must be Margaret Spencer," the tall woman said as she came up behind the child and placed her hands on the girl's shoulders. Maggie estimated that the woman, who had a blond braid that circled her head, was in her mid- to late thirties, and the resemblance to the figurines in the studio was remarkable.

Maggie nodded and turned toward Nat. "And this is my partner, Nat Southby." Maggie extended one of her business cards. "As I said on the phone, we won't keep you long."

"What's it about?" the woman asked warily, glancing at the card. She drew her daughter closer to her. "What is it you want?"

"Can we come in and we'll explain," Nat said smilingly. "We're not here to harm you. We just want to talk to you about Jonathan Standish."

"What has he to do with you?"

"We've been hired to look into his death."

"You told me over the phone that he was murdered," she said flatly.

"Please let us come in and talk to you about it," Maggie said.

The woman hesitated a moment longer before opening the door wider. She led them past a small waiting room furnished with miniature chairs, tables, and shelves packed with toys and books, and into a bright living room that looked over a garden full of spring flowers and pink roses.

"Who hired you?"

"Alice Standish and her sister Jane hired us. They weren't happy with the suicide verdict."

A small smile curved the woman's lips. "She couldn't collect the insurance, you mean. And I guess it was Aaron Standish who gave you my number?" She looked over to her young daughter who, although playing with the dog on the rug, was obviously taking in the conversation. "Jenny, take Rex outside in the garden to play."

"Aw, mom . . ."

"Go." She walked over to the French doors and opened them. "We'll take him for a long walk later." She waited until her daughter had left the room and then turned back to say, "You didn't answer my question. Was it Aaron who gave you my number?"

"No," Maggie answered. "His wife." Maggie related the telephone conversation she'd had with Irma that morning. "She seems very frightened of her husband."

"She didn't even tell him I'd called?" she said then shook her head. "I can't say that I'm surprised. It's hard to believe that Jonathan, who was such a gentle person, could have sired such a nasty piece of work as Aaron."

"I didn't think you'd met."

"We haven't, but Jonathan told me about his son *and* Catherine his first wife *and* Alice his second." She sighed. "He made some very bad choices in his life." Then she laughed derisively. "Apart from Jenny and me, that is."

"Can you tell us about it?"

"Will it help find his murderer?"

"It might."

"I don't want Jenny dragged into a sordid murder enquiry."

"We'll do our best," Nat answered. "When did you first meet Jonathan Standish?"

"About twelve years ago. I was a very hard-up medical student, interning at the hospital where his wife was being treated for lung cancer. He visited her most days and I just happened to be assigned to her ward." She shrugged. "We got to talking . . . and it sort of went from there."

"So what happened to end it?"

"About the time I was graduating his wife became very ill and I guess he felt guilty . . . Anyway . . . we stopped seeing each other."

"Was that his idea or yours?" Nat asked.

"His. I was heartbroken at the time, and as soon as I graduated, I went back to Toronto and took a job at the children's hospital there. Then," she laughed, "I found out I was pregnant."

"Whatever did you do?" Maggie asked.

"Luckily for me my parents live in Toronto. After Jenny was born, they took care of her so that I could find work in a medical clinic. It was tough, though."

"Did you let Jonathan know about the baby?"

Judith shook her head. "No."

"But you came back to Vancouver?" Nat asked.

"Yes, three years ago. I thought it was time Jonathan met his daughter. But I might have thought twice about returning if I'd known he'd remarried."

"You hadn't corresponded at all?" Maggie asked.

"No. I waited until I had established a practice here before contacting him. I didn't want him to think he was obligated to look after us." She walked over to the window where she could see her daughter.

"Jonathan must've been very surprised," Nat remarked wryly.

"He was. Very! And so was I when he told me he'd remarried."

"But you started seeing him again?" Maggie said.

"It was Jenny. He fell in love with his daughter."

"Why did you try to contact Aaron?" Maggie asked.

Judith, still looking pensively out of the window, took a few moments before replying. "I wanted to talk to Aaron about his father. I knew Jonathan well. And he would never have taken his own life, especially under the circumstances."

"What do you mean, *under the circumstances?*"

"Didn't that woman tell you that Jonathan had started divorce proceedings?" She gave a bitter laugh. "No, of course she didn't."

"Alice knew about you?" Maggie asked, surprised.

"Jonathan kept our identity secret but she must have suspected when he asked for a divorce."

"Do you have the name of the divorce lawyer?" Nat asked.

"No. Jonathan kept all that to himself." She pondered for a moment. "He got the name from his business lawyer . . . some funny name . . . Snood . . . Snod . . . Snodgrass. That was it . . . Snodgrass. But I haven't a clue where he's located."

But I do, Maggie thought.

Maggie stood and opened her handbag. "This is the reason we came looking for you." She pulled out the photographs of Judith and her daughter. "We found them in his studio."

"Has that woman seen them?" Judith asked fearfully, thrusting them back into Maggie's hands.

Maggie nodded. "She said you were just models for the figurines in the studio. But," Maggie added, "she's getting curious about the person leaving pink roses on Jonathan's grave and asked us to look into it."

"I . . . oh, dear." Judith looked stricken. "Please don't tell her where we live."

"We won't," Nat answered. "But it's a murder case now, and since *we* managed to find you, others could as well. You've got our card," he added as he rose to stand beside Maggie. "Please call if you think of anything that will help us find his killer."

"You haven't told us your name," Maggie said.

The woman hesitated before replying, "I guess you'll find out anyway. It's Sloan, Doctor Judith Sloan."

"I RATHER LIKED her," Maggie remarked as she slid into the passenger's seat. "She's naturally scared for her daughter's sake, but she's got guts to come back to Vancouver and open a practice."

"But *why* is she so scared?" Nat asked as he pulled out into the traffic.

Maggie was quiet for a moment before posing a question of her own. "And if she wanted to keep a low profile, why go to see Aaron? After all, she's waited this long. And what do we tell Alice? She asked us to find out who was leaving those roses."

"M-m-m. We'll tell her that Jane was right and she's just a model that Jonathan used for the figurines."

"But she's going to find out eventually."

"We can do a bit more digging in the meantime. Now," he added, "are you really going over to Harry's tomorrow?"

CHAPTER TWENTY

Harry greeted her at the door and led her into the living room. The house in Kerrisdale looked just the same, even the same faint smell of lavender furniture polish, and she found herself automatically sitting in her favourite chair opposite Harry by the fireside.

"Midge is making tea," he announced.

"She's here already?"

"Of course she's here. After all, it's her wedding. Mother should be arriving soon, too."

"Your mother! Why is she coming?" Honoria Spencer had never approved of her only son's choice—and their separation had proved her point.

"Now, Margaret," Harry said defensively, "Midge *is* her granddaughter and she wants to be part of the planning." The doorbell rang as if on cue. "Ah, there she is now."

Harry went to open the door for his mother as Midge appeared from the kitchen carrying a loaded tea tray. She raised her eyebrows at Maggie as she bent to place the tray on the coffee table. "Inviting Grandma was not my idea," she hissed.

Honoria, dressed in a beige silk suit, matching straw hat, and sensible brown oxfords, leaned heavily on a silver-knobbed cane as she walked into the room. "Margaret! What a surprise to see you here. You've managed to find time to get away from that . . . that place where you work?"

Don't let her get to you. Maggie rose from her chair. "Why don't you sit here? Midge has just brought in the tea and some delicious-looking scones."

"And before you ask, Grandmother," Midge cut in, "I didn't make them. I'm not a good cook like my mother."

"Mrs. Jennings, my housekeeper, made them," Harry cut in quickly. "And I'm sure you are an excellent cook, Matilda." He looked anxiously at the three women. "Now shall we get on with the arrangements?" He produced a lined legal pad and a pen. "I've ordered three cars . . ."

Why did he ask me here? Maggie thought, listening to his pompous voice droning on. *He's made all the necessary arrangements.*

"Now is there anything I've left out?" Harry eventually asked, picking up his cup of now cold tea.

"I'm so glad you took my advice and the wedding is going to be at Christ Church Cathedral." Honoria beamed at her son. "That's where your father and I were married."

"I know, Mother. It is also very handy to the Hotel Vancouver where the reception is to be held."

"Did you tell the car service that I need to be picked up in plenty of time, Harry?" Honoria banged her cane on the floor. "My girl will help me get ready." She turned to Maggie. "What colour are you wearing? My dress is a soft rose silk with matching accessories, and as we'll be sitting next to each other, we certainly don't want to clash."

Maggie felt like telling her she was wearing mustard yellow and lime green, but managed to bite her tongue. "We won't clash," she said, thinking of the beautiful blue lace gown she and Midge had picked out—perfect for the mother-of-the-bride.

"And that reminds me," Harry's mother continued, "What are you doing about Barbara?"

"What about her?" Maggie asked, mystified.

"What will she wear to cover her ... her ... pregnancy? Perhaps she should stay home."

"Why would she stay home?" Midge asked incredulously. "It's quite a normal thing to be expecting a baby."

"In my day," Honoria said haughtily, "women in that delicate condition didn't show themselves in public."

"Thank God times have changed," Midge answered. "And my sister is welcome at my wedding even if she's the size of an elephant."

Good for you, Midge, Maggie thought. She had never known Midge to answer back to the old battle-axe, but she thought she had better break the tension. "I must be going. Do you want a lift home, Honoria?"

"My taxi will be here at four." Maggie could tell the old girl was still nettled. She turned to her son. "Of course, you've placed me at the head table ..."

"Yes, of course, Mother," Harry answered her absently. "I'll see you out, Margaret."

"I'll kill her if she spoils Midge's day," Maggie warned Harry as she slipped on her coat in the hallway.

"My mother means well, Margaret." He bent to kiss her on the cheek. "You will make sure you're here on time, won't you? After all, a girl needs her mother on her wedding day, and ... and ... I need you, Margaret. I miss you very much, you know."

Harry, looking forlorn, stood in the open doorway and watched Maggie back her car out of the driveway. She discovered she had quite a lump in her throat.

CHAPTER TWENTY-ONE

It's a pity I have to go to the office on a day like today, Maggie thought. It was still before seven in the morning and she was walking Oscar through the leafy paths of the park close to her home on 5th Avenue in Kitsilano. Apart from Kent, England, where Maggie grew up, she thought there was no other place to be than Vancouver in the spring. They passed several other dogs and walkers and Oscar did his best to greet every one of them. As she turned for home, Maggie thought about her visit to Harry the day before and tried to analyze her feelings toward him. They had been very close through the first years of their marriage, though like many other young couples they had gone through some very rough times. By the time the two girls were born, Harry had become so mired in his job that they had slowly drifted apart and she had become totally bored with being the dutiful housewife. She smiled to herself—she certainly couldn't complain of being bored now!

AS USUAL, HENNY had arrived in the office first. The coffee was on and she had brought in a fresh batch of her infamous cookies.

"It is lucky I made these," she said proudly, setting eight of her overdone delicacies on a plate. "Sergeant George is coming to see you and Mr. Nat."

"He is? Did he say why?"

"No. But it is police business," she stated.

"How do you know it is police business if he didn't tell you why he was coming?"

"Because he said another policeman coming, too. Funny fishy name . . ."

"You didn't write it down?"

"No." Henny wrinkled her brows in concentration. "Herring? Salmon?"

"Haddock?" Maggie said.

"Yes, Haddock. I knew it was fish." She smiled triumphantly at Maggie.

"Constable Haddock. Sergeant George say you know him."

Maggie nodded. "Forgotten all about that man. He was Inspector Farthing's old sidekick."

THE DUO ARRIVED slightly after ten.

"Gone up in the world, I see," Haddock remarked, scanning the enlarged office space. "Very nice. George tells me you're some kind of partner and got your own office." He shifted a wad of chewing gum from one cheek to the other. "So where's the big boss?"

"In his own big office," Maggie replied sarcastically. "Henny, would you ask Nat to join us in *my* office." She turned back to the two men. "After you, gentlemen." She pointed to her own domain.

"Are those cookies for us?" George stage-whispered to Henny just as Nat walked in. Maggie could see George was having trouble keeping a straight face.

Henny blushed. "Yes, Mr. George. I must have known you come today."

"So what's up?" Nat asked breezily as he toted an extra chair into Maggie's room.

"Ah, we have the honour of Stan Haddock's company, as well." He looked expectantly at George.

"I've been officially assigned to the Donitz murder and Stan's my new partner."

"What happened to Luigi?"

"Taken an early retirement. I'm going to miss him," George replied in a doleful voice. "We'd been together since you and I were partners."

"Long time ago," Nat answered. "Now why do you want to see us?"

"You went to the deceased's apartment." Haddock had addressed his remark to Maggie, and he followed this up by reaching over to pick up a glass paperweight from her desk and then proceeded to heft it from one hand to the other.

Maggie nodded. "So?"

"Farthing says you're both meddling in police business . . . again."

Now Maggie remembered how irritating Haddock had been the first time he came to the agency with Farthing. The man couldn't keep still for a second. "Officer, would you please put that down before you drop it. And yes I did visit the apartment in the company of Alex Donitz's girlfriend."

"What was she doing there?" George asked. He looked up to smile at Henny who had placed a cup of coffee and a couple of cookies on the edge of Maggie's desk directly in front of him.

"You want coffee?" Henny asked George's partner.

"Never touch the stuff."

"A cookie?" Hennie persisted.

Haddock took one look at the overdone and misshapen lumps on the plate, then shuddered and shook his head. "No thank you."

"She was looking after the dead man's cats," Maggie answered George.

"You didn't go there to see cats," Haddock said sarcastically. "What did you go there for?"

"Probably the same reason you went, Mr. Haddock. I wanted to have a look around."

"We didn't find anything of any real interest—in fact, the apartment was pretty sparsely furnished." George took a bite of his burnt offering. "Did you find something we missed?"

Maggie glanced at Nat and he gave a slight nod. "Okay. This is what happened . . ." and she told him all that had occurred at Donitz's apartment the day before.

"Sounds as if you had a very close call," George said when Maggie had finished. "And these paintings—do you think they were genuine . . . what did you call them?"

"Krieghoff, Cornelius Krieghoff. I can't say for sure, George, as I'm no expert. But they weren't prints, and why would the man take a chance and come into the apartment and grab them like that if they weren't originals?" The four of them were silent for a few moments and then Maggie added, "They could be the reason that Alex was killed."

"You mean that he was the real target and it wasn't a case of mistaken identity, as we surmised?"

"But no one would be killed for just a bunch of paintings by some unknown," Haddock cut in. "Now if they'd been painted by that Frenchie Mo-nette, then you could understand somebody snatching them." Maggie squirmed at the mispronunciation of Monet. "No, it has to be something else."

"Cornelius Krieghoff's work sells for thousands of dollars," Maggie said, glaring at Haddock.

"In that case," George placed his empty cup on the desk before continuing, "the guy who snatched them must've been watching the place, just waiting for an opportunity to get inside."

"And he knew that Gloria would be no match for him," Nat cut in.

"Do you think these paintings were stolen from that Unicorn

place?" Haddock asked. He fished the wad of gum out of his mouth and stuck it under the seat of his chair. "You know, the one where that art dealer offed himself."

"It's called the Silver Unicorn and Jonathan Standish was murdered," Maggie stated firmly.

Haddock folded another stick of gum into his mouth. "You didn't answer my question."

"There's a possibility the Silver Unicorn might sell Krieghoff prints, but I think originals would be way out of their league."

"Well, they had to be pinched from somewhere," Haddock persisted, "and it's now obvious that the murder of this Donitz character and Standish's suicide are connected somehow. And I'm sure that White character is mixed up in this, too."

George, raising his eyebrows at Maggie, stood up and reached for his jacket from the back of his chair. "Let's go, Stan."

"You going to caution them?"

"I don't have to spell it out to these folks." He waited until his sidekick had left the room and then turned back to Maggie and Nat. "Do either of you have any idea how those paintings ended up in Donitz's apartment?"

"No. But we intend to find out," Nat answered.

"I'm really sorry you've been saddled with Haddock," Maggie whispered to George as they walked back into the main room.

"You and me both," George said with a wry grin. "Thanks for the cookies, Henny. Really must get the recipe for my wife."

"I WONDER WHAT prompted that visit?" Nat followed Maggie back into her room.

"I wondered that, too. Especially as they seem to know nothing about the paintings. I was even of two minds whether to tell George about them, but I thought they may come back to haunt us if we didn't. I noticed you didn't mention the key you found, either," she added.

"We should find out if it belongs to that girl, Gloria, first," Nat answered. He paused for a moment before continuing, "But we do need to talk to Sheldon and Alice ASAP."

Maggie nodded and reached for the telephone. "The gallery is closed on Mondays. You got anything on this afternoon?"

"Nothing I can't put off. Let's do Sheldon first and then Alice."

A short while later Maggie placed a memo slip in front of Nat. "Sheldon at one. He has students coming around two, and Alice and Jane will be delighted to see us at two-thirty. Oh, one other thing." Nat looked up expectantly. "The key you found. It doesn't belong to Gloria. And she insists that if it had been on the floor before that thug attached her, she would have found it."

"Then I'll cross her off the list. Remind me to ask Sheldon about it."

"SHELDON SAID HE would be in his studio," Maggie remarked as Nat parked in the driveway. "I don't know if I could work there myself."

"You mean because of the murder?"

"Yes. It's even going to be hard for me to go in there." Maggie led the way around the side of the house and then up the gravel path to the studio. The door was open and they could see Sheldon busy setting up easels. She hesitated at the open door before walking in.

"You have news about Alex?" he asked.

"Nothing new," Nat answered. "We have a few questions, but we won't keep you long."

"I told Mrs. Spencer that I'm expecting students at two."

"I'm glad they're beginning to come back to you," Maggie said as she perched on one of the high stools.

"They realize that I'm an excellent teacher. Now what's happened?"

"Cornelius Krieghoff."

Sheldon gave a start in a way that Maggie thought was too casual. "What about him?"

"You have any of his paintings?"

"Don't be ridiculous. How could I possibly afford them?"

"Your friend Alex Donitz seemed to have done."

"What do you mean?"

"Maggie—or rather Alex's girlfriend—found a couple Krieghoffs in his apartment . . ." Nat waited a few seconds before ending, ". . . and then someone rushed in, pushed the girl down, and grabbed them."

"Grabbed them?" he stuttered. He seemed to be visibly shaken. "Were . . . were these Krieghoffs the reason he was murdered?"

"Could be," Maggie answered. "But Sheldon, Donitz was murdered in this very room."

"It wasn't you who grabbed them, by any chance?" Nat asked.

Sheldon pulled himself together. "I know nothing about stolen paintings," he answered firmly.

"Who said anything about them being stolen?" Nat asked quickly.

"Alex wouldn't be able to afford a Krieghoff any more than I would. Besides, very few of them ever come on the market so it stands to reason they were stolen." He paused for a few moments before continuing, "Have you told the police about them?"

"The police came round to see us this morning," Maggie answered, not mentioning the fact that the police appeared to be totally in the dark about any stolen paintings.

"Well, I know absolutely nothing about them. And anyway, I didn't know Alex Donitz that well."

"Enough to rent him space in your studio," Nat answered. "By the way," he continued, fishing the key out of his pocket, "is this yours?"

"No. Where did you find it?"

"You sure it's not your front door key?" he answered, ignoring Sheldon's query.

"No, man. All the keys to this house are completely different to that one. Check if you like."

"We'll do just that," he said as he walked toward the door. "Come on, Maggie." Then he turned and called back to Sheldon, "Perhaps you'd better watch your back."

"You think I'm in danger?" Sheldon cried, running after them. "I told you I needed police protection."

"You've got our number. Call if you think of anything that will help us solve Alex's murder."

"NAT, SOMETHING HAS just come back to me," Maggie, who had waited in the car while Nat had tried all the locks, said to him as he slid behind the wheel.

"What's that?"

"Do you remember the day we discovered Alex dead in the studio . . . ?"

"How could I forget?"

". . . and I was checking out the dining room downstairs while you were upstairs. Well, there was this art book open on the table and I thought the pictures were familiar. Now I realize they were Krieghoffs."

"And," Nat said slowly. "Do you remember way back when Sheldon said his place had been ransacked and told us he'd had a couple of weird calls asking where the Krieghoffs were?"

"You're right. I'd completely forgotten that," Maggie answered. "So contrary to what he's been trying to make us believe, he *is* interested in Krieghoff. Perhaps we should go back and have another go at him."

"No," Nat answered slowly. "We've got him worried. Let him stew for a bit."

"HAVE YOU MADE any progress?" Alice asked as she led them into the sun-filled living room. "Jane is making tea and will be with us shortly."

Ever the hostess, Maggie thought, sinking into one of the plush armchairs. She waited until Nat had seated himself before asking, "Do you sell many originals in the gallery?"

"They are all originals." Alice seemed amused by the question. "We sell works by many artists on consignment."

"I mean paintings by long-dead Canadian artists—Krieghoff, for instance."

"Krieghoff? I'm afraid very few of his pictures ever come on the market these days—except in the case of a bankruptcy or estate sale. Besides, he's well out of our range, though we have sold a few of his prints. Why do you ask?"

Jane entered with a tray and began pouring the tea.

"We think that three of Krieghoff's paintings were taken from Donitz's apartment."

"Who's Donitz? And what has this to do with my gallery?"

"You know, Alice," Jane said, handing cups of tea around. "The young man who was murdered. The one we thought was Sheldon."

"Oh, that young man. Came into the gallery a couple of times." She looked puzzled. "But he was only a Polish immigrant!" She paused. "So he must have stolen them." She took a sip of tea out of the thin china cup. "Now, to change the subject, have you located that young woman who's been leaving those flowers on Jonathan's grave?"

Maggie, still surprised by Alice's snobbish remark, took a moment before answering. "We've made a little progress, and it looks as if Jane could be right and the girl did some modelling for Jonathan for the figurines in the gallery."

"Told you so, Alice," Jane said triumphantly. "All that worry for nothing."

"Worry?" Nat asked quickly. "You thought there was more to it?"

Alice gave a nervous laugh. "Well, you know there was that suicide note."

"Which we now know that Jonathan didn't write," Jane cut in, "and you know that husband of yours just adored you."

Maggie, thinking back to their conversation with Judith, wondered how true that statement was.

"I really would like to have the young woman's name and address," Alice continued, "so that I could thank her for the flowers."

"We'll see what we can find out and let you know," Nat hedged.

"Alice," Maggie cut in quickly, "I know we've asked this before, but have you any idea what was worrying Jonathan? You see," she continued, "Sheldon said he was very worried about something at the time of his death."

"Don't believe anything that man says," Jane said briskly. "Mark my words, he's mixed up in both the murders."

"Now, Jane," Alice had reverted to her soft, placating voice, "he was a great help after Jonathan's death." She turned back to Maggie and Nat. "Jonathan didn't seem all that worried to me. Of course, January is always slow in the art business, but he knew it would pick up once the tourist season began." She looked thoughtful. "It's odd finding those paintings in that young man's apartment . . . and you say he was a friend of Sheldon's."

"Now we've spoiled your day off from the gallery long enough." Nat rose from his chair.

"I know this is going to be a hard question," Maggie said, also rising. She looked straight into Alice's eyes. "But are you absolutely sure everything was okay between you and your husband at the time of his death?"

"Of course it was," Jane answered for her sister. "That's why we couldn't believe that terrible suicide note."

As Maggie started to follow Alice to the door, she saw that Jane had cornered Nat and they were talking quite earnestly about something.

"He was absolutely devoted and faithful to me," Alice said, fishing a small lace hanky out of her pocket and dabbing her eyes. "I know you're doing your best, dear . . ." She patted Maggie on the arm as she led her to the entrance door. "But I sometimes wish that we'd left well enough alone."

"Don't you want to find his murderer?"

"I had accepted his suicide and was getting on with my life . . . Now . . . you and Nat are delving into our lives . . . and the police are back asking questions. Where's it all going to end? Jane," she called, "Maggie is ready to leave." She turned back to Maggie, "Sheldon's coming back to the gallery tomorrow," she said in a conspiratorial whisper. "He wants us to get back to normal—if that's at all possible."

"How does Jane feel about that?" Maggie asked with a smile.

"Not happy. But he's much better than Jane with our clientele."

"I was just commenting to Jane about the wonderful view you have here, Alice," Nat said as he joined Maggie by the door. "By the way, this couldn't be the spare key to the studio, could it?" he held the key out for Alice to look at.

"No. The studio ones are completely different. That's a Yale. Similar to the ones to this apartment." She took it from him and tried to fit it into her entrance door. "It's not mine. Where did you find it?"

"Among the dead young man's effects," he answered.

"I see." Alice pondered for a few moments. "If it had been the studio key," she said, "it could have meant that he was the one who murdered my Jonathan."

"But he hardly knew Jonathan," Jane cut in, "and what possible motive would he have had to do such a terrible thing?"

Alice sighed as she opened the door. "You're right as usual, Jane."

"SO WHAT WERE you and Jane chatting about?" Maggie asked as they walked down the concrete steps leading to the street.

"She wants to come and see us privately. I told her tomorrow about ten. Does that fit your schedule?"

"That's okay with me. Did she say what's on her mind?"

"No. But she doesn't seem to be a happy camper staying with her sister."

"I can't imagine why." Maggie's voice had a sardonic tone to it and Nat gave his partner a quizzical look as he bent to fit the key into the passenger door.

"What do you mean?"

Maggie slipped into the seat. "Let's just say that Alice is not all peaches and cream."

CHAPTER TWENTY-TWO

"Is Mr. Southby going to join us?" Jane asked as she settled into the chair across from Maggie.

"He'll be here in a few minutes." Maggie drew a lined pad toward her. "He had a last-minute call so asked if you'd mind meeting in my office." She smiled at Jane. "It's a bit smaller," she added, spreading her arms, "but cosy."

Jane laughed. "Give me cosy all the time. I'm interested—do you *really* like doing this kind of job?"

"It's stimulating, sometimes dangerous but never boring."

"I think I envy you." Jane looked up as Nat came into the room.

"Sorry about that," he said with a grin as he grabbed a chair, slewed it around and faced the two women. "Now what's on your mind?"

Jane sat for a moment gathering her thoughts. "I'm worried about my sister."

"In what way?" Maggie asked.

"I thought I was being useful, but honestly, I don't think she wants me here. There's been . . . well . . . several hints about when I will be returning to Victoria."

"It could mean she's ready to get on with her life."

"I suppose."

"There's something else, isn't there?" Maggie said gently.

Jane looked miserable. "She's been receiving quite a few phone calls from some man . . . She's very secretive about them, and when I ask, she says they're business calls. Then there's that woman leaving the flowers. She tries to pass that off, but I know she's very upset about them."

"Any idea why?" Nat leaned forward.

"She seems almost afraid. I keep trying to assure her it's some lovesick admirer, but I know she doesn't believe that any more than I do. After all, Jonathan passed away over four months ago."

Maggie leaned over her desk. "Jane, going back to the phone calls. Have you any idea who the man is?"

Jane looked abashed. "I've eavesdropped a few times," she admitted. "I think it's that Saul Wingate. I did hear her mention some woman called Tricia."

"Saul *was* one of Jonathan's friends," Nat cut in, "and he and Tricia are shareholders in that studio on Quebec Street."

"Oh! Then that would explain him calling. But why so secretive?" She paused. "And she was very angry about something he'd done." She sat gazing past Maggie at the view outside her window before suddenly bringing her attention back to Nat. "I guess you think I'm worrying about nothing. But Jonathan *was* murdered. Do you think Alice's life is in danger, too?"

"Are you planning on going back to Victoria?" Maggie asked.

She nodded. "I'm leaving at the end of next week." She stood up. "Oh, about the flower woman. Was she one of Jonathan's lady friends?"

"We're a bit closer to solving that mystery," Nat hedged. "I'm sure she's no threat to Alice."

Maggie accompanied Jane to the outer office where the older woman thanked her for all they had done. "And in spite of what Alice says, I still think I was right in bringing you two in to investigate." She reached out for the door handle and then stopped.

"Oh, I forgot, here's my address and phone number in Victoria." She handed Maggie a neatly folded piece of paper. "Please keep me informed."

When Maggie returned to her office, she found Nat gazing out of the window. "What's with the view out there?" Maggie laughed.

He shook his head. "Just thinking. There are so many loose ends that are leading us nowhere."

"We deserve a break in this case," Maggie answered, leaning back against her desk. "What about us having another talk with that artistic crowd." She turned and pulled her desk calendar toward her. "They're all there on Thursdays, aren't they?"

Nat nodded. "Let's turn up for coffee and surprise them."

THE PHONE CALL came just as Maggie was about to sit down to a supper of canned salmon salad, and she thought briefly of ignoring it. *Probably Harry with another one of his things-to-do lists. But on the other hand it could be something important.*

"I am so sorry to call you in the evening." Maggie recognized Irma's panicky voice.

"What's wrong, Irma?"

"I'm so stupid. I know I shouldn't have told him."

"Told him what?"

"I told Aaron about that woman who claims her daughter is his step-sister and he yelled and yelled and told me I was lying." She paused for breath. "I had to give him her telephone number."

"Did he call her?"

"Yes, and then he left."

"How long ago?"

"A few minutes ago. I'm really scared what he might do."

"Did you warn Judith?"

"Aaron took her phone number and . . . and I don't know her full name," her voice trailed off.

Maggie glanced at the clock and did a quick calculation. "He left about six then?"

"Yes."

"I'll call Judith and warn her. Anyway, stop worrying . . . after all, he is a pastor."

There was a pause before Irma answered. "He's not a happy pastor, Mrs. Spencer. In fact, he should never have become one."

"I'm beginning to see that. Anyway, as I said, I'll get in touch with Judith and warn her that he's on his way."

"Thank you," Irma whispered.

But although Maggie tried several times, there was no answer at Doctor Sloan's clinic, and to make matters worse, Nat's phone went unanswered, too.

"There goes my leisurely supper and peaceful evening." Quickly buttering two pieces of bread, she made herself a salmon sandwich to go.

A GUST OF wind and cold, slanting rain met Maggie when she opened her back door. "Blast!" Retracing her steps to the hall closet, she grabbed her hooded raincoat and prepared for the run down the garden path to the garage that faced onto the back alley. She tried to pull the hood over her face but the wind just snatched it from her hands, letting cold rain run in rivulets down her neck.

The door, wet and swollen with the endless rain, rasped as she pulled it open. "Thank God the garage doesn't leak," she muttered as she thrust the key into the lock of her car and then rammed it into gear. The little car was very reluctant to move. Maggie realized it was well down on the right front. Climbing out she walked around the back and then squeezed up the right side so that she could peer at the front wheel. "Damn and blast! Damn! Damn!" The tire was as flat as a pancake, and the car was such a tight fit for the garage there was absolutely no room to change it.

Walking back to the rear she lifted the trunk and found the spare—inflated, thank goodness—then the jack and the spider wrench. All she needed was someone, anyone to help push the car backward into the alley. Pulling her hood more tightly over her face, she made a dash for the house and telephone. But Nat still wasn't home. She decided to call Judith again to warn her, but the answering service informed her to call again or if it was an emergency to go straight to the hospital. There was only one thing to do: call a taxi. She grabbed the directory.

"It's the weather," the dispatcher at the Ace Taxi Service explained. "All our vehicles are out."

Yellow Taxi Service put her on hold, and then informed her it would be at least an hour's wait.

"I guess I'll have to fix it myself and hope to God I get to Judith in time." Pulling her hood up once again, she prepared for the return run down the garden path. *I'll just have to try and back it out even if the blasted tire is flat.*

Back in the garage, Maggie put the car into reverse and gave it a tentative spurt of gas. It lurched slowly backward until it was nearly out of the garage and across the narrow alleyway. Then, wrenching hard on the steering wheel, she began to manoeuvre the unresponsive vehicle. After a lot of to-ing and fro-ing, a lot of swear words, and a completely ruined tire, she made it. Now came the hard part: changing the tire. *Where are all the men when you need them?*

She knelt in the muddy lane and after several attempts managed to get the jack to raise the car. Then the nuts on the wheel seemed to be welded on, the spider wrench had a mind of its own, and the tires were heavy. But by the time she had lifted the spare into place and had tightened the very last nut, a feeling of triumph took away the misery of being thoroughly soaked, caked in mud, and aching all over. She returned to the house to wash and change.

Nat still wasn't answering his phone, and to her dismay she realized that the time was now seven forty-five. She would have to get a move on if she was going to get to Judith's house before Aaron got there.

MAGGIE DREW UP behind the rusty pick-up and, wasting no time, ran up the path to Judith Sloan's front door. Even before she pushed the doorbell she could hear the raised voices inside the house. Obviously, no one was going to answer the damned bell but she pushed it several times anyway. She waited a few seconds before turning to walk quickly toward the right side of the house to see if there was a way to the backyard. Tall lilac bushes barred her way. *The other side then.* Although bushes had been planted close to it, there was a narrow wooden gate that looked as if it hadn't been opened for years. Using her shoulder, she pushed until she had enough room to squeeze through the gate, only to fall headlong over a large prickly bush. Blood oozing down her face, she struggled to her feet and staggered to the back of the house.

Lights were ablaze in the living area, showing a tableau of a frightened little girl sitting in a large armchair, clutching the spaniel, Rex, to her chest. Both child and dog were gazing in alarm at Judith, who was yelling at Aaron Standish. Maggie, completely forgetting what a sight she must look with her blood-streaked face and tangled hair, tapped on the glass of the French doors to get the girl's attention. The child turned, saw the apparition, and screamed.

At least, Maggie realized, the two adults had stopped yelling at each other and turned to look at her instead. "Open the door," she yelled. It took a few seconds before Judith finally recognized her and slid the door open.

"What the hell are you doing here?" Judith shouted at her, then looking more closely at the blood on Maggie's face, asked, "Whatever's happened to you?"

The dog, making the most of the confusion, managed to break away from Jenny's tight embrace and made a mad dash for Maggie, sending her flying back into the wet garden. Maggie, beginning to feel like a yo-yo, struggled to her feet once again.

Judith grabbed the exuberant spaniel by his collar. "You'd better come in."

"It's that busybody detective woman," Aaron sneered. "I suppose my stupid wife called you."

Judith's medical training took over. "Come with me and I'll clean you up." She turned back to Aaron, "You, sit down and keep that mouth shut. We'll continue this discussion in a normal way when I return. Rex, you keep an eye on him."

The dog obediently settled on the middle of the carpet, a low growl emanating from his throat.

Satisfied, Judith beckoned to her daughter. "Come with us, Jenny."

"They're only scratches," Maggie said, as Judith led her into her surgery. "I'm so sorry I frightened you," she said, turning to Jenny.

"I'm actually glad you did turn up," Judith said, pointing to a chair. "He won't listen to a thing I have to say. Just keeps calling me a whore."

"Aren't you worried he'll hurt the dog?" Maggie asked, remembering Irma's fear of her husband. "He can be very violent."

"He won't hurt Rex, will he?" Jenny cried, and turned to run back into the living room.

"Jenny, stay here," her mother ordered. "Rex will be just fine." But Maggie heard the doubt in Judith's voice. "We'll only be a minute."

"At least my barging in stopped him yelling," Maggie said as Judith applied some salve to the scratches.

Judith stood back and looked at her handiwork. "That should stop the bleeding. Now let's go and talk some sense into that imbecile."

"What's an imbecile?" Jenny asked.

"Jenny," her mother said, squatting down in front of the child. "I have to talk some adult stuff with that man in there. Do you think you and Rex could do me a great big favour and go up to your room for a while?"

"I don't like him, Mommy. I'm scared he'll hurt Rex."

"I'm sure the dog can look after himself."

"But suppose he hurts you and then . . . then he comes after me."

Maggie, who had seen how scared his own family were of him, was of the same mind. "Don't worry, Jenny." She tried to put some confidence in her voice. "Your mommy and I will deal with him."

"You promise? I'm really scared of him."

"I'm sure he's just a bit mixed up." Judith stood up and took Jenny's hand. "Let's go and get Rex."

"I'm glad you have a good watchdog," Maggie said, following behind.

Judith laughed. "Little does he know that Rex is all bark and no bite. I'm sure he'd even welcome a burglar in."

Aaron was sitting in an upright dining-room chair and the fearless dog Rex was still standing guard over him.

"Does he bite?" Aaron nodded fearfully toward the dog.

"He is very protective of us." Judith took the dog by the collar and led him to the door. "You go upstairs with Jenny." She shut the door firmly behind her daughter and the dog and returned to sit opposite Aaron. "All right, Aaron, what is wrong?" she continued. "Why all the anger?"

"How would you feel if one of your father's women turned up . . . with . . . with an illegitimate child?"

Maggie could see Judith taking a firm grip on herself before answering. "I was not one of your father's women. I know it's hard for you to understand, but we were very much in love. But your mother was dying and we parted."

"How could you have had an affair when my mother was so ill? That's what I can't understand. And then you trapped him by getting pregnant."

Judith laughed. "Trapped him! He only found out about Jenny a couple of years before his death." She looked sadly at Aaron. "It's a pity that you never *really* knew your father. He was a very kind and considerate man."

"Kind! Considerate! He never loved either my mother or me."

"Sometimes marriages don't work."

"So if he loved you so much, why did he marry that . . . Alice?"

"I guess he and Alice were both lonely." She looked steadily at Aaron. "I had no idea he had remarried. I just came back to the Coast because I thought he should get to know his daughter."

"There's no money, if that's what you're after. She got all that."

"I don't need your money, Aaron. I had hoped we could be friends." She shrugged. "There is just one other matter."

"What's that?" He stood up and reached for his raincoat.

"Don't let Alice know our name or where we live."

"Why not? You said you're not after his money."

She spoke very calmly. "Your father was murdered, Aaron. He didn't commit suicide." She walked him to the door leading into the hallway.

"But why are you afraid? His murder has nothing to do with you, has it?"

Without answering him, she opened the front door to let him out. "Look after those precious daughters of yours."

"I'm sorry you've got caught up in this horrible mess," Judith said to Maggie when she returned to the living room.

"That's my job, so don't worry about it. But," Maggie added as she reached for her coat, "I feel very sorry for that man's wife and kids."

Judith nodded. "Me, too. But I mean to keep in touch with them."

"NOW FOR MY belated supper." Maggie let herself in the back door of her house and reached for the light switch. Oscar, sitting in his basket and looking very guilty, gave a few thuds with his tail, and Emily, in her usual place on the window sill, was fastidiously preening her whiskers. "Okay, what have you two been up to?"

The broken plate on the floor told her all. It still had bits of lettuce, cucumber, and tomato clinging to it, but the salmon had completely disappeared. There were only torn bits of wax paper left of the sandwich she had forgotten to take with her. She was too exhausted to scold.

She walked disconsolately to the hall closet to hang up her raincoat and caught sight of her bedraggled figure in the hall mirror. Wet, stringy hair, scratches on both cheeks and hands, and a wet and filthy raincoat. "You're some detective, Maggie!" And she began to laugh.

"THAT CAT SCRATCH you?" Henny demanded on seeing Maggie's face the next morning. "You have to take care, you could get that . . . that . . . tetsie-something."

"Tetanus," Maggie supplied. "This was a rosebush. I fell in it." Not waiting for Henny to give dire warnings on the diseases that could be caught by falling into rosebushes, she asked, "Is Nat in?"

Henny nodded. "Mr. Nat come in early."

"WHAT THE HELL happened to you?"

"And good morning to you, too, Nat. And where were you last night when I needed you?" she asked, ignoring his question.

"Had an urgent call from Nancy."

"And what did she want *this time?*" Although Maggie had come to know Nat's ex-wife, Nancy, on a case the previous year, she'd also come to know they could never be real buddies.

"The kitchen tap sprang a leak and flooded the place," he explained with one of his lopsided grins.

"What's wrong with calling a plumber?" Maggie's face was sore and she was not feeling at all charitable toward mankind and Nancy in particular.

"On a Tuesday night? Anyway, what *did* happen to you?"

Maggie leaned against the doorjamb and told him.

Nat burst out laughing. "I can just see you changing a tire in that narrow alleyway." The look on his partner's face stopped him getting in any deeper. "Do you think Judith was scared by Aaron's visit?"

"Yes, very. But she was even more scared that he would tell Alice about her and Jenny's existence. But I can't see that being a problem—he has very little to do with his stepmother."

Nat leaned back in his swivel chair. "Depends how vindictive he wants to be. I have a feeling he would love to get one over on Alice."

"You may be right," she said, settling into the chair in front of his desk. "He's a strange character, and I know that Irma is scared of him—she told me he has an awful temper."

He leaned over the desk to touch her face very gently. "Will these be gone by Midge's big day?"

"Hope so. I've got slightly over three weeks."

"You still okay for our visit to Saul Wingate's studio on Thursday?"

Maggie nodded. "I did have another appointment but changed it to Friday. Any idea what excuse we're giving for us calling on them unannounced?"

Nat stared into space for a few moments. "You know, Maggie, I think that bunch knows more than they're letting on. Perhaps we can shake them by just turning up."

CHAPTER TWENTY-THREE

Maggie and Nat hesitated in front of the studio door, which stood wide open to the fine June afternoon sunshine.

"Do we ring the bell or just walk in?" Maggie asked.

"What are you doing here?" They turned to see Saul Wingate with his arms full of papers and sketchbooks and a leather satchel slung over one shoulder.

"We were in the neighbourhood and wondered if any of you had any new thoughts on Jonathan's murder."

"I haven't. Don't know about the rest of the gang. At least," he continued, pushing the books into Nat's arms, "you can help me with these." And he went back to his car, parked at the curb, and emerged with another armload of supplies.

"Are the others here?" Maggie asked.

"I've no idea," Saul answered as he led the way inside. "One never knows who'll turn up." But with the exception of Adele Rousseau, they were all in the studio. "Look who's come to visit us," he said, throwing his satchel onto the nearest scarred table.

"Hope you don't mind us barging in like this," Nat said as he placed the sketchbooks beside Saul's satchel. "We've just a few things to ask."

Nobody answered. The atmosphere seemed almost hostile to Maggie as she moved into the room and sat down on one of the stools.

"I guess you've heard by now that Maggie came across some original Cornelius Krieghoff paintings in Alex Donitz's apartment?" Nat asked, moving to a position behind Maggie's stool.

"Alice did mention something about it to me," Saul Wingate answered, "but I don't think anyone else here knows about it."

"Alex Donitz?" Tricia Forbes asked in her lazy voice. "Do I know him?"

"For God's sake," Saul answered her. "The young man who was killed. You know ... in Sheldon's studio."

"Oh, *that* young man." She turned back to Maggie. "So what were you doing in his apartment?"

"The same as the police. Looking around."

"Can't see how finding some paintings has anything to do with Jonathan's death," she said.

"I'd like to see them, though," Chris Barfield said.

"I don't have them," Maggie answered.

"That's right." Saul began unfastening the buckles on his satchel. "Alice mentioned that you were attacked and they were snatched from you."

"Not me. I was using the phone downstairs when somebody snatched them from Gloria." Maggie didn't go into any other details.

"Who's Gloria?"

"For God's sake, Tricia, don't you remember anything? She was Alex's girl friend."

"Oh, yes, that Gloria. What a ghastly name. Then he must have stolen them in the first place," she added petulantly. "Stands to reason, Polish immigrant, no money, no prospects."

So much for not knowing who Alex Donitz was, Maggie mused, thinking how she'd like to swipe the cat-like smile off the woman's face.

"But how would he know where to steal them?" Chris asked. "Had to be from a private collection of some sort."

"You're all artists," Nat said, looking around. "Perhaps one of you might have heard of an art theft—"

"Oh, come on," Ian Buckle, who had been silent up to then, interrupted. "We make pots and sculptures, mostly for our own edification, I might add, and of course hoping we're going to make it big one day. But none of us move in the circles of the rich collectors."

"I hope you're not implying that we're thieves?" Chris pulled his briar pipe and a can of tobacco out of his pocket, filled the bowl, tamped it, and then struck a match before continuing. "My art and my private life are quite enough for me."

"I see that Adele isn't here today." Maggie nodded to the potter's wheel the woman had been using on their last visit, which stood empty.

"She got all huffy and left us," Tricia answered. "Just as well. She didn't fit in."

Saul looked uncomfortable. "She really joined the group because she was a close friend of Jonathan's," he explained. "I think she's planning to organize a group of her own."

"Do you have her address?" Nat asked.

Saul nodded. "Here, I'll write it out for you."

"Just one other thing," Nat turned to face all of them. "Have any of you lost a key."

"What kind of key?" Ian asked.

Once again Nat pulled it from his pocket and showed it to him. "Looks like an ordinary door key."

"Didn't you say that you'd lost your front door key, Tricia?" Chris asked.

"It was just misplaced," she answered tersely, and then turning to Nat asked, "Where did you find this one?"

"In Alex Donitz's apartment," he replied.

"What in heaven's name would any one of us be doing in that man's sleazy apartment?" Tricia asked.

"How do you know it's sleazy?" Maggie asked quickly.

"What else could he have afforded?" Chris answered for her. "You told us he was a young Polish emigrant with no money." He turned back to his potting wheel.

"SO WHAT DO you think of that charming little group?" Nat asked before pulling away from the curb.

"That Tricia is really something, and I think she's only playing dumb. She knows much more than she lets on."

"What makes you say that?"

"She said she knew nothing about the theft of the paintings, but then she said there were three of them. I have a strong feeling that artsy little group is mixed up in all this."

"And she knew what kind of apartment Donitz lived in," Nat mused.

"And the key?"

"Perhaps she was lying and she's the one who grabbed the paintings from Gloria," Nat answered. "It doesn't fit the potting studio, I tried it on the way out."

"But we've no way of proving it was her." Maggie was thoughtful for a moment. "Gloria did say the person smelt faintly of flowers—it could have been talc powder."

"I can't see her as a thug." Nat laughed. "She'd be worried that she would break one of her fingernails."

"It *is* hard to imagine," Maggie agreed with a grin. "Okay, where to now?"

Nat handed her the slip of paper with Adele's address on it. "Let's go potting."

THE HOUSE ON Maple was a small one-storied stucco, and both house and scrubby front yard were in urgent need of care. When Adele finally opened the door, Maggie wasn't sure whether the look on her face was fear or astonishment.

"What do you want?" She peered myopically at them before fumbling for the glasses that were hanging around her neck. "Oh! It's you." She looked up and down the street and then opened the door wider. "I suppose you'd better come in."

"Is anything the matter?" Maggie and Nat followed Adele into what should have been her living room but which had been converted into a studio. It was a typical potter's studio—two wheels, bags of clay, shelves with pots, jugs, mugs, odd-looking teapots drying or waiting to be fired, and glass jam jars full of shaping implements. Mounds of clay sat under a damp towel on a low table at one end of the room, waiting to be readied for the wheel. Adele pushed the piles of books on pottery, pencil sketches, and other bits of paper off a couple of stools and indicated they should sit down. Maggie resisted the urge to take a handkerchief out of her pocket and dust the stool first.

"Why should there be anything the matter?" Adele sat on the seat of the nearest wheel where a lump of clay had been centred. She peered at Maggie.

"You left the other studio and Tricia said you were . . . a bit huffy."

"She would, the bitch. I needed to move back into my own space."

"Why did you work there, anyway?" Nat asked. "You've got everything you need right here."

"You mean why did I lower myself to use the Quebec Street studio? I did it to be near my dear Jonathan." Adele answered in such a defiant manner that Maggie turned to see if Nat was as startled as she was. "Sorry, didn't mean to sound off like that." And to their astonishment the woman suddenly burst into tears.

Maggie moved over to Adele and put her arm around her shoulder. Brusquely pushing her away, the woman fished into her clay-smeared apron pocket, pulled out a crumpled handkerchief, and buried her face in it. Feeling very uncomfortable, Maggie and Nat waited for the sobs to subside.

Giving her eyes a final wipe, Adele stood up, staggered over to the sink, washed her face under the running tap, and dried her face on a towel. "I'm sorry about that," she hiccupped as she returned to her seat. "It's just I miss him so damned much."

While Nat was still trying to think *who* she missed, Maggie said quietly, "You loved him dearly."

Adele nodded. "I suppose you think I'm a silly old fool. He was at least ten years younger than me, but he was such a gentle soul. How could anyone have killed him like that?" Dabbing her eyes, she looked straight at Maggie. "That bunch of morons have no feelings, just carried on as if nothing had happened, even . . . even laughed at me."

Nat, who had suddenly caught on that Adele was talking about Jonathan, decided to let Maggie carry the ball.

"What could they find to laugh at?" Maggie asked.

"I tried to hide my feelings but that bitch—and I'm sorry, but she is a bitch—realized I was in love with him. And even after he was gone, there were the nasty little digs. I just couldn't stand it anymore."

"Did Jonathan know?"

"I don't think so. I sort of hoped when his first wife died . . . but then he met Alice, which to my mind was another mistake. He really wasn't a good judge of women, you know."

"So I gathered," Nat cut in dryly.

"But he trusted me," she said proudly. "He told me about the girl he'd loved years before. Did you know he had a daughter?"

"You know about Judith and Jenny?" Nat asked in astonishment. "Why didn't you say so when we showed you their photographs?"

"Jonathan didn't want anyone at the studio to know about

them. But," she added proudly, "he took me into his confidence." She twisted the sodden towel between her hands before carrying on. "He needed someone to talk to. He was terrified that Alice would find out about them."

"Did she?" Maggie asked.

"She knew there was someone, especially after Jonathan asked for a divorce. She absolutely refused to give him one."

"I can't understand why Jonathan was so terrified she'd find out." Nat gazed across the room for a moment. "After all, what could she have done about it?"

"Made life miserable for the poor man. She threatened she'd take him to the cleaners if he left her." She paused and gazed out of the window. "I often wonder about her first husband's death . . . After all, no one saw him fall down the basement steps."

"Is that how he died?"

"You didn't know? Alice is a black widow spider where husbands are concerned."

"SORRY TO CALL you so late," Maggie said after Jane Weatherby lifted the receiver. "Hope you weren't watching anything exciting on TV?"

"Maggie! How nice to hear your voice. No, only a show about a talking horse. Actually," she gave an apologetic laugh, "it's quite funny."

"You mean Mr. Ed, the talking horse, and his pal, Wilbur Post? Oh, I enjoy that program, too."

"Don't let on to Alice, will you? She only watches intellectual programs."

Maggie laughed. "Your secret is safe with me. Actually, I'm calling about Alice's first husband."

"First husband? Do you mean Hugo or her very first one? Hugo was actually her second."

"Second! Do you mean she's been married three times?" Maggie asked incredulously.

"Well, the first one hardly counted, as it only lasted a year." There was a pause on the line before Jane continued. "She's been very unlucky in her choice of partners. It makes me glad I chose the single life."

Maggie was speechless for a moment. "So what happened to the first one?"

"It was one of those teenage romances, and they soon realized it was a mistake. I did hear that he'd remarried. Can't even remember his name . . . Charlie something . . . Bracken . . . that's right . . . Charlie Bracken."

"And the second one, Hugo?"

"Alice worked at a firm that did picture restoration, reframing, silk-screening—all kinds of things to do with art. Hugo was a recent widower, and he brought some pictures in to be cleaned. They dated and a few months later they were married. Between you and me, Maggie, I'm sure he was looking for an unpaid housekeeper with all the frills."

"How long were they married?"

"About five years and then he had that tragic accident."

"He fell down some stairs?"

"Yes. He seems to have tripped over their pet dog. It was terrible for my sister because she'd been the one to leave the door open. She went down to get a jar of canned fruit for our dinner and forgot to close the door. It's still hard for her to talk about it."

"I can imagine. Was he . . . was he . . . dead when she got to him?"

"He'd fallen head first onto the concrete floor. She was in shock for days."

"You said *our* dinner. Were you there at the time?"

Jane sighed audibly. "Not when he fell. I was attending a two-day conference at UBC—I always stayed with my sister and her husband when I was in Vancouver—and the session had run over-time so the ambulance had come and gone by the time I got to their place."

"Alice mentioned that he left her pretty badly off—financially."

"The bugger left all his money to his two daughters from his previous marriage. Alice just got the house."

"I guess that was something."

"It was mortgaged up to the hilt," Jane said dryly.

"And then she lost Jonathan," Maggie said softly.

"She thought things were at last going right for her. She loved that man."

"Alice is very lucky to have a sister who is so protective."

"Our parents died when she was ten—so I practically brought her up."

"It must've been very hard for you to stand by and see her last two marriages end in tragedy," Maggie said sympathetically.

"And not be able to do a damn thing about them," Jane answered tersely. There was something of a deeper meaning here, but Maggie couldn't quite put her finger on it. After she got off the phone, she sat for quite a while pondering the conversation she'd just had with Jane, and wondered why she had this feeling of disquiet.

CHAPTER TWENTY-FOUR

The next morning Maggie peered into Nat's office and announced, "Alice has been married three times. One year to number one and five years to Hugo Smyth. He apparently tripped over his dog and fell down the basement stairs and was pronounced DOA when he arrived at Emergency."

"Where did you get all that info so early in the morning? Come in here and explain yourself, woman."

Maggie laughed and looked over to where their girl Friday was sitting at her desk with her mouth open. "Do you think I should demean myself, Henny?"

"Mr. Nat is only yoking," Being Dutch, Henny sometimes had a hard time with the letter J. "You want me to take notes?"

"You're busy. I'll fill you in later."

"SO SHE DIVORCED number one, and number two only left her a mortgaged house. At least she did better with Jonathan."

"M-m-m. But did she do all that well?" Nat said. "Granted, she got the apartment in English Bay, though she says that was already hers. But the gallery sells on consignment and the artists have to be really well known for her to make money on them. There is Jonathan's work, of course."

"As far as I could see there's only the Silver Unicorn and a few of his figurines left," Maggie mused. "And I can't see her selling the unicorn, can you?"

"No. It's the gallery's logo."

"And he only left $5,000 to his son," Maggie added. "I wonder if he left anything to Judith and Jenny?"

"And how do we find out?"

"Let's ask Judith." Maggie arose from her chair and headed for the door. "There's no time like the present."

"You're going to ask her on the telephone?"

"No. I'm not that insensitive. I'll call and ask when it would be convenient for her to see me."

As it happened Judith only had morning office hours on Fridays and she would—rather reluctantly—see Maggie at noon.

"SO WHAT'S SO urgent?" Judith led Maggie into her office and indicated the chair that faced her across a very tidy desk.

"A rather delicate question."

"Okay . . ." Judith said carefully. "What do you want to know?"

"Jonathan's estate. Did he leave you or Jenny anything in his will?"

"Why are you asking that?" Then a look of consternation crossed her face. "My God, this isn't coming from Alice, is it?"

"No." Maggie looked sharply at the woman across the desk. "Are you sure she doesn't know about you and Jenny?"

Judith buried her face in her hands. "I honestly don't know."

Maggie waited a few moments before pressing her for an answer. "About the will. Did he leave you anything in it?"

"No." She sat looking through the window at her garden. "But you know, it was as if he knew something was going to happen to him."

"Why?"

"It was about three months before . . . before he died. He

took me to see his lawyer . . . Humphrey Crumbie . . ." She gave a rare smile before continuing. "Such a funny name. Anyway, he told me if ever I found myself in any kind of difficulty, I was to call Mr. Crumbie."

"So Jonathan was helping you financially?"

"Not me . . . Jenny. He insisted on paying for her school fees. She's a pupil at York House, you see."

"Great school," Maggie said. "I wish my two girls could have gone there, but the fees were beyond us at the time."

"To be perfectly blunt, Maggie, I couldn't have afforded it either without his help."

"So it's a trust fund? And there's no way Alice could have found out about it?"

Judith shook her head again. "It was just between us and the lawyer—and there's no way Mr. Crumbie would tell anybody."

Maggie smiled. "You're right there. I know him very well."

"You do?"

"He's one of my husband's law partners. And although I've left Harry, I can say in all sincerity that you can put all your trust in that firm." She got up to leave. "Just one other thing, Judith . . . You haven't noticed anyone following you or received strange phone calls?"

"No phone calls, but sometimes I'm sure I'm being followed." She laughed lightly. "But maybe I'm just paranoid."

AFTER LEAVING JUDITH'S house, Maggie sat in her car for a few minutes to gather her thoughts. Then glancing at her watch, she realized that there was no point in going back to the office. After all, it was a Friday and she was meeting Nat around seven-thirty at Monty's Seafood restaurant on West Hastings—she could fill him in on her conversation with Judith over dinner.

After parking the car in her garage, she walked slowly up

through her mix-and-matched garden and thought it was time she did some urgent weeding and pruning. The dandelions' fluffy white heads were ready and waiting to send their glorious parachutes of seeds to all her neighbours' gardens. As she entered the house, she heard the phone ringing. Emily, crouching by the back door waiting to escape outside, was almost trampled as Maggie lunged for the instrument.

"It's me, Adele Rousseau. Oh, dear. You sound out of breath. I do hope I didn't interrupt you getting supper . . . or anything."

"No, it's okay." Maggie laughed. "I just missed squashing my cat, that's all."

"You have a cat? How nice."

"What can I do for you, Adele?"

"You did leave your card, and you did say if I thought of anything . . ."

"Yes," Maggie said encouragingly.

"It was before Jonathan . . . died. I knew he was worried about something."

"It was something he said?"

"No, not really. It was something he hid."

"Hid? What?"

"He didn't tell me what it was. Only the location . . . in case something happened . . . to him. I was so unhappy that I forgot all about it."

"What did he say to you exactly?"

Adele was quiet for a few moments. "He said—'If anything should happen to me, old girl'—that's what he used to call me," she added with a little giggle, "'you'll find something,' I think he said a note, hidden in the studio."

"And he didn't tell you what it was?"

"No. He said if he was dead, I'd know what to do."

"Did he mean his studio at the gallery?"

"I took it to be the one where we all worked—on Quebec Street."

"And you've only just remembered this?"

"I told you I completely forgot."

"But he died over four months ago . . ."

"You sound just like that lot at the studio," she snapped. "You think I'm past it and eccentric. But I'm not making this up."

Maggie, who was thinking just that, jumped in quickly. "I'm only surprised that you've just remembered, that's all, Adele."

"I've had a lot on my mind. Now what do we do about this?"

"We can go to the police, but they'd want more information, and they wouldn't search a place without a valid reason. After all, you don't even know what it is that Jonathan's hidden."

"I was thinking more on the lines that you and I should go and have a look."

"What? We can't do that." Maggie knew from experience that Nat would absolutely veto that suggestion. She'd been in too many unauthorized scrapes in the past.

"I've still got my key," Adele said quietly. "Of course, I could go on my own, but . . . two pairs of eyes and all that . . . and there's never anyone there on a Friday night," she added, as if that clinched it.

"What about the people in that café next to the studio?"

"They close at six. You pick me up around six-thirty?"

"It's not a good idea, Adele. Besides, I'm meeting Mr. Southby for dinner at seven-thirty."

"M-m-m. That would be a bit tight. Let me see, it's five-thirty now. Make it six o'clock then. That'll give you plenty of time to make your date. You have my address."

"I really don't think this is a good idea . . ." But Adele had put her phone down. Maggie sat down hard on the nearest chair and buried her head in her hands. *Her fellow artists are right—she's batty.* She considered calling Nat but decided it would be better after the deed was done, and then she and Nat could have a good laugh about it. Though somehow Maggie knew he wouldn't consider it something to laugh about. *I've got to call her back.* But as usual, her curiosity got the better of her.

Adele, a large tapestry bag slung over her shoulder, her body encased in black slacks and black shirt with a squashed black felt hat on her head, was waiting as Maggie drew up outside the shabby, paint-peeled house. Opening the passenger door, she slid in and smiled at Maggie.

"Hard to hide this car. Whatever possessed you to buy a red one?" She settled herself down in the passenger seat and pulled her hat over her face. "We'll just have to park a bit before the studio and walk. This is quite an adventure, isn't it?"

Maggie, surprised at the difference between the tearful woman she had last seen and this one eager for adventure, said, "This isn't a very good idea, Adele. It's still light and we could be seen by someone."

"And I had you pegged for the adventurous type! Don't worry—just follow my lead. We'll just ad lib if one of those buggers turn up."

Maggie was also surprised at the language of this new Adele.

AS ADELE SUGGESTED, Maggie pulled into the curb a few shops before the studio and waited until Adele had hauled herself out of the passenger seat.

"Don't worry. No one will be there."

"But there's someone in *there*," Maggie hissed as they came abreast of the café.

"That's only Cristobel Jennings. She's the owner and I think she's Swedish."

"You said they closed at six."

"They do, but they have to clear up, you know." And to

Maggie's horror, Adele tapped on the window and waved to the apron-clad woman who immediately came to the door.

"Thought you'd finished with that lot next door." Topping six feet, Cristobel Jennings peered down at Adele. "I told you that you'd miss my baking."

"It's your baking that's caused this." Adele laughed and patted her stomach. "This is my friend, Maggie, and we've come to collect the rest of my things. In case you think the noises next door are ghosts."

"It will be more like a herd of elephants," she answered, glancing down at the lace-up boots Adele was wearing.

"The others don't need to know I've been back," Adele said conspiratorially.

"Okay by me." Cristobel turned and re-entered the café, locking the door behind her.

"She's a good friend." Adele slipped her key into the lock of the studio's door.

"I hope so." Maggie had visions of the entire group of artists and the police arriving at the studio to find out what was going on.

Maggie soon understood the reason for Adele's large tapestry bag. First a coffee-stained misshapen mug disappeared into it, followed by tools, brushes, a pair of black wool socks, numerous pencils, pens and erasers, and, after scrutinizing the bookshelf, a couple of dog-eared books. "I wondered where they'd got to," she exclaimed, stuffing them in the bag.

"Aren't we supposed to be looking for something?" Maggie asked as she watched the bag get fatter and fatter.

"Quite forgot for the moment. You start that side." She pointed to a row of pot-drying racks mounted on casters.

"But I don't know what I'm looking for."

Adele looked into the distance for a few moments. "Well, it can't be very big or someone would have discovered it already."

"'They probably have," Maggie snapped back. "Sit down, Adele, and tell me again what Jonathan said to you."

Adele sat. "It was a long time ago, you know . . ."

"And I haven't got time to search a room without some idea what I'm looking for."

She looked at the row of racks absently. "He said—'If something funny should happen to me, old girl'—I told you that's what he called me—'I've left something in the studio.' Or perhaps he said he'd left a note in the studio . . . I told you, it was a long time ago."

"Oh! For God's sake, think!"

"No need to get all shirty. I think he said it was a note."

"And he was referring to this studio?"

"I told you before he was."

"Okay." Maggie took a firm hold of herself. "Where did he keep his things?"

"Nowhere in particular. We sort of shared the space." Then, seeing Maggie's face, she quickly added, "He kept some of his things on that shelf over there."

"There's nothing much on it now."

"There's his tea caddy." She pointed to a tin adorned with roses intertwined with the words LIPTON TEA, and then, looking wistfully at the tin, she grabbed a clay-stained rag from the table set under the shelf and wiped her eyes. "He only drank tea made with real tea leaves, you know." When Maggie looked blankly at her, she clarified by saying, "Loose tea leaves."

Maggie reached for the tin and tried to pry off the lid but only succeeded in breaking one of her fingernails. "Damn!"

"Give it to me." Adele took the tin and then grabbed a screwdriver from a nearby shelf. "He kept it tightly sealed so the tea didn't get stale." She dug the blade into the groove. "There you go."

Maggie peered inside the tin. "There's only tea," she said, disappointed.

"You sure?" Adele grabbed back the tin and pushed her plump hand down into the tea leaves and felt around. "You're right. I guess we'll have to look somewhere else."

"After you've picked up the tea you've spilled," Maggie said firmly.

"There's a brush and dustpan in that closet."

"Adele, I'll have to leave soon." Maggie sat back on her heels after sweeping up the last of the tea.

"Let's give it a few more minutes."

Maggie glanced around the room. They had searched all of the shelves, pulled racks away from the walls, riffled through every art book and magazine. There was nothing left to search. "That's it! We've exhausted all the hiding places in this godforsaken hole." She couldn't help sounding testy.

Adele shrugged. "I guess one of the others must've found it."

"Or you misunderstood what Jonathan said to you." After washing her dusty hands under the tap, Maggie looked around for a towel, but the only things available were the clay-smeared towels draped over drying sculptures. "Whose coat is that?" She nodded toward a corduroy jacket with leather elbows hanging on a hook by the door.

Adele, who was standing precariously on a stool to search the top of a bookcase, looked down at Maggie, "That? Jonathan kept it here as a spare. The studio gets cold in winter. Nothing up here," she added.

"That's it, then." Maggie watched in trepidation as Adele clutched her way down the bookcase. She breathed a sigh of relief when the woman landed safely on her feet. All she needed was to have to call an ambulance for a broken limb. "Where did I put my purse? Ah! There it is. Come on, Adele, I really must be going." She reached for the door handle and then stopped and looked at the jacket.

"Well, go on then," Adele said behind her.

"Wait a sec." Maggie plunged her hand into each of the jacket's pockets, but apart from a few toffee wrappers, accumulated crumbs, and a book of matches advertising some restaurant, there was nothing. Maggie sighed, "Oh, well, just a thought. Nice lining," she added as she started to return the jacket to its hook. "Ah!" There were two inside pockets and in one of them was a tightly folded piece of paper.

Adele peered excitedly over Maggie's shoulder. "Silly me. He must've have said 'coat,' not 'note.' What does it say?"

"It seems to be a list," Maggie replied, as she carefully spread it open. "But it doesn't seem to make much sense." She handed it over to Adele. "What do you make of it?"

"I've no idea." She sounded so disappointed. "I thought it might tell us who murdered him."

Maggie smiled. "He'd hardly know that in advance. Would you mind if I took it with me?"

"Why not? Perhaps your partner will be able to help you unravel it."

CHAPTER TWENTY-FIVE

"And that's why I'm late."

Maggie waited until they'd ordered—sole stuffed with baby shrimp in a creamy wine sauce for her, and fish and chips for Nat—before filling him in on her "adventure" with Adele. She waited for the explosion.

"You could have called me," he said quietly.

She would rather have had the explosion. "I know. Anyway, here's the piece of paper."

"It's probably his laundry list," Nat commented dryly, not even glancing at it.

Maggie knew he was very miffed, but she wasn't about to let it spoil her appetite. She was starved and the food looked wonderful. She let the list lay between them while they ate.

Finally Nat pushed his empty plate away, reached for his coffee, and picked up the piece of paper. "This doesn't mean I'm happy about you going off with that crazy woman without telling me. Just a phone call, Maggie—that's all it takes."

"You would have said no."

"Maybe. But it's because I love you and I'm so scared of you getting hurt again." He leaned over the table and covered her hand with his. "Now let's look at that piece of paper."

Jonathan—Some suggestions that I think might be going on.

SW—paintings, probably copies.

CB?—IB?

Adele—No.

TF—small stuff: miniatures, inlaid snuff boxes, paper weights, etc.

AS—keeps accounts, finds buyers.

The three CKs you found (Have them safe but want them out of my place ASAP.)

SW

"What do you make of it?" she asked

"I have absolutely no idea. Obviously, peoples' initials and works of art." He sat looking at it for a few more moments. "Off hand I'd say that SW could be either Sheldon White or Saul Wingate, TF could be Tricia Forbes, CB Chris Barfield. And all of them use the Quebec Street studio."

"I don't recall an AS there."

"Me either. Whoever AS is, he or she kept the books and moved the stuff."

"Moved! This could be a list of stolen stuff, Nat."

"Or it could all be legitimate. The group could be buying from people who want to sell their art and other valuables. Or," Nat said quietly, "you're right and they are stealing the stuff."

"But how? I can't imagine any of them being cat burglars like Raffles. But perhaps this explains Jonathan's murder. Maybe he found out."

"And AS could be Alice Standish, though I have a job seeing her mixed up in art theft."

"And I can't see her murdering Jonathan," Maggie answered. "Jane told me she really loved him."

Nat sat thinking for a moment before answering. "I'll put my money on the SW being Sheldon White. Perhaps he will be able to answer some pertinent questions on this note. What about first thing in the morning?"

"Can't. It's Saturday tomorrow and I'm meeting with the caterers and having a final fitting for my dress."

"Oh, the wedding! But I thought you said you'd already bought a dress."

"I did. But it was too long and it had to be altered to fit properly. Anyway," she added, "it would be better to see Sheldon at his house on Monday."

"You could be right." He looked up as the waiter deftly removed their empty plates and placed the dessert menu in front of them. "Dessert?" he asked.

"Of course. Raspberry swirl cheesecake—we can share."

They left the restaurant feeling well fed—or in Maggie's case, a bit overstuffed—and walked to the rear car park.

"My place for coffee?" Maggie asked as she climbed into the ancient Chevy.

"Where else?" Nat put the car into gear.

MAGGIE WAS UP, showered, dressed, and making breakfast when Nat made his appearance the next morning. "You look like you've had a night on the tiles," she commented, grinning.

Coming up behind her, he slipped his arms around her waist and pulled her tightly against him. "Can't you forget your dress fitting and come back to bed?"

Turning to face him, she kissed him gently on the lips before pulling away. "Love to, but the wedding is only a couple of weeks away."

"Will you be seeing Harry at the caterers, too?" he asked just a trifle petulantly.

"No. Just me. So you can take that jealous look off your face," she answered with a laugh. "I have to give them the final count and the printed cards for the seating arrangements—after that, it will be in the lap of the gods. Now sit and enjoy the breakfast I've made you."

"You've seen a lot of Harry lately. Has he been getting on to you about going back to him?"

"Oh, Nat dear, he gave up a long time ago. Now pass the marmalade."

"Harry will never give up. I love your daughter Midge, but I'll be damn glad when she's safely married to Jason and we can get back to normal."

Taking a last sip of her coffee, Maggie swept up her dishes and walked to the sink. "I want her day to be wonderful and it will be over so quickly, and if that means putting up with Harry and his detestable mother to achieve that, then so be it."

"I'm sorry to be so . . ."

". . . Jealous?" she finished the sentence for him. "But you've no need to feel jealous. Now," she added, "to change the subject, don't forget we're going to see Swan Lake at the Queen Elizabeth tonight."

"How could I forget?" Ballet wasn't really Nat's thing, but he knew that Maggie adored it. She had even managed to drag him to several performances since the big theatre had been built just three years earlier.

"Oh, blast, look at the time. Be a dear and take Oscar for a run before you leave, okay?"

Oscar, hearing his name, looked expectantly from one to the other.

"By the way, I might go and see Sheldon myself," he called to her as she stepped out the back door.

"Okay. But be careful."

NAT'S CLEANING LADY was in his apartment and washing the kitchen floor when he arrived home.

"I've stripped and put clean sheets on your bed, Mr. Southby," she greeted him. "You need a new can of Vim and washing-up soap. I've told you already it's time you bought yourself some new towels—the ones you got are a disgrace, and your tea towels . . ."

"I'll try and remember, Mrs. Waters," he answered as he skirted around the metal bucket. "Next time I shop," he added making a dash for his bedroom to change his clothes.

"You said that the last time," she called after him.

"Oh, you do look smart," she commented when Nat reappeared a short time later wearing a grey pinstriped suit, white shirt, and blue tie. "You going somewhere nice with your lady friend?"

"To the ballet this evening."

"How nice. Didn't think you were the ballet type."

"I've left your money on the table. Don't forget to lock up," he added, making his escape.

SHELDON WHITE'S HOUSE on William Street looked just as drab as the first time he and Maggie had called there and found the body. It was late afternoon, a bit later than Nat had intended, and he sincerely hoped there wouldn't be any unpleasant surprises on this visit. Slamming and locking his car door, he walked up the cracked concrete path and rang the bell several times before he decided to try the back.

Sheldon, paintbrush in his hand and wearing a long-sleeved paint-daubed shirt, opened the studio door to Nat's repeated knocking. It was obvious he was not at all pleased to see his visitor.

"What is it this time . . . another dead body?"

"Just want you to look at something."

"Can't it wait until Monday? I'm very busy . . ."

"This won't take a minute." Nat pushed his way into Sheldon's studio.

"What is it?" Sheldon demanded.

Nat withdrew the paper from his pocket and handed it to him. "Did you write this?"

"No," he said, barely glancing at it before thrusting the list back into Nat's hands. "Now get out of my . . ."

"Look again," Nat said through gritted teeth.

"Where did it come from?"

"Came to light among Jonathan's things."

"It did? Gimme. I'll have another look. No, never seen it before."

"You're saying that the SW who signed it isn't you?"

"I keep telling you and the cops that I had nothing to do with Jonathan or Alex's murders."

"I didn't say anything about murders. All I want to know is if you wrote this list and gave it to Jonathan."

"I told you I know nothing about it. Now look what you've made me do!" he said as, in his agitation, he knocked over the easel at which he had been working. When Nat knocked at the door, he had thrown a sheet over the painting, and now easel, painting and sheet were all on the floor. Bending down, he quickly picked up the easel then the painting and threw the sheet back over it, but not before Nat saw that the painting was an exact replica of the one on the page pinned to an adjoining easel. It had obviously been cut from a book of art illustrations.

"You copy paintings?" Nat asked, nodding toward the covered easel.

"All artists copy paintings," Sheldon said scathingly. "It's the only way to understand the techniques of the old masters."

"But I think that you are the SW on this list because it says here, 'SW—copies or originals.' And while we're discussing this list, I think that the CKs it mentions are the Cornelius Krieghoffs that were stolen from Alex's apartment. And I think," Nat said enunciating each word very clearly and advancing toward the hapless Sheldon, "that Jonathan gave the Krieghoffs to you for safekeeping, and when he was killed, you panicked and slipped them to Alex."

"No! No!" he screamed. "Why don't you all leave me alone?"

"And," Nat went on relentlessly, "someone wanted them so badly that they were prepared to kill for them. In fact, Alex was killed instead of you."

"Stop it! Stop it!" Sheldon screamed again, and then to Nat's complete surprise the man lunged at him and landed a vicious uppercut to his jaw.

Finding himself flying backward, Nat grabbed at the covered easel to try to stop his momentum, but he and the stand went crashing onto the concrete floor followed by an enraged Sheldon still throwing wild punches. Nat tried to fight back but Sheldon, now sitting astride his chest, grabbed a hunk of Nat's hair and gave his head a sickening bash against the floor.

When Nat didn't move again, Sheldon, spent and sobbing, got slowly to his feet to look down in absolute horror at his victim. "I told you and you wouldn't listen," he whimpered. "You should've let me alone."

Nat groaned while Sheldon, looking around in a panic, grabbed a wad of paint rags. He knelt down beside Nat again, stuffed one of them into his mouth, and used another to tie the gag in place. When Nat tried feebly to pull the gag from his mouth, Sheldon bashed his head on the concrete floor again. This time when Nat was motionless, Sheldon, muttering and crying, began unfastening Nat's tie. "I'm sorry but I've got to do this . . . it's your own fault . . . you wouldn't leave me alone . . ." A few minutes later Nat was lying on his side with his hands trussed firmly behind him with his own blue silk tie. Sheldon then secured Nat's ankles with a piece of string that had been wrapped around a large painting ready to be shipped.

Then, making sure all the lights were out, Sheldon locked and bolted the studio door behind him, and fled.

CHAPTER TWENTY-SIX

Maggie waited impatiently outside the Queen Elizabeth theatre. "Where in heaven's name are you, Nat?" Glancing again at her watch, she realized there were only about five minutes left to curtain time, and she was not going to miss the start of the ballet just because he couldn't get there on time. Giving an exasperated sigh, she walked over to the box office and handed Nat's ticket to the attendant. "Would you tell my friend that I've gone in?"

It took a while before she could relax, but once the poignant strains of the ballet's overture began to fill the theatre, she gave into Tchaikovsky's soothing music. It was only when the first intermission came that Maggie, turning to speak to Nat, remembered he had been late. She knew that if he arrived after the ballet started, he would have had to wait for the intermission before he would be allowed to enter. She was confident he would arrive any minute now, smiling and full of apologies. Standing up, she turned to face the back of the theatre, ready to wave to him when he eventually appeared through the throng who were either making for one of the bars or a washroom. But when the place finally cleared, there was still no Nat, and she debated staying in her seat or struggling through the cocktail crowd in the foyer to look for him. But when the warning bell announcing that the second act was about to start, her own warning bell went off. *Something bad has happened!* She walked quickly up the aisle before everyone surged back to their seats.

"No, madam." The girl, flawlessly made up and beautifully coiffed, peered at her through the half-glassed window. "The ticket is still unclaimed."

"Is there a message for me—Maggie Spencer?"

"I'm sorry, madam. No messages for that name." Maggie knew the girl thought she'd been stood up.

A few minutes later she was sitting behind the wheel of her car and wondering what to do. *He's had an accident! He's in the hospital!* Climbing out of the car again, she made her way back to the auditorium to use one of the public telephones, but although she let Nat's telephone ring eight or nine times, there was still no answer. *He would have got a message to me somehow—unless he just plain forgot about going to the ballet. He's probably waiting for me at home.* She reinserted the returned dime to dial her home number. But the ringing just continued. Maggie's imagination ran on overtime as one scenario after another flashed before her.

She was lucky to find a parking space outside Nat's apartment building. She slammed her car door then raced up the steps into the foyer, up the two flights of stairs, and inserted her key into his door. The place smelled too clean. In fact, it was so tidy that even his clothes were in his closet and not on the floor. There weren't even any dirty dishes—and then she remembered that Nat's cleaning lady came in on Saturdays. On the table there was a handwritten note under the saltshaker:

I've done fridge, put clean sheets on bed, see you next week. Doris Waters. P.S. Nancy wants you to call her back. DW.

"Nancy! That's it! Another one of her everlasting emergencies. I'll kill that wretched woman!" Her number was on a list pinned over the telephone.

"Nat? No, he's not here. I left a message with his cleaning lady to tell him to call me back ASAP. Why hasn't he called me?"

"What's wrong this time?" Maggie, who'd got to know Nat's ex a lot better in the past year, still found the woman irritating.

"Well, I gave up waiting and had to call a real plumber. He's probably gone out with that George Whatshisname—Sawasky."

George! Maggie knew his number.

"Hi, Maggie. How's things?" It was Lucille, George's wife, who answered.

"Is George there?"

"Afraid not. He's been on one of those everlasting courses this week. Should be home soon, though. Can I help?"

"I'm so sorry to have bothered you, Lucille, but Nat was supposed to meet me at the theatre . . . He didn't turn up and I'm afraid something awful has happened . . ." Suddenly she found herself blubbering. "I'm so sorry."

"Don't apologize, Maggie. But you know Nat, he'll turn up as if absolutely nothing's happened—but that's men for you, isn't it?" she added with a laugh. When she didn't get an answering laugh from Maggie, she said, "I'll get George to call you as soon as he gets in."

"I'm at Nat's place. Please get him to call me here."

A HALF HOUR later George was sitting across Nat's kitchen table from Maggie. "Okay, when was the last time you spoke to him?"

"This morning. You see, I had to go to the caterers and then the dressmakers . . ." Her voice trailed off.

"And he left your house the same time you did?"

She nodded. "He had some errands to run before coming back here."

"Did he say where he was going exactly?"

"No." She picked up the scrap of paper with the message written on it and passed it over to him. "His cleaning lady comes on Saturdays."

"That's a place to start. Do you know her number?"

"Doris Waters. She's on that list over there."

"He left before me," Doris Waters said when George called. "Oh, dear, I hope nothing's happened to him. He's in a bad kind of business, you know ... sees all sorts of criminals ... never know when one of them will turn on you, do you? Could be lying wounded somewhere." Doris was enjoying the prospect of relaying a horrifying crime scene to the rest of her clients.

"What time did he leave the apartment?" George asked patiently.

"Let me see ... I'd finished the kitchen floor and done the living room. Oh, that's right, he left just before I changed his bed. I do that each week. He looked so smart, too. Said he was taking his lady friend out."

"And the time, Mrs. Waters?"

"About two, I'd say ... but ..."

"Thank you." He replaced the receiver before she could continue her tirade. "She said he left here around two this afternoon and he was all dressed up to meet you." He sat back at the table and then leaned toward Maggie. "Are you sure he didn't mention where he might go before catching up with you?"

"I was running late and we sort of rushed breakfast." She buried her face in her hands. "If only I could remember what we talked about."

"Anything about the case—you know the Silver Unicorn Gallery, Alice Standish, Sheldon White?"

"That's it! Sheldon White. He said he might visit him this afternoon. There was this list, you see."

"List. What list?"

"It was only a short one," and Maggie related what had been on the paper and where they had found it.

George glanced at his watch. "It's a bit late but I think I should call White and see if Nat's been there." But the phone rang on and on.

"Do you think we should call any of the hospitals?" Maggie's voice held a trace of the panic she was trying hard now to keep down.

"Let me check in at the station first to make sure he wasn't in an accident."

Maggie paced up and down the small kitchen while she waited for him to place the call.

"No report of him being involved in any accident," George said as he replaced the receiver. "The duty sergeant is going to check the hospitals for us and call back."

It was a long fifteen minutes before the phone rang and both Maggie and George made a lunge for it. George got to it first and listened before turning to Maggie. "He hasn't been admitted to any of the hospitals."

"I'm going to Sheldon White's place."

"But there's no answer there . . ."

"Are you coming with me, George?"

He nodded. "I'll drive."

"I DON'T SEE Nat's car," Maggie said as they pulled up in front of Sheldon White's house.

"We'll check with White anyway," George said, but Maggie was already heading up the path to the house.

It was very obvious that Sheldon White had been drinking. "What do you want?" His voice was slurred and his naturally pale face was ashen. "Why can't you all let me alone?"

"Where's Nat Southby?" George pushed Sheldon back into

the house. The overwhelming smell of liquor and vomit made Maggie retch as she followed close behind.

"Here! Who do you think you are?" Sheldon tried to fight back but his puny attempts against George's bulk was no contest. Staggering against the newel post at the bottom of the stairs, he wrapped his arms around it. "I haven't seen him. Go away."

George took Sheldon by the arm and frog-marched him down the hall and into the kitchen while Maggie headed up the stairs to check the bedrooms. When she returned to the kitchen, George said, "See if there's any coffee, Maggie." He dumped White onto a kitchen chair. "Let's try and get some sense out of this scumbag."

"What about putting his head under the cold water tap?" she said unsympathetically as she searched for and found a jar of instant coffee in the pantry.

"Good idea."

Five minutes later a wet and still protesting Sheldon slowly and reluctantly drank the now tepid brew. "I keep telling you, I don't know where that fucking detective is. I want to go to bed."

"And I don't believe you."

Maggie gazed out of the kitchen window onto the dark backyard. The wind had risen and the moon, peeping momentarily through the scudding clouds, reflected the branches of the swaying trees onto the studio windows. "Have you got a flashlight, George?"

"In the car. Why?"

"Whereabouts?"

"Glove compartment. Do you want me to get it?"

"No. Give me your keys. You keep an eye on our friend here."

Minutes later she was walking toward the studio and playing the light over the door. The place was dark and locked up tight. Weeds, nettles, and blackberry bushes grew in abandon along each side of the studio, making it impossible for her to get close enough to see through the windows. She went back and rattled the padlock that was fastened through a metal hasp, but it was obviously new and didn't give at all. Laying her head against the door surface, she listened for signs of life. "Nat! Are you in there?" Nothing! She had to get inside.

She returned to the kitchen. "Where's the key to the studio?" she asked Sheldon.

"Don't know."

"Answer the lady," George ordered. He grabbed Sheldon's arm and twisted it behind him.

"You're hurting me. I don't know where it is."

George gave the arm another twist. "Tell her, you little weasel."

Sheldon started to cry. "It's in the laundry room. On a board."

There were several keys hanging on the board, and gathering them up, she ran back to the studio. It was difficult to hold the flashlight and try forcing each key into the lock, but at last she felt the padlock give and she was tugging open the double doors.

"Nat! Are you in here?" She advanced a step inside, sweeping the beam of the flashlight ahead of her. Nothing! "Where's the damned light?" She played the flashlight onto the wall until she located the switch. "Oh, my God!"

Nat, gagged and tied, was lying on his side, but at least he was alive, and his eyes beseeched her to untie him. Maggie knelt down beside him and unfastened the paint rag around his head and then pulled the other rag from his mouth.

"What took you so long?" he croaked.

Sheldon had done a good tying job and it took several frantic minutes—accompanied by Nat's coughing and cursing—to undo the knots in his beautiful silk tie and set him free.

"Where is that sonofabitch? God, I desperately need to go to the john—Help me up, Maggie—I'll kill that little . . ." Leaning heavily on his partner, he staggered outside. He took a deep, satisfying breath before heading for the side of the studio building to pee on the blackberries. "I'm going to kill that bastard!—right after I've had a good stiff drink."

"George is in the house looking after Sheldon." She guided him to the back entrance of the house and held the door open for him. "I suggest the drink first and Sheldon second."

"I keep telling you I don't *know* who killed them." Sheldon, still looking a mess, was at least coherent. He looked shamefaced at the bedraggled and furious Nat. "I'm sorry I tied you up, but what else could I do?"

"What were you going to do—leave me there to die?" Fortunately, Sheldon hadn't consumed all the liquor in his house, and Nat now had a large glass of rye whisky in hand.

"I hadn't thought that far . . ."

Nat balled his fist and loomed over the terrified Sheldon. "I'd like to . . ."

"Cool down, Nat. Mr. White is going to tell us what's going on here, aren't you, Mr. White?" George looked expectantly at Sheldon.

"I don't know nothing, man. How many more times do I have to tell you . . . ?" The menace on the faces of both of the men looming over him stopped him in mid-sentence. "I just copy the pictures I'm told to copy."

"Sounds exactly like fraud to me," Maggie interjected. "And who tells you to copy them?"

He gave a short bark of a laugh. "I don't know. I just get my orders . . ."

"The lady asked you who gives the orders, Sheldon." George spoke very quietly but Sheldon got the point, and they watched him wrestling with whether to spill the beans or try to bluff his way out of this corner.

Finally Sheldon said, "The snooty one—Forbes—that Forbes woman."

"Tricia Forbes? But why?" Maggie asked.

"It was just before Jonathan died. She came round here one day to look over the studio and caught me copying a Khouri."

"The impressionist?" Maggie asked. Nat and George looked blank.

Sheldon nodded. "I like doing his stuff."

"And you sell these things?" George asked incredulously.

"I did until Forbes caught me at it."

"Who did you sell them to?"

"People who are too dumb to tell a fake from the real thing." He added bitterly, "Then Alice and that Forbes woman took over."

"And they sell them for a lot more money, but now you just get a cut?"

"Thirty percent. You don't think I make much being Alice's dogsbody, do you?"

"And that's what you were doing when I barged in this afternoon?" Nat said.

"That was a Saffy. Not up to a Khouri, to my mind." He looked from George to Nat. "So what's going to happen to me?"

"I am going to charge you with unlawful confinement and assault and battery," George answered.

Nat looked thoughtful for a few moments. "No. As much as I'd like to put you behind bars for assault and battery," he felt the bump on the back of his head, "I'm willing to let you go."

"What?" George and Maggie said together.

"What's the catch?" Sheldon asked suspiciously.

"The catch is you tell us who, apart from Tricia Forbes and Alice Standish, is in on this art scam."

"There isn't anyone else."

"Oh, come on, Sheldon, there have to be others in on it."

"I tell you," Sheldon shouted back, "Forbes is the only one who's been here. And," his face paled, "she'll kill me if she knows I've told on her—look what happened to Alex!"

"Then," Nat continued, ignoring Sheldon's protests, "you carry on painting as if nothing has happened—you don't tell Tricia Forbes or Alice Standish. But if I find out you've breathed a word to either of them," he paused to let the full effect of his words wash over Sheldon, "I will give Sergeant Sawasky the go-ahead to issue that warrant. Understood?"

"Has Forbes ever mentioned Saul Wingate being in on this?" Maggie asked.

Sheldon shook his head. "No."

"Does Alice Standish do some of the fraudulent painting?" Nat asked.

"Alice Standish," he said witheringly, "knows nothing about art. She's all show."

Nat started for the door. "I think we're about finished here."

"You're actually going to trust this skunk?" George said, glaring at Sheldon. "I still think you should let me charge him."

"He knows better than to cross me again. Don't you, Sheldon?" Nat asked, towering over the quivering man. "And I don't advise running away again." He turned to George. "Can you get an unmarked patrol car to keep an eye on him?"

George saw Nat's wink. "Sure can. I'll get them to start right away. Tonight."

"DO YOU THINK he'll keep quiet?" Maggie asked as she climbed into the passenger seat of Nat's car. It had taken a while to locate the Chevy in the dark as Sheldon had taken Nat's keys and parked his car down the street and around the corner.

"It depends on what he's most scared of—the fear of being charged or Tricia Forbes." He backed carefully over the scrubby grass of the road allowance and around the corner where George was waiting for him.

George stuck his head into the open window. "You okay to drive?"

"Yeh! Don't worry."

"Still think I should have charged that creep and taken him downtown," George muttered as he turned away.

"I'll call you in the morning." Nat put the car into gear and eased away from the curb. "Where did you leave your car, Maggie?"

CHAPTER TWENTY-SEVEN

Sheldon's attack had left Nat with one enormous headache, but as was typical, he wouldn't entertain the idea of getting medical help.

"Stop fussing, Maggie. A couple of aspirins will do it," he muttered irritably when she insisted on inspecting his head. "Go on home. I'll call you in the morning."

She had complied, albeit reluctantly, but she spent a restless night waiting for the telephone to ring and thinking about missing the second half of *Swan Lake*. Perhaps she could pick up a ticket and see the whole ballet later in the week. When the phone finally *did* ring on Sunday morning, it took her quite a while to come to and pick up.

"How about visiting Saul Wingate this morning?" Nat sounded annoyingly awake and surprisingly chipper.

"You okay?"

"Of course I am. Takes a lot to get me down. I've called Wingate," he went on, "and he's expecting us for coffee around eleven. I'll pick you up about ten-thirty."

"Have you heard from George?"

"He called early this morning," Nat replied. "Still thinks I'm a fool for not letting him charge Sheldon."

"He's right, you know."

"No. I want that little bugger truly scared. He knows a lot more about both Jonathan's and Alex's deaths than he's telling us."

SAUL MET THEM at the door and led them into his large bright living room and nodded toward a sofa. Nat opted instead for a wingback chair—he remembered the struggle he'd had to get out of that sofa on his last visit.

"Nat told me about your wonderful view . . . would you mind?"

"Of course not, my dear." Putting an arm around Maggie's shoulders, he led her to the floor-to-ceiling windows. "Be my guest. I'm very proud of our view."

Although Nat had given her a good description, she wasn't prepared for the magnificent panorama that lay before her. It was a perfect early summer day and the North Shore Mountains and the Lions were flooded with bright sunlight. "Oh, my God! I'd stand and look out of these windows all day if I lived here."

Saul smiled. "We try not to get too blasé and take our view for granted." He made it sound as if he had created the scene all by himself. "Ah, here's Leslie."

Leslie, in his mid-thirties, tall with tightly curled blond hair, eyelashes that any girl would give a fortune for, and—to Maggie— devastatingly good-looking, was bending to place a large silver tray on the walnut coffee table. "There's cream and sugar and I've warmed some heavenly croissants that I picked up from the French bakery down the street. The strawberry jam's homemade, of course. Please do help yourself." He sank down on the sofa beside Saul.

"You wanted to talk to me about Jonathan's death?" Saul had waited until they'd helped themselves before speaking.

"Not directly." Nat wiped his jammy fingers on the small linen napkin—he always found balancing small plates and coffee cups very difficult. "Did you write this?" He passed over the list.

Saul read it and then looked up. "Wherever did you find it?"

"Actually, Maggie found it."

"I did write it, but that was way before Jonathan was killed." He turned to Maggie. "Where did you *find* it?"

"In an old jacket that had belonged to Jonathan." She paused for a moment. "It was in your studio on Quebec Street."

Saul looked nonplussed. "The studio? When was this?"

Looking embarrassed, Maggie replied, "A few days ago. I was with Adele."

"Adele! What were you doing there?" Maggie could tell he wasn't pleased. "It's a long story . . ."

He nodded, waiting.

"Adele Rousseau called to tell me she had remembered something Jonathan had told her . . ."

"Adele? But she's no longer a member of our group."

"I know."

"Sorry. I won't interrupt again." True to his word, he listened until Maggie had finished her narrative and then said, "And you found this list in that old jacket of Jonathan's. To think it's been hanging there all these months."

"So what's it all about?" Nat asked.

Saul waited until Leslie had refilled the coffee cups before he answered. "It was a couple of months before dear Jonathan died. He had called me—you see, I was his closest friend and he knew he could talk to me. He told me that something . . . how did he put it . . . something very *fishy* was going on. First off, Alice and Sheldon had become very close and secretive and, what was most unusual, Tricia Forbes was becoming quite a frequent visitor to the gallery—even though Alice had always professed her dislike for the woman."

"Perhaps they'd buried the hatchet," Maggie said.

"Very unlikely," Saul said drily. "Anyway, Jonathan got suspicious when he noticed that most times Tricia would arrive carrying either a large bag or small flat parcels—that's the way he described it—like small framed paintings. Alice would wait until he was busy in his studio and then the two women would disappear into that little workroom at the back of the building between the studio and Jonathan's office. Tricia would always leave the gallery empty-handed."

"She could have been bringing in pre-ordered pictures or pottery of some kind," Nat said.

Saul nodded. "And that's what Alice answered when Jonathan tackled her about it. But Jonathan knew his stock, kept methodical accounts of the consignments and the art he had ordered and bought. There was no pay-out to Tricia Forbes or, when he searched the workroom, no canvases or whatever else she was bringing in."

"So they were doing some private transactions." Nat reached for another croissant. "These are very good. So what was Alice doing with this stuff?"

"He came to the sad realization that Alice was passing them on to Sheldon to smuggle out the back way, and he was delivering the stuff to private buyers."

"But I don't understand," Maggie said. "Where was Tricia getting the work that she was passing on to Alice?"

"She was stealing it."

"How did you come to that conclusion?" Nat asked. "She could have been picking the stuff up cheaply at estate sales or auctions, places like that. Then Alice simply sold it for a profit."

Saul stood up and walked over to a tall rosewood cabinet. "Come over here." When Maggie and Nat joined him, he took a keychain from his trouser pocket and unlocked the bevelled glass doors. The cabinet contained dozens of delicate snuffboxes artfully displayed on a bed of black velvet. "The majority of these boxes are very valuable."

Maggie leaned closer to see them. "They are *really* beautiful."

"I never tire of looking at them. Leslie's a consulting engineer, you know, and is often away on business—and many of these are gifts he's brought back for me." He smiled at his partner. "About six months before Jonathan died, Leslie had just returned from a trip to Germany and brought me that exquisite enamelled box right there. I was making room for it in the cabinet when I realized that three very old and valuable boxes were missing. Two were silver and inlaid with mother-of-pearl and the other was carved ivory—a beautiful piece of art."

"And you suspected Tricia Forbes?"

"Not at the time. But after Jonathan called with his suspicions about her, I realized that she'd been the only visitor the week they must have gone missing. You see, I was home with a wretched cold and she came to visit with some fruit and a bunch of flowers—I guess she stole them while I was in the kitchen getting a vase."

"But you keep the case locked . . ."

"I didn't in those days."

"Saul was absolutely devastated," Leslie said from the sofa.

"Did you call the police?" Nat asked, returning to the wing-back chair.

"What was the use? It had happened at least three weeks prior to my finding they were missing and I couldn't believe it of her. I now keep the cabinet firmly locked and the key is always with me."

"What about the Krieghoffs?"

"That's when Jonathan knew that serious stuff was going on—he found the three paintings wrapped in brown paper and stuffed behind some boxes in that workroom next to his office."

"Did he ask Alice about them?" Maggie asked.

"No. But what he *did* do was pass them over to me for safe-keeping."

"So that's what you were referring to in the note?" Nat chimed in. "But at some point you gave them back to him . . ."

"Unfortunately, yes. They'd obviously been stolen from some private collector and I was very worried about having them in my possession. I gave them back to Jonathan just two days before he was murdered. I often wonder if he'd still be alive if I'd kept them."

"But then you could have been murdered, too!" Leslie cried out. "Oh, Saul, why didn't you tell me about this?"

"Because I didn't want you getting worked up and worried, too."

Nat spread the note on his knee. "So can you explain these other initials to us? I guess they're CB for Chris Barfield and IB for Ian Buckle."

"You'll see that I put question marks against them. At the time I thought they might have been mixed up with Tricia."

"Do you still think so?" Maggie asked.

Saul shook his head. "No."

"And Adele?"

Saul laughed. "You've met Adele. Enough said."

"Do you think that's why Jonathan was killed?" Maggie asked.

"I do hope not," Saul answered sadly. "I can't see Alice or Tricia killing him over three small paintings—even if they are Krieghoffs."

"We'll get going," Nat said a few minutes later. "Sorry to have messed up your peaceful Sunday morning."

"I only hope I've been a help in finding Jonathan's murderer." Saul led them to the door and shook hands with them.

"A VISIT TO Adele?" Maggie suggested, slipping into Nat's Chevy.

"Good thinking." He glanced at the clock on the dash. "We've just time before lunch."

"Lunch! You've just eaten three croissants with strawberry jam!"

"They're very light and airy—there's nothing to 'em."

"OH, IT'S YOU." Adele didn't seem too keen on seeing them. "It's Sunday."

"Won't keep you long. Only want to ask you a couple of questions."

Adele reluctantly led the way into her living room-cum-potter's studio. "Just got up and the place is a mess. Worked late last night and left it all to clear up this morning." She handed them each a rag. "Dust off the worst and take a seat." She waited until they'd complied before turning to Maggie. "Did you make head or tail of that bit of paper we found?"

"We came to the conclusion that the initials referred to your artist friends on Quebec Street."

"Any fool could've seen that! But what did it mean?"

"Could refer to fraud, stealing, or unlawful copying. We're not sure. Did you notice anything—uh, unusual going on while you were there?"

"I told you that the place changed after my . . . Jonathan died."

Maggie nodded. "But while he was still alive?"

Adele gazed mournfully out the window. A strong wind had suddenly arisen, and the huge maple beside the house began swaying so that its branches scraped against the windowpane. She shuddered before returning her gaze on to her visitors. "There was a . . . a . . . coldness between Jonathan, Saul, and Tricia. It was so palpable it made one feel very uncomfortable. Then Jonathan stopped coming to the studio and even that pompous ass Barfield seemed to breathe easier."

"When did Jonathan stop coming?" Nat asked.

"About a month or so before he died."

"Did he tell you what was wrong?"

"All he would say was there was something bad going on at the studio and the gallery, and that he was determined to get to the bottom of it—and then he was murdered!"

"Did you notice anything suspicious going on with Tricia Forbes?" Maggie asked.

"Tricia Forbes? I told you she's a bitch."

"Apart from her being a bitch." Maggie waited. She didn't want to put words in the woman's mouth.

"I can't think of anything really suspicious. She was just her nasty self."

"WELL, THAT WAS a wasted effort," Nat said, pulling away from the curb. "Where to now?"

"Back to my place. I'll make lunch."

"Thought you'd never ask."

THE TELEPHONE WAS ringing when they entered the house. "They'll call back if it's important," Nat yelled at Maggie as she made her usual dash to get it.

"Might be Midge."

But it wasn't Midge.

"You see what's happened with your constant meddling?" Judith Sloan screamed over the telephone. "Jenny's gone!"

"What do you mean, gone?"

"That's what I'm trying to tell you! She didn't come home . . ."

"From where?"

"Saint Thomas's. She sings in the junior choir. Oh, my God! I should have been there to pick her up . . ."

"Judith, take a deep breath. Now, did she walk there? Did she get a lift?"

"I took her, but she said she would get a ride home with one of her friends."

"Have you called the church?"

"That's where I am now. No one saw her leave . . ."

"Give me the address."

"Wait a minute." Maggie could hear voices and then Judith came back onto the phone. "It's 2444 East 41st Avenue."

"2444 East 41st. Okay, Judith, I know where that is. We'll be there as fast as we can." Maggie replaced the receiver and turned to Nat. "Jenny's gone missing. Her mother's in one hell of a state."

CHAPTER TWENTY-EIGHT

As Nat and Maggie drew up outside Saint Thomas's, Judith rushed to meet them. She was followed by a very young, dog-collared, sandy-haired cleric and an elderly, mustached, grey-haired man, both wearing black cassocks that were flying in the wind.

"Any news?" Maggie asked.

The look on Judith's face answered her question. "This is David Henderson—he's the rector and . . ." Judith turned to the other man.

"Norman Lambert," he supplied. "Choir master."

"Let's go inside," Nat said, pointing to the church entrance.

"I drove her here at ten o'clock this morning—she's in the junior choir—but I couldn't stay as I had an emergency." Holding on to the back of a chair, she took a shuddering breath. "Jenny said she would get a lift back with Lillian."

"Have you spoken to Lillian?" Maggie asked

"Right away, when Jenny didn't turn up for lunch. She said Jenny had told her that I would be picking her up, after all. Oh, my God! Who's taken her? What am I going to do?"

Nat turned to the two men. "Did either of you see her get into a car or walk away with anyone?"

Both men shook their heads. "The young people are always in

a hurry to leave, and there's the coffee hour for the adults after the service. Everyone had gone by the time I locked up."

"Have you called the police?"

"They said she's most likely with some friend and I should call around."

"First thing is to question Jenny's friend again." Maggie moved toward the outer door. "We'll follow behind you," she added to Judith.

"Please call me when you find her," David Henderson pleaded. "I feel so . . . so responsible."

"THIS IS SO terrible." Morag and Bill McPherson stood at the entrance to their large two-storey house on Oak Street. The smell of the Sunday roast permeated through to Nat, Maggie, and Judith as they stood in the porch, reminding Nat that he hadn't had lunch. "You'd better come in," Morag said. "We always have our main meal at midday on Sundays," she explained, leading the way into the dining room. "I'm sure she'll turn up at any minute."

The family, two girls around ten and twelve and a small boy in a wooden highchair, were seated around the oval table. Nat noticed with envy that they had got to the apple pie and ice cream stage of the meal.

"You must be Lillian." Maggie smiled at the eldest of the three children.

"I'm Sheila. She," she said, pointing to the other girl, "is Lillian."

Maggie turned to the younger child. "Can you tell me what happened?"

"Nothing happened."

"When did Jenny tell you that her mother would pick her up?"

"We were getting out of those stupid choir gowns in the changing room and she told me her mom was going to pick her up."

"How did she know that?" Nat asked gently.

The girl shook her head. "I dunno."

"Did someone come to the church for her?"

"No. I don't think so."

"So how did she know that her mother would be coming for her after all?" Maggie asked.

"There was a note pinned on her coat."

"A note. Do you know how it got there?"

The girl shrugged. "We were singing in the church."

"What did the note say?" Judith cried out in a shrill voice. "For God's sake, what did it say?"

Lillian burst into tears. "I don't *know* what it said."

"I'm sorry, Lillian. I didn't mean to shout at you."

"Did you see her get into a car?"

"She left before I did."

"I know you're worried," Morag McPherson said as she escorted them back to the front door, "but Lillian's only a little girl."

"I'm sorry. I shouldn't have shouted. I just want to know what happened."

"Thank you for your time," Nat said, and taking Judith by the elbow, he steered her toward her car. "We'll follow you home," he told her.

"I'D LIKE TO use your phone," Nat said as soon as they were inside Judith's house. "I'm going to call Sergeant Sawasky—he's a friend of mine—and get him to light a fire under Missing Persons."

Maggie headed for Judith's kitchen to make coffee. When she returned to the living room, Nat announced, "They'll be here as soon as possible."

"George, too?" Maggie asked.

"Later, but as a friend. He has no jurisdiction with Missing Persons."

GEORGE MUST, INDEED, have started a fire under Missing Persons because Sergeant Cadbury, a tall, dark man in his early forties, turned up in no time flat. "You said you were called out on an emergency," he said, sitting across the table from Judith.

"I was," Judith answered. "But they told me at Children's Hospital that they hadn't called me. My God! It was all planned, wasn't it?"

"Have you any idea who would take your daughter?" Constable Deirdre Jones, Cadbury's partner, asked. Short and plump with black hair pulled back into a bun and round tortoiseshell glasses perched on a button nose, she stood behind Cadbury's chair. "Any enemies?"

"Of course not . . ."

"Are you sure, Doctor Sloan?" Cadbury had caught the slight hesitation. "Estranged husband, for instance?"

"I'm not married."

"Divorced then?"

"No."

"The child's father?"

"He's dead."

There was a silence while the two digested this information before Cadbury asked, "Any other relatives?"

"Apart from Jenny's step-brother, we're on our own."

"Step-brother? Who does he live with?"

"He's a grown man with small children of his own. And I can't see him taking Jenny."

"Are you on good terms with him?"

"Not really. He's not terribly happy about having a step-sister the same age as his own daughters."

The ringing of the telephone saved her from Cadbury's next question. Judith went into the office to answer it. She returned a short time later and sat down hard on a chair.

"That was the rector. He's been calling his parishioners, and a Mrs. Hollister thought she saw Jenny getting into a car."

"Whose car?" Maggie and Nat were both on their feet.

"She didn't see the driver, but she recognized Jenny's long, blond hair. She said the child seemed to hang back a moment before getting in. The rector's still on the phone if you want to speak to him."

"I'll take it." Cadbury strode into the office.

"Constable," he said when he returned, "you stay here with the doctor. I'm going to have a talk with this Mrs. Hollister."

"Did he say what kind of car?" Nat asked.

"Black or maybe dark blue."

"What about some coffee?" Maggie suggested to Judith after the officer had left. "And I'll make some sandwiches."

"I can't eat a thing," Judith replied. "I should've gone with him," she added as she started pacing up and down the room.

"Come on. It will keep our minds occupied until the sergeant comes back."

Nat was very relieved that there would be food.

A half hour later the ringing of the doorbell sent Judith flying to the door. "What did she say?" Judith grabbed Cadbury's arm. "Did she see who was in the car? Did she get the number?"

Cadbury gently disentangled his arm before leading her back into the house.

"I'm sorry. But her eyesight isn't all that good and she only noticed that the car was dark and that the little girl didn't want to get in. I've put out an APB but right now we're not positive it was your daughter, and they could be anywhere by now."

George Sawasky, who had arrived just minutes before the return of Cadbury, turned to Judith. "Tell us more about this step-brother."

"He only found out about us a short while ago. You see, he

wasn't on good relations with his father, and then to find out he had a young step-sister ... !"

"He was jealous?"

"Very."

"Enough to hurt her?"

"He's a pastor—not that being a pastor would mean anything," she added bitterly.

"What do you mean?" Cadbury looked sharply at her. "Perhaps you'd better tell us what you know about this man."

Cadbury and Jones listened intently while Judith related the visit she'd made to Aaron's place in Mission where she'd met his wife and children and the subsequent visit from Aaron himself. "I have the distinct feeling that he would like me and my daughter to just disappear," she finished up.

"Was he violent?"

Judith thought for a moment before answering. "He could be, I suppose."

Cadbury stood up. "I'll leave Constable Jones with you just in case you receive a phone call from the kidnapper."

"You mean a ransom?" She gave a bitter laugh. "I don't have any money."

"I'm going back to the station to make arrangements for the Abbotsford detachment to search the Standish place in Mission," he continued without answering her question.

Soon after the sergeant's departure, George gave Maggie and Nat a slight nod and the three of them got up to leave.

"We're not abandoning you," Maggie said, touching Judith on the shoulder. "But we need to go over things a bit more."

"Can't you do that here?" her voice was edging on the hysterical.

"You have Constable Jones here and she can call us if anything happens. We're not that far away."

Reluctantly, she saw them to the front door. "If that creep has taken Jenny . . . I'll . . . I'll kill him," she said as she closed the door on them.

The three of them stood beside Nat's car. "I can't see Aaron taking Jenny," Maggie said. "For one thing, he hasn't got the guts."

"Although from what you've told me, he has one hell of a temper," Nat answered.

"Yes, but after Judith gave him a tongue-lashing, he slunk out of her house like a whipped puppy. And I saw him with his own family. He loves his children."

"Jealousy can be the basis of many a serious crime," George cut in. "Anyway, there's nothing we can do until we hear from the Abbotsford RCMP. By the way," he added before stepping into his own vehicle, "have you heard from our Sheldon?"

"No. Perhaps he's at the gallery."

"Are they open on a Sunday?" George asked.

"I'm not sure."

"He's a slippery one, Nat. My advice is to make sure that he is where he's supposed to be, and then keep an eye on him."

They watched George drive away. "Perhaps we should call in at the gallery." Maggie slipped into the passenger seat of Nat's car.

"Maggie, it's after five. Even if they were open today, Sheldon would be on his way home by now."

"Let's go and make sure, okay?"

CHAPTER TWENTY-NINE

The Silver Unicorn Gallery *was* open, and luckily Maggie and Nat found a parking spot right outside. A grey-haired woman assistant—totally unknown to either of them—flashed them a smile. "We're just about to close. But you're welcome to look around."

"We would like to speak to either Alice or Sheldon," Nat asked.

"Neither of them came in today. Perhaps I can help you?"

"Is Alice ill?" Maggie asked with concern.

"No. She called me early this morning and asked if I would fill in for her. I wasn't busy so I was happy to oblige."

"Do you know where she's gone?"

"She just said that she wanted to attend a special estate sale."

"And Sheldon White?"

The woman shook her head. "I was expecting him but he didn't turn up. I rang him at home but there was no answer."

"Any idea when Mrs. Standish will be back?"

"The gallery isn't open Mondays, so I guess it'll be Tuesday. Is it urgent?"

"Yes, very," Maggie answered shortly. "And you don't have *any idea* where she is? What if you have an emergency?"

The woman shrugged. "It's Sunday and it's only for one day so she didn't leave an emergency number for me." She fumbled beside the cash register and produced a pencil and paper. "If you'd like to leave your name and phone number . . ."

"We'll try and get her at home."

"Mrs. Standish told me she wouldn't be back in town until tomorrow."

The assistant waited until they had left the gallery and watched them warily through the glass door as they walked toward Nat's old Chevy. The sound of the lock and bolt of the door made them turn back to gaze at the building. The woman gave them a curt nod as she firmly pulled down both the door and window blinds. They were still standing by the car when she reappeared from the side alleyway and, after giving them a very suspicious look, marched down the road.

"I've got a bad feeling about this." Maggie slid into the passenger seat. "Let's get over to Sheldon's place."

SHELDON'S HOUSE WAS enveloped in dark shadows. The blinds were down on all the front windows, and when they went round to the back of the place, the back door was locked tight. Nat hurried over to the studio but it was locked, too.

When he returned, Maggie was standing on tiptoe peering into the kitchen. "Where could they have gone?"

"The woman back at the gallery could be right, I suppose."

"An estate sale? Come off it, Nat. Sheldon's up to his eyeballs in some kind of fraud involving forged art, he almost killed you when you confronted him, and . . ."

"And Alice owns an art gallery and is most likely just as involved," Nat added slowly.

"And Jonathan was murdered and now his little daughter is missing . . ." Maggie stopped and stared over at the studio. "Nat! You don't think Jenny's tied up in there, too?"

"We'll soon find out." He took off his jacket and wrapped

it around a large stone. The glass windowpane in the laundry room door shattered inward, and within seconds he had slipped his hand through the hole and unlocked the door and entered. "Which key was it?" he whispered. Maggie took the keys from him and selected the one that opened the studio door.

There was no sign of the little girl ever having been in the studio. Even Nat's struggle with the ropes that had bound him, the fallen easel and the painting that he'd knocked over had been completely cleared away. Easels and canvases were all neatly folded and leaning against the one blank wall. The worktable was bare.

"The house!" Nat rushed out of the studio.

"Wait." Maggie caught up to him and grabbed him by the arm. "Let's call the police."

"And tell them what? That we think Sheldon has kidnapped Jenny? What proof do we have? For all we know he's never laid eyes on the child."

"Okay." She followed him into the dark and now very familiar house. There was nothing to show that Jenny had ever been there either.

"ALICE AND SHELDON are both mixed up in Jenny's abduction," Nat said grimly, sitting down at the kitchen table. "I can feel it in my bones."

Maggie couldn't help smiling. "And you scoff at my *woman's intuition*. But where could they have taken the child?"

"Well, there's nothing more we can do tonight," Nat said, dispiritedly. "I can't imagine what that poor woman's going through. She must be out of her mind."

Maggie stood up and stretched her arms above her head. "I'm just about all in. Let's go back to my place and I'll fix us supper."

"That's one of the nicest suggestions I've heard today. But not until we've been to Alice's apartment."

"Do you think she would have risked taking Jenny there?"

"No. But it's worth a look."

As they expected, the apartment was in complete darkness, and their repeated pressing of the doorbell went unanswered.

"I HAVE AN idea," Maggie said an hour later as she set a bowl of homemade soup before him. "Galiano!"

"And that's just what I was thinking, too! When's the first ferry in the morning?"

CHAPTER THIRTY

In the morning they were up at six to catch the ferry, and to Maggie's surprise, Nat didn't even grumble about the early hour.

"Sorry, Oscar." Maggie bent down and undid his leash after a very hurried walk around the block. "We can't take you this time."

"Why not?" Nat poured them each a coffee. "He might be a help."

"Nat, he's not a guard dog. Remember how he ran away when I had that break-in last year?"

"He had only just become part of the family. Now he's very devoted and protective. Anyway," he glanced up at the kitchen clock, "we'd better get our skates on if we want to catch that first ferry."

Oscar, giving Nat one of his lopsided grins, knew he would be going.

"What about George?" Maggie asked, pulling on her raincoat.

"I hate to disturb his day off. After all, we may be totally wrong."

"But just suppose we're not?"

"There are phones on the island, you know."

"It might be a bit late by then." She picked up the prepared picnic basket from the table. "Would you mind stowing this in the trunk and getting this very spoilt animal into the back seat?" She headed upstairs.

"Where are you going?"

"I'm grabbing some towels. I've a feeling we're going to need them."

Nat drummed his fingers on the steering wheel as he watched the windshield wipers making ineffectual swipes at the downpour. "Why do women always take such a long time, Oscar?"

THERE WERE ONLY a few cars and trucks lined up for the Galiano ferry on this drizzly day, and Nat found himself thinking that sensible people stayed in bed on days like this. When their turn came, Nat followed a pick-up onto the ferry.

On their last visit the sun had been shining and Galiano had been inviting. Today, as they drove off the ferry and into Montague Harbour, low clouds scudded overhead, trees and bushes dripped rain, and the unpaved road squelched beneath the Chevy's tires.

Nat drew up outside the general store and climbed out of the car. Pulling the brim of his fedora down and turning his raincoat collar up, he made a dash for the door. Maggie watched as he rattled the latch, peered through the shuttered door, and then the window.

"It's not open," he said unnecessarily as he climbed back into the car. "What now?"

Their first idea had been to ask the owner of the store if he'd seen anything of Sheldon in the past couple of days and if he had noticed any visitors with him.

"Perhaps it's best if we keep a low profile ourselves, anyway. I think we should drive up Burrill, find a place to hide the Chevy, and walk the rest of the way to White's place."

Maggie remembered the gravel road from their last visit, but this time the rain had turned the road into a slippery, potholed hazard.

They were about two-thirds of the way up the slope when Maggie suddenly yelled, "Stop!"

Nat jammed on the brakes, which sent Maggie sharply forward and Oscar flying off the back seat. "What's the matter?"

"There's a place to pull off." She pointed to a narrow track.

"My God! I thought something was wrong."

"Sorry. Didn't want you to pass it."

"Suppose someone lives up there?"

"It's overgrown. Nothing's been up that track in years."

Nat drove to a bend in the track, pulled to the side, and parked under a large oak. Oscar was the first to jump out and, whimpering with excitement, jumped up and down while waiting for Maggie to attach his leash.

"I thought we were closer to Sheldon's place than this," Nat gasped as they negotiated the narrow strip of grass between the gravel road and the near-to-overflowing ditch.

"We're almost there." Maggie found she was whispering. "I recognize that huge maple." She pointed ahead. "It's on the edge of the property with White's name nailed to it."

"Thank you, God!"

She waited until he'd caught up to her before walking the last few steps. "I'd forgotten that the land had been cleared between the log cabin and the cottage." She peered cautiously around the maple.

"They cut the trees to build the cabin," Nat whispered back. "Doesn't look as if any work has been done on it since our last visit."

"If we keep to the bushes on the left side and then make a dash for the cabin," Maggie suggested, "we should be able to see if there's any sign of life in the cottage."

Oscar thought it was a great game and gave an excited yelp when they made the dash for the unfinished construction. There were cutouts intended for windows and doors on either side of the cabin, but spindly alders, bracken, and thimbleberry bushes had grown up across them, barring the way in. Glancing anxiously toward the cottage, Nat barged through the tangle and into the log cabin, and Maggie and Oscar followed close behind. Before abandoning work on it, the builders had installed logs to the height of the ceiling of the first floor. There were no divisions for separate rooms, but several rafters were in place for either a ceiling or a second storey.

The dog gave another whimper, and Maggie bent down to pet him. "S-h-h-h, Oscar." The brush gave them ample coverage as they peered through one of the cabin's window spaces at the cottage, but it seemed oddly quiet and unoccupied. The windows and doors were shut, not a whisper of smoke came from the chimney, and there was no sign of any type of vehicle. "What kind of car does Sheldon drive?" she asked.

"The only vehicle I saw at his place was an ancient blue Ford parked right up against the fence."

"I don't remember seeing a blue Ford."

"I saw it when we were retrieving my Chevy on Friday. It didn't look as if it had been driven for years."

"So," she said slowly, "if he's the one who kidnapped Jenny, how would he get her here?"

"He must have had help. Shall we try and get closer to the cottage?"

They had reached the back of the cottage without mishap when Maggie whispered, "Let's see if there's a window or a door open."

"What's the point?" Nat sounded thoroughly dejected.

"They might have been here."

The blinds of the cottage were up so it was quite easy to look into the rooms on the ground floor. It was a typical two up and two down cottage, the rooms going from front to back with the front door leading into a very small foyer, stairs straight ahead, and a door each side into the living and kitchen areas. The back door led straight into the kitchen. They tried the door but, as expected, it was locked.

"Just as well," Maggie commented. "We're soaking wet from the rain and Sheldon would easily see our footprints on the tiled floor."

They were circling the house, looking for any sign of recent occupancy when Nat suddenly bent down. "Look at this, Maggie!" He knelt in the wet gravel for a closer look. "Tire marks! And they're fairly recent."

"How can you tell?" She bent down to peer at the tread marks.

"There's very little rainwater in them." He stood and pulled Maggie to her feet. "And the edges of the tracks are sharp and fresh-looking. We'd better get the hell out of here before they come back."

"You're right. Come on, Oscar." The three of them sprinted for the log cabin. "It won't keep the rain off us but at least we can't be seen," she said when they were safely inside again. "What have you got, Oscar?" Bending down, she pulled a piece of sodden material out of his mouth. "Oh my God, Nat! They've definitely got Jenny!"

"What makes you say that?"

"The last time I saw her she had her hair tied back with a piece of black ribbon." Maggie held out her hand. "Just like this!" She stopped talking. "Listen! It's a car! Nat, they're coming back!"

Peering over the rim of the window opening they saw Sheldon get out of a large black car and scurry around to the driver's side to hold the door open for Alice Standish. Disregarding his helping hand, she emerged from the car dressed as if she was on a business trip—black raincoat, leather gloves, and high boots—rather than on a casual visit to one of the Gulf Islands.

Opening a large black umbrella, she elbowed Sheldon out of the way. "Why don't you have a telephone in the house, for God's sake?" she demanded.

"I don't use the place enough."

"But I need to use a telephone—now!"

"The store will be open in an hour. You can leave me and the kid and try again later."

"No way am I leaving you two here alone. I don't trust you any further than I can see you."

"Where's Jenny?" Maggie whispered.

"Get the kid, and hurry up before I get soaked." Alice walked to the back of the car and waited for Sheldon to join her.

Maggie and Nat watched in horror as Sheldon opened the trunk and the two of them leaned in and pulled a struggling child from its depths. It was Jenny and her mouth was covered with duct tape. "Hold still, you little bastard!" Alice hit the little girl so hard that she crumpled backward onto the ground where she lay sobbing and visibly quaking in fear.

Sheldon immediately ran to the child and helped her to her feet, but Jenny was so terrified that she cringed away from him, her eyes wild with horror.

"You're such a wimp, Sheldon. Get the brat inside."

"Wait," Maggie whispered, grabbing hold of Nat's sleeve. "Let's think this through. If we make the wrong move, that woman could kill Jenny." They watched in silence as Jenny was dragged, still struggling against her captors, to the back of the cottage.

"I should have alerted George," Nat said.

"It's all right. He'll be here on the next ferry."

"What?"

"Before we left this morning I called him and told him of our suspicions."

"You did that?" Nat couldn't help grinning at his partner.

"Maggie," he said, pulling her close, "what would I do without you? Does he know how to find us?"

"I told him we'd meet his ferry." She glanced at her watch. "We'd better do a careful retreat."

"I hate to leave Jenny with those two," Nat said, moving slowly and cautiously toward the doorway where they had entered the cabin earlier.

"At least she's out of that trunk," Maggie whispered as she began to follow him. Suddenly she stopped. "Wait. You go and meet George. I'll stay here and keep an eye on things."

"I don't think that's a very good idea."

"Take Oscar with you. I don't want him barking or something."

"But Maggie . . ."

"Just go!"

"No. It's too dangerous. We stay together."

"It's that child's life that is in danger. Just go!"

"Maggie, if that woman discovers you here, she won't hesitate . . ." his voice trailed away.

"She won't discover me. Now, get going before it's too late."

Nat could see Maggie was adamant. He said reluctantly, "As long as you promise to stay put and not try any heroic rescues or anything."

"As if I would!"

She watched as Nat and Oscar raced for the grove of the trees on the edge of the property and breathed a sigh of relief when there was no hue and cry from the cottage. She looked around the unfinished cabin for something that would make her wait more comfortable but realized that apart from the sawn ends of logs and a couple of trestles there was very little in the line of furnishings. She chose a fat, two-foot-high chunk of log, rolled it across the floor, and sat below the window opening to wait. There was an eerie feeling about the place—the grey smoke lazily curling out of the stone chimney of the cottage, the constant drip, drip, drip from trees, and the little rustling sounds as small, invisible animals scurried about in the bushes. Maggie shivered. She stood up and peered through the window and wished she could be a little closer to hear what was going on inside the cottage.

After a while the rain stopped and the shake roof of the cottage steamed in the warmth of the weak sun that slid in and out of the clouds. She sank back down onto the log and leaned her head against the wall. It had been a long day. Her eyelids began to droop.

NAT, DOING HIS best to hurry, had the option of slipping on the grassy edge of the narrow road into the water-filled ditch or staying in the middle of the track and skidding onto his rear end in one of the rivulets of water rolling down its middle. Oscar enjoyed both venues and joyously pulled on his leash, eager to make Nat run faster. Fortunately, the car was still parked where they'd left it, and he backed up the track until he found a place wide enough to turn.

When he reached the ferry terminal, he was told it wouldn't be in for at least another half hour. *Thank God Maggie put that thermos of coffee within easy reach.* He settled down, a steaming cup of coffee in hand, to wait for George. "Please don't do anything stupid, Maggie."

"I KNEW YOU would be a problem the moment I set eyes on you. Turn and face me . . . slowly."

Maggie opened her eyes and turned slowly to see Alice Standish pointing a gun at her.

"Don't even think of doing anything silly. I know how to use this gun. Now stand up and walk in front of me."

Maggie thought about making a run for it, but Alice's hand

was steady and her face grim. She meant every word she was saying. Cursing herself for being caught so easily, Maggie did as she was told.

"Well, I can't offer you tea and cookies here, Mrs. Spencer, but I think we can provide you with some entertainment," Alice said sarcastically as she pushed Maggie into the kitchen. "Get the rope out of the car, Sheldon." She turned back to Maggie, waving the gun to indicate a stool in the middle of the kitchen. "Sit!" she ordered. "And don't try anything funny! Unlike the wimp, I'm not afraid to use this."

"You've killed before," Maggie stated.

The woman didn't answer. "Where's your partner?"

"Gone for help."

"Help?" she sneered. "I don't think he'll get much help from the local sheep or any of the artsy lot that live around here. We'll be long gone by the time he finds any help. Okay, Sheldon," she said as he returned with a coil of rope, "tie her arms behind her back and then bring the brat down here."

"Why are you doing this, Alice?" Maggie asked. "What have you got against that child?"

"That money should have been mine!"

"Money? Judith and her daughter don't have any money."

"He gave her $25,000! And that money should have been mine!" She turned to Sheldon, who was standing with his mouth open. "What are you standing there for? I said tie her arms behind her back!"

Sheldon didn't move. "Is that what this is about?" he asked.

"Tie her up!" she ordered and waved the gun at him.

Sheldon knelt behind the stool that Maggie was sitting on and began tying her wrists together.

"What makes you think he gave it to Judith and her daughter?" Maggie asked.

"I've gone over the books and that's how much is missing. He certainly didn't leave it to me, and that son of his sure as hell didn't get it." She put the gun down on the table and inspected Sheldon's knots. Satisfied, she picked up the gun again. "So that woman and her bastard must have it," she continued, "and if she wants her daughter back, she'll hand the money over. Go and get the kid, Sheldon! We've got to get going."

WHEN THE FERRY came in sight Nat hauled himself out of the car and walked quickly down to meet George. To Nat's surprise, Sergeant Cadbury was with him. As they walked off the ferry and got within hearing distance, Nat shouted, "They're here! Come on, I left Maggie keeping watch on them!"

"Is the little girl all right?" Cadbury demanded.

"She was the last we saw of her," Nat said as he hustled the two men into his old Chevy.

"Where did you say Maggie was?" George asked as he settled himself into the front passenger seat.

"Keeping an eye on the place. I warned her not to do anything silly."

"I hope she listened," George answered dubiously, as he pushed Oscar's wet tongue away from his face. "Down, Oscar."

"Me, too," Nat answered grimly, thrusting the car into first gear.

"Aaron Standish doesn't appear to have had any hand in this," Cadbury said from the back seat. "He could vouch for every hour of the day and we searched his place from top to bottom."

"I'm afraid we have to walk it from here." Nat had driven the car to the spot where he had left it earlier.

"How far?" Cadbury asked, pulling his coat collar up.

"A few minutes."

"Ah! They're still here." Nat pointed to the black car still parked next to the cottage. "Follow me." Holding tight to the leash of the excited dog, he led the way through the trees and bushes along the side of the property. "The tricky part is to get over to that log cabin."

"Won't they see us?" George whispered.

"It's pretty hard to see anyone inside as the holes for the windows are overgrown with brush and weeds. Just follow me." One by one they sprinted for the derelict cabin.

But Maggie was not waiting for them when they arrived.

"Where's your sidekick?" Cadbury whispered.

"Don't tell me she's taken things into her own hands." George glared at Nat.

"She promised she'd stay put." Nat's voice was grim. "She promised."

"That child's life is at stake." Cadbury walked to the door opening. "I'm taking charge. You two stay behind me."

MEANWHILE, MAGGIE, HER mouth taped and hands tied behind her back, was stumbling over tree roots and boulders as Sheldon pushed her through the dense brush. The route they were following could hardly be called a path—just a steep, narrow animal track. Alice and a terrified Jenny were close behind. Before leaving the cottage, the child had begged Alice not to tape her mouth again, but the woman took no notice and made Sheldon hold her fast while she applied the duct tape.

"How much farther?" Alice demanded.

"Around the next bend." He pushed Maggie harder and they suddenly burst through the bush and onto a stony beach. "There she is." He pointed to a twenty-foot cabin cruiser that was moored to a wooden dock.

"Quick. Put the kid on board. I'll deal with this one." Maggie tensed as Alice pointed the gun at her, but to her relief she nodded toward the boat instead. "Get in. I'd like nothing better than to shoot you now, but I'd have to drag your body down to the boat. It'll be less messy out at sea."

CADBURY MADE A run for the windowless side of the cottage and beckoned the other two to join him. Drawing his gun, he then led the way to the back of the house, ducked under the kitchen window, and flattened his body against the wall to reach for the doorknob. "It's locked," he mouthed.

Nat, still on the other side of the window, took a quick peek inside. The place looked deserted. "They've gone," he whispered.

"The car's still here." Cadbury banged on the door. "Open up. Police! Open up."

"They've gone," Nat repeated.

Cadbury's answer was to crash the door with his shoulder. All he got for his effort was a very sore shoulder, as the door was made of solid wood and didn't give an inch. Nat sighed, picked up a hefty rock, and removed his jacket.

"Allow me, gentlemen." He gave the kitchen window a sharp tap with the covered rock, widened the resulting hole, reached in for the catch, and opened the window. "You're younger and thinner," he said to Cadbury. "Will you do us the honour?"

"You've done this before," the younger man grumbled as he climbed in.

"Many times."

"So where have they disappeared to?" George asked. "There's plenty of food in the fridge, the beds have been slept in, and . . ." He pointed silently to a length of rope on the floor.

"And," Cadbury added ominously, "this roll of duct tape."

"But no sign of Maggie. She's either followed them somewhere or they've rumbled her." He headed outside.

"They've definitely gone this way." George pointed to the

scuffed, narrow track leading downward toward the water. "They must have a boat. Hurry!"

"Listen! That's a boat engine." Nat unclipped Oscar's leash and pushed his way to the front of the line. Slipping and sliding on the muddy surface, he and the dog ran as fast as they could downhill, but the boat was already fifty feet from shore as he and the other two, who had drawn their weapons, burst onto the rocky beach.

"Stop!" he yelled. His answer was a bullet ricocheting off the twisted trunk of the arbutus tree beside him. Instinctively the three of them ducked, but Oscar ran to the edge of the water to bark at the fleeing boat. Another shot rang out and Nat watched helplessly as splinters of rock flew close to the dog. Pushing Cadbury's restraining hand away, he raced down the beach, and scooping the frantic animal into his arms, ran back with him to the shelter of the trees. George and Cadbury slowly lowered their weapons and Nat, wondering why, looked back at the boat to see that Alice was holding Jenny in front of her as a shield. They watched helplessly as the boat rounded the point.

"And not another bloody boat in sight when you need one!" George holstered his gun. "We'd better get back to the car. Where's the nearest telephone, Nat?"

"The general store."

CHAPTER THIRTY-ONE

"Down there." Alice pushed Maggie and Jenny down the steps into the small cabin. "I'll deal with you later."

Maggie, missing the last two steps, crashed into the table that was fixed to the floor. Regaining her feet, she sat down on the long bunk and nodded to Jenny to sit beside her. *If only I could get this damned tape off.*

Alice had left the door to the cabin slightly open. "How far to this place?" they heard her ask.

"Not far. It's in a small cove and well hidden."

"Good." They heard her laugh. "The stupid bastards will think we've left Galiano. And you're sure he has a telephone?"

"Yes. Here's the entrance." He cut the engine speed to a slow crawl. "Keep your eye out for hidden rocks."

"You're sure he's away?"

"He only comes over on Fridays and leaves first thing Sunday mornings. Look out!" he yelled as the boat scraped against something solid. "I told you to watch for rocks!"

"Don't boss me around, Sheldon."

"Sorry." A few seconds later and the boat bumped against a wooden dock. "You stay put while I make sure he's gone."

"You're bossing me again, Sheldon! Tie this thing up securely before you go."

The boat tipped as Sheldon jumped off onto the dock. Maggie was so intent on listening to the conversation going on above that the sudden tug on her wrist bindings made her jump. To her astonishment Jenny had somehow freed herself and torn the duct tape off her mouth.

"He doesn't do good Girl Guide knots," the girl whispered and she began working at the rope binding Maggie's wrists.

Maggie felt rising panic as she divided her attention between trying to hear what was going on above them and willing Jenny to hurry up and untie her before Alice turned her attention back to her prisoners.

"They're tighter than mine," Jenny whispered.

"Take the tape off my mouth," Maggie tried to mumble, but Jenny was too engrossed in trying to undo the rope to understand what she was trying to say.

"How far is this damned house?" Alice yelled.

Maggie couldn't make out Sheldon's answer, and she realized that he was already on his way to "the damned house."

"Be quick about it. I'll just take a peek at our guests to make sure they're comfortable."

Maggie moved her tied hands to get Jenny's attention.

"What . . . ?"

Maggie nodded her head toward the steps and then to the discarded tape.

"The tape!" Jenny grabbed it and tried to stick it back on her mouth.

Then Maggie nodded her head to the pile of rope hoping that the child would understand.

"The rope!" Jenny picked it up and had just pushed it behind one of the back cushions and placed her own hands behind her back when Alice wrenched the door open to peer down at them.

Too late, Maggie realized that the tape covering the child's mouth was obviously becoming unstuck. *Perhaps Alice won't notice.*

"You've been chewing on that tape," Alice growled at Jenny. "Cut it out or I'll put a bigger and much tighter piece across your face."

"Alice!" Sheldon's voice came from far away.

"Don't go away," Alice ordered, and she disappeared from sight.

"The coast's clear." Sheldon's voice sounded closer to the dock now.

Alice's face appeared again above the cabin staircase. "I've got to make an urgent phone call to your mother, little girl. Let's hope she thinks you're worth $25,000. As for you, Mrs. Spencer," she laughed scornfully, "I don't think your boyfriend can lay his hands on $75 let alone $25,000. But perhaps Doctor Sloan will chip in some extra for you. I'll be back to let you know the verdict."

Jenny pressed closer to Maggie but remained silent until they felt the boat rock again, indicating that the woman had gone ashore. "What are we going to do?" she whispered.

Maggie could feel the little girl shaking with fear. "I'm thinking," she mumbled through her taped mouth.

"Sorry, I forgot the tape." Reaching over, Jenny picked at the edge of the tape then gave it a yank. "Sorry," she said again when Maggie stifled a yelp of pain. "My mother always says it's better to do it quickly."

"Never mind. Just undo the rope!"

From outside they suddenly heard Alice shrieking in anger, "What are you following me for? I told you to stay on the dock and keep your eyes peeled in case that detective manages to find a boat and come looking for his girlfriend!"

"I was just coming up to show you where the telephone is," Sheldon whined.

"I'm not stupid! I can recognize a telephone when I see one! I'll be back as soon as I've phoned that woman. I'm going to put the fear of God in her."

"I'VE DONE IT!" Jenny whispered.

Maggie felt the ropes drop away. *Thank God for one very bright little girl!* She rose quickly from the bench and, after giving the child a hug, risked a peek out of the small side window of the launch.

Alice had negotiated the ramp leading from the dock and was now teetering on her high heels up a path strewn with crushed oyster shells. Maggie flexed her wrists and hands to bring life back into them before she climbed the three steps to the cabin door. When she carefully cracked the door open, she could see Sheldon leaning on the rail on the other side of the dock, peering despondently down into the glassy, calm depths.

Maggie backed down into the cabin. "Somehow, we've got to untie the mooring lines on the dock." She moved forward and peeked out at the bow. "No, it's all right. We can do this." What she saw was a rope that had been pulled through a metal ring to form a loop that had then been slipped over a cleat on the bow. And on this windless afternoon the line leading from the bow hung slackly to another cleat on the dock.

Maggie beckoned Jenny to come forward. "See. All you need to do is loosen that loop of rope and slip it off the cleat."

"He'll see me," Jenny replied fearfully.

CADBURY REACHED THE top of the track first and waited impatiently for Nat, the dog, and George to catch up.

"Come on, you two. I've got to get on to the Coast Guard before that boat disappears onto one of the other islands. There's a thousand places where they can hide. Give me your car keys, Nat. I'll have it turned around and ready to go by the time you get there."

"Nice to be young, gung-ho, and fit," Nat gasped as he and George ran down the hill to where the Chevy was waiting. They piled in, and Nat cringed as Cadbury mangled the gears.

The general store was open. Cadbury threw himself out of the vehicle and rushed inside. Nat and George were just in time to hear his one-sided exchange as he alerted the Coast Guard on Vancouver Island to the kidnapping.

"Vancouver Island!" Nat gasped. "It will take ages for them to get here, and that boat could be holed up anywhere by then. We'll never be able to find them."

"They can't have gone that far," George said hopefully.

Nat hoped George was right, but when he thought of the time that had elapsed and of all the hidden bays, coves, and inlets around the Gulf Islands, he knew that even if they were close by, they could stay hidden forever. "We can't wait for the Coast Guard to get here," he burst out. "We need a boat." He turned to the startled storeowner. "Where can we find a boat?"

"What's going on? Who are you people?"

"Police officers." He didn't bother to explain that he was ex-police. "A woman and child have been kidnapped and we need a boat—urgently."

"I've got one. But I'll have to come with you as she's a bit temperamental."

"That's great." As the storekeeper headed into the back to grab a coat and the keys to his boat, Nat rushed over to Cadbury, who was in the act of replacing the telephone receiver. "We've got a boat. Come on."

"I think we should wait for the Coast Guard." Cadbury grabbed Nat's arm. "We shouldn't take things into our own hands."

"That's okay, if you want to stay behind," Nat answered curtly. "But I'm not waiting."

"Now you wait a second and listen to me," Cadbury insisted. "Alice Standish has just called the girl's mother and demanded a ransom of $25,000 for her safe return."

"Where would Doctor Sloan get that kind of money?"

"Standish claims her husband gave it to the doctor and it's rightfully hers. She's given her twelve hours to come up with it."

"What about Maggie?"

"She's being held hostage, too."

"That settles it. That means they're not far away and we need to be out on the water searching for that cruiser."

"The telephone company is trying to get a fix on the call."

"I'm not waiting. You coming, George?"

"Yes. Anything's better than waiting around here."

"Okay, we'll give it a try." Cadbury turned to the owner of the store. "Mr. . . . ?"

"Charlie Wilkes. Follow me."

Nat rushed back to the car and collected the dog. *Oh, Maggie. Why didn't I insist we stay together?* "Don't worry, Oscar, we'll find her. I promise."

"YOU JUST HAVE to slip the loop on the end of that rope over that little cleat on the bow," Maggie whispered as she slid the window open on the far side of the cabin. She was about to boost the child up so that she could climb through the window when she glanced back toward the dock. "No, wait!" She grabbed the child's arm and together they ducked down below window height. Sheldon had turned to lean back on the rail while he fished for a cigarette and matches from his jacket pocket. She raised her head and watched him light up before he turned back to flick the match into the water. "Okay! Go . . . and don't make a sound!" She could feel Jenny trembling with fear as she boosted her through the window, and she watched her crawl forward on hands and knees along the narrow strip between the cabin and the gunwale.

Jenny had reached the bow and had her hands on the rope when there was a cry from the path leading down to the dock.

"Stop them! Sheldon, you stupid idiot! Stop them!" Alice, hampered by her high heels, was running down the crushed oyster shell path.

"Flip it off, Jenny! Quick! Flip it over the cleat!"

Then suddenly the bow was free and swinging outward, and Jenny was slithering backward across the bow toward the safety of the cabin. But the boat was still tethered by the stern and it was Maggie's job to deal with that line. She had just exited the cabin and was reaching for the stern line when there was a fresh outcry from Alice.

"Help me, you stupid idiot! Help me!" The heel of her boot had caught in the slats at the top of the ramp, and she had gone sprawling headlong down it.

Sheldon didn't know which way to go. For a moment he dithered, and then, unwilling to risk Alice's further fury, he rushed to help her up.

It took Maggie only a few seconds to leap from the boat, unwind the stern line from the cleat on the dock, and give the boat a mighty push as she leapt back on board.

"Get them, you fool! Don't let them get away!"

Sheldon was in a quandary. Should he leave Alice struggling to get to her feet or rescue his boat?

"Go after them, you fool!"

Sheldon ran back down the ramp and onto the dock and made a flying leap, but Maggie, oar in hand, was ready for him and she joyfully hit him in midriff.

"Oo-o-o-f-f!" There was a huge splash as he landed in the water.

"Come back or I'll shoot!"

Maggie, knowing that Alice meant what she said, dashed up the stairs to the controls. The keys were still in the ignition. "I'm sure driving a boat can't be any harder than driving a car," she muttered to herself. She turned on the ignition and looked for the gearshift. She gave it an experimental push and instantly realized her mistake. They were going backward. "Oh my God!" Quickly she pushed it the other way and they surged rapidly ahead. "Jenny," she yelled, "get down into the cabin." Another shot rang out. "That's close!" But at least she was getting the hang of the steering. It was a bit wobbly, which in the long run, spoiled Alice's aim. "I just hope to God I miss those rocks," she muttered.

"IS THAT IT?" Cadbury looked in disbelief at the old wooden boat. "Does it leak?"

"Not much. And there's a bucket."

"Oh, for chrissake, let's get going." Nat picked Oscar up in his arms. "Where do you want us to sit?" he asked, looking dubiously at the meagre seating. Apart from a bench seat in the prow, there were only two small seats on either side facing the stern.

Charlie looked him up and down. "You and him," he nodded at Nat and George, "are a bit on the big side. Better if you sit in those two seats. You," he added to Cadbury, "get up in the prow to balance her." The boat rocked precariously as each of the men stepped into it and sat down. "Okay, here we go. Which way?" Charlie stood in the stern and pulled the starter on the ancient Evinrude two-stroke outboard. Three pulls later and the motor roared into life, then spluttered and quit.

"What's wrong with it?" Cadbury yelled.

"Told you it's a bit on the temperamental side." The three men watched impatiently while he fiddled with the motor. "Got a bit flooded, I guess. Have to wait a few minutes while it dries out." He reached over the stern, unfastened the cover on the motor, and lifted it off.

"Bloody hell!" Nat started to get to his feet. "We need to get going."

"Keep your socks on." Charlie turned his attention back to the motor, fiddled a bit, then carefully replaced the cover. To Nat's amazement, he patted it gently and whispered, "Come on, old girl. You can do it." And with the next pull the thing flared into life.

"YOU CAN COME up here now," Maggie called to Jenny over the noise of the engine.

"Has she stopped shooting?" Jenny asked tremulously as she peered around the door.

"Yes. See if you can find us some lifejackets, will you, dear?"

"Why? Are we going to sink?"

"No, of course not." Maggie tried to put some confidence in her voice. "But we have to get out of this narrow channel and there are a lot of rocks around."

"But you can miss them, can't you?"

"Yes. Just go and find yourself a jacket, okay?"

Jenny disappeared into the cabin and a few minutes later climbed back to the upper deck with a lifejacket in her hand. "I could only find one."

"Fine. Do you think you can put it on yourself?" The mouth of the cove was tantalizingly close but Maggie's steering was still a bit erratic. "All I have to do is stay away from those slimy looking rocks," she muttered.

"WHAT'S WITH THE dog?" Charlie Wilkes yelled over the noisy engine. Oscar, ears flying in the wind, was sitting on Nat's lap and peering out to sea.

"He belongs to Maggie—the woman who's been kidnapped," Nat yelled back.

"Oh! Any idea what we're looking for?" Wilkes yelled again.

Nat leaned toward the man as he steered from the stern of

the boat. "It's a twenty-foot launch and it's holed up somewhere quite close—probably in a small inlet or cove."

"There are several along here leading to private docks. Do you want to go into each of them?"

"Just far enough to see if the launch is there."

"I didn't realize there were so many private docks on the island," George yelled after they had negotiated five small coves without success.

"There's another one coming up." Cadbury stood up in his seat to point over the bow. "And look! There's a boat coming out of it."

"It's them," Nat yelled. "Careful! That woman knows how to use a gun." They ducked down as they watched the launch shoot out of the inlet.

"Gun? You didn't say anything about being shot at," Charlie yelled back. He cut the engine to a crawl. "What do we do now?"

"Get ready to chase it," Cadbury yelled at him.

"Chase it? That's a powerful boat."

At that moment Oscar wriggled out of Nat's arms and began barking ecstatically.

"What is it, Oscar?" He stood to look more closely at the launch. "It's Maggie!" he yelled and began waving frantically, making the boat tip ominously. "She's steering it! What a girl! Maggie! Maggie!"

Oscar continued to bark furiously, racing round and over all the men in the boat.

"It's Nat!" Tears cascading down her face, Maggie turned to Jenny. "We're all right now. Everything's okay. It's Nat." She throttled the engine down until the boat slowed and came to a halt, rocking gently in the waves. "We're safe now." She put her arms around the little girl and held her tight.

"I want my mommy!" Jenny cried.

"Of course you do. And I promise you will be with her very soon. And I am going to tell her what a brave and clever girl you are."

CHARLIE WILKES, AFTER he had been assured the woman steering the boat wasn't toting a gun, manoeuvred close to the launch. Oscar didn't wait but leapt from one boat to the other and in no time was jumping up and down, trying to lick Maggie's face. Nat wanted to follow, but as Cadbury pointed out, his bulk was a bit of a deterrent for safe boarding and, he added, Nat was likely to fall into the drink.

"I'll pilot it back," Cadbury announced firmly as he prepared to climb over to join Maggie and Jenny. "We'll see you back at Mr. Wilkes' dock."

Nat had to be satisfied. At least his Maggie was safe and sound.

THE COAST GUARD was waiting for them when they docked and Cadbury quickly apprised them of the situation. "We haven't much time," he said as he jumped aboard. "The owner of that place is bound to have another boat of some kind moored nearby and they could get away. I'll show you where the place is."

Maggie, her arm around Jenny, stood on the wooden dock and watched the powerful launch speed away.

"I want to go home."

"So do I," Maggie laughed. "Look, there's Mr. Wilkes' boat coming in. Let's go down and meet them."

"Maggie!" That's all Nat had to say as he drew her close to him.

"I want to go home," Jenny said again.

"And so you shall." George, who had followed Nat out of the boat, took the little girl's hand in his large one. "Let's go and phone your mother."

CHAPTER THIRTY-TWO

"So Cadbury was in time to nab those two?" It was a week after their seafaring adventures and George had arrived at the agency to bring Maggie, Nat, and Henny up to speed on the latest development.

"Yes," George answered. "But only just! Sheldon White had managed to get the little Seagull motor going on the owner's dinghy, and they had almost reached the mouth of the cove when Cadbury and the Coast Guard arrived."

"Did Alice shoot at them, too?" Maggie asked.

George shook his head. "She'd run out of bullets firing at you."

"That lady shoot at you?" Henny gasped. "You could have been killed!"

"She missed, Henny." Maggie patted Henny's hand comfortingly, but she had vivid memories of how scared she had been as the bullets flew.

"And the little girl was in the boat with you," Henny persisted. "She could have been shot, too."

"We were lucky," Maggie answered. "And it was wonderful to see Jenny reunited with her mother," she added wistfully.

"Who arranged for the helicopter?" Nat asked.

"You'll never guess—your old friend Inspector Farthing!"

"Do you mean to say that he actually has a soft heart?" Nat laughed. "Earning Brownie points, more like it."

"Have you spoken to Judith since the kidnapping?" George asked.

"She came in Tuesday morning to thank us for our part in the rescue."

"She had a lot to thank you for," George commented. "I don't know what would have happened to that little girl if it hadn't been for you two." He reached for the coffee that Henny had put on the desk. "Still don't know where Alice Standish got the idea that Doctor Sloan had $25,000 that belonged to her."

"Alice told me that was the amount that was missing from the gallery assets," Maggie said, "so she decided that Jonathan had given it to Judith. But Judith was totally mystified, so she called Jonathan's lawyer, Humphrey Crumbie, and asked him about it. He was reluctant to tell her at first but quickly changed his mind when told of the kidnapping. Apparently, Jonathan, already unhappy with his marriage, had put the money into trust funds for his daughter Jenny and his two grandchildren—Aaron's daughters, for when they reached the age of eighteen—for their education."

"So why hadn't Standish told her about it himself?"

"He was waiting until after the divorce. But then, of course, he was killed."

"But how did Alice Standish know her husband had money?" Henny asked, pushing the plate of her famous cookies closer to George.

"I asked Jane Weatherby the same question when she came in to see us yesterday," Maggie answered. "She said her sister knew how much he was worth because he had hired her to do his book-keeping before they were married. Jane was quite honest about her sister—told me that all she ever thought about was money."

"You know Alice Standish has been charged with her husband's murder, don't you?" George asked.

"Jane told us. She is terribly upset, but I think deep down she knew her sister had killed him—and probably husband number two as well, although we'll never be able to prove that. He supposedly tripped and fell down the basement stairs."

"Poor man," Henny said sadly. "To think she marry him for his money and then kill him to get it."

"There was a bit more to it than that, Henny," George answered. "Jonathan had discovered that Alice and the Forbes woman were using his gallery for fraud and a front for stolen art. He had demanded that they stop immediately and he wanted Alice out of his life permanently. She couldn't let that happen because she had quite a ring going and it had become a very lucrative business. So, Jonathan had to go. She tried to make it look like suicide, and if it hadn't been for your keen eye, Nat," George added, "she would have got away with it."

"And then to find out there was no money," Nat added.

George nodded. "She knew that her late husband had been involved with some woman and, putting two and two together, came to the conclusion that the money had gone to his lady friend."

"And that's why she was so anxious for Nat and me to find Judith."

George nodded. "Jonathan had managed to keep her identity a close secret."

"I guess she killed that poor boy, Alex Donitz, too," Maggie said sadly.

"Sheldon White helped us with that one," George answered. "Alex was just what he seemed, a poor immigrant artist from Poland, out of work and hungry but also light-fingered. Sheldon introduced him to Alice and she immediately recruited him into her fraudulent scheme of copying and stealing. Sheldon rented him space in his studio to do the work, and that was where Alex found the three Krieghoffs that Sheldon had stolen and hidden away because he planned to copy them and sell the copies himself."

"So Sheldon realized that Alex was the one who had taken them and he told Alice," Nat commented as he absent-mindedly picked up one of Henny's burnt offerings.

"Yes. Alice already suspected that Alex was two-timing her and was selling paintings on the side. And, I guess, by that time killing came easy to her."

"So Sheldon suspected Alice had killed Alex?"

"Oh, he knew darned well she had done it. That was why he was so scared. He thought he would be next."

"Was Tricia Forbes in on Alex's murder?" Maggie asked.

"She admits to art fraud but absolutely denies having anything to do with either of the murders," George answered.

"But Forbes must have been the one who grabbed the paintings from Alex's apartment," Maggie mused. "Gloria said the person who bashed her in the mouth and took the paintings was tall and slim and left behind a slight trace of perfume."

"Gloria didn't see the person's face?"

"It was well hidden behind a scarf."

George pushed his chair away from the desk and stood up. "It's early days, so I know I don't have to ask you to keep all this quiet. Farthing would have my badge if he found out I'd given you all this info."

"You don't have to ask, George. Our lips are sealed."

"I'll walk you to the door." Maggie followed George out of Nat's office.

"So when's the big day?" he asked as he opened the outside door.

"This coming Saturday."

"You know, you had us very worried, Maggie." He put his arm around her and gave a gentle squeeze. "So glad to have you back with us safe and sound. I hope you enjoy every minute of Midge's wedding."

CHAPTER THIRTY-THREE

The wedding was set for eleven that morning, and Maggie made sure that she arrived at Harry's house a good two hours beforehand. She wanted, more than anything else, for this day to be one of the most cherished memories for her daughter.

"So glad you made it in good time." Harry, already impeccably dressed in his black morning suit, opened the door, gave her a peck on the cheek, and then took the garment bag containing her dress from her hands. "Midge is getting dressed in our bedroom," he said, leading the way inside, "and you can dress in the adjacent spare room. Is that all right with you?"

"That is so thoughtful of you, Harry." She was determined to be as nice as possible. "The connecting bathroom will make it so much easier for me to help Midge get dressed. And all that giggling must be the bridesmaids?"

"They're in the back bedroom. Why does Midge need four of them?"

"They're her friends. Flowers arrived?"

"Yes, and the hairdresser." Maggie could detect a little hysteria in his voice. "Thank God, Mother decided to go straight to the church."

Maggie also thanked God.

As she put her foot on the first stair, she was immediately

taken back four years—it had been her fiftieth birthday and she had climbed these self-same stairs to the bedroom she had shared with Harry, looked in the mirror, and knew she needed more out of life. That fateful decision changed her life forever. She walked along the landing to the familiar room and pushed the door open.

"You're just in time to help me into my dress." Midge, her chestnut hair piled high, smiled at her mother. "Isn't it a wonderful day?"

CHRIST CHURCH CATHEDRAL never looked lovelier. Sunshine flooded through the stained glass windows to bathe the interior of the church, masses of spring flowers overflowed their vases to decorate the sanctuary, and white ribbons had been tied to each of the pews. Maggie, escorted by her son-in-law Charles, walked proudly up the aisle to slip into the pew beside Honoria. She had to admit that Harry's mother looked regal in her soft rose silk dress with matching hat and shoes.

"I must say, Margaret," her mother-in-law said, leaning close to whisper in Maggie's ear, "that your blue lace complements my ensemble."

Maggie smiled and then leaned over to speak to her daughter Barbara, who was sitting on the other side of her grandmother. "You okay, dear?"

Barbara gave her mother a wan smile. "As well as can be expected, considering that this child," she patted her bulging stomach, "is continuingly kicking my insides out. Must be a girl!"

Honoria straightened her back and glared at her granddaughter. "Barbara, lower you voice. People will hear you." She shook her head in disapproval. "There's a time and place for everything."

"Look, Mom, Jason and the best man have arrived," Barbara

said, completely ignoring her grandmother. "Midge should be here any moment."

The excitement in the church was palpable as the guests waited for the arrival of the bride. Maggie turned in her seat to glance toward the back of the church, and her heart beat a little faster when she saw a familiar, dear face. Nat, as promised, had arrived. Charles, finished with his ushering duties, came to claim his seat next to his wife. Maggie smiled at him as she stood to let him pass, but Honoria, still miffed, remained seated.

"Just watch your feet, young man."

"Sorry," he mumbled before sinking down onto the pew.

"Young people these days," Honoria mumbled.

Then the music of the organ suddenly changed from a cantata to "Here Comes the Bride" and the congregation rose to its feet.

The procession began with the four bridesmaids dressed in lavender velvet and carrying bouquets of lilac and baby's breath, and then came five-year-old Oliver, dressed in a white velvet suit and precariously carrying a white satin cushion with the wedding rings pinned firmly to it.

Midge, her face covered in the veil Maggie had worn at her own wedding, was radiant as she walked down the aisle on the arm of a very proud Harry. The bouffant dress of creamy lace decorated with seed pearls had a heart-shaped neckline and, Maggie saw, provided a frame for the gold and diamond pendant Honoria had graciously lent her granddaughter for the occasion. Instead of a bouquet Midge carried a simple white prayer book with cascading purple orchids.

There were tears on Harry's face when, after giving his daughter away, he joined Maggie in the front pew. She automatically reached out and patted his hand.

"Thank you for this day, Margaret," he whispered. "We are a family."

THE RECEPTION, HELD in the Hotel Vancouver just across the way, went without a hitch. The food was excellent and the speeches long. Maggie dutifully danced with Jason's father—a doctor of the old school—and then was claimed by one of Harry's business partners.

"You look very lovely, my dear," Snodgrass said, and Maggie felt the old coot's hand slipping down below her waist. "Harry should never have let you go."

"Thank you." She gently lifted his hand higher. "Ah, here is one of the bridesmaids, who, I'm sure, would love to dance with you." And Maggie skillfully grabbed the startled girl and guided her into the man's arms. She turned to make her escape only to find that Harry was waiting for her.

"What was Snodgrass saying to you?" he asked as he guided her onto the small dance area.

"He said I looked lovely."

"And you do, Margaret. What a wonderful day, and we are back as a family again."

"I'm glad Barbara is having a good time," Maggie said as Charles and his very pregnant wife danced by.

"And that's our next big family event," Harry answered proudly. "Perhaps she'll have another boy."

"Harry, please go and dance with your mother." Maggie could see her mother-in-law bearing down on them. "I must get a breath of fresh air."

"I'll come with you."

"No," she answered, slipping out of his arms. "Your mother's waiting for you."

Maggie passed through the double doors of the reception room and out into the corridor. She walked up to the balustrade above the staircase leading down to the lobby. Leaning over, she gazed at the throng of people milling below, and she found herself smiling as the laughter from all these well-dressed people drifted up the staircase.

Then she saw him. Nat was sitting in one of the plush arm-chairs that were scattered around the huge reception area. As if he sensed her presence, he glanced up to where she was standing. He smiled and got to his feet. They met halfway down the sweep-ing staircase, and taking her by the hand, he led her gently down to the main floor and into a small alcove.

He drew her to him. "Midge made a beautiful bride—but nowhere as beautiful as her mother." He paused for a moment. "I know how tough it must be for you not to be a real part of all that going on upstairs, Maggie. There're your daughters, Harry's business associates, friends of the family . . ." his voice trailed off.

She leaned forward and kissed him on the lips. "Nat, you are my life. And," she added, "I realize that I haven't been fair to you. I am going to wait until the excitement of the wedding has worn off, then I am going to ask Harry for a divorce."

More in the Margaret Spencer Mystery Series

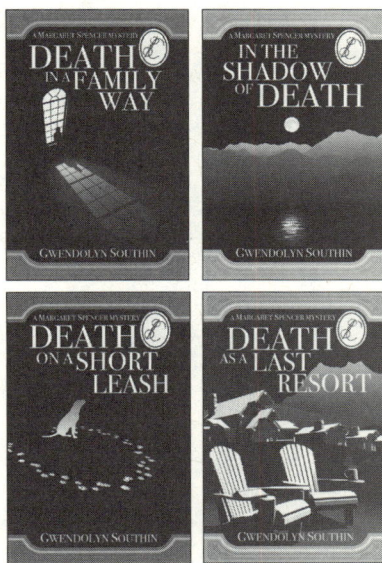

At age fifty, Margaret Spencer's empty nest and empty marriage prompt her to answer an ad for part-time work at the office of private investigator Nat Southby. Suddenly, she is deep in the most unlikely of adventures for a woman in 1950s and '60s Vancouver. Gwendolyn Southin blends the charm of gumshoe techniques with the fresh perspective of a developing female detective.

"The flow is smooth, the action well-paced." —*Quill & Quire*

"This is a clever series, and puzzle-plot fans will adore it." —*The Globe and Mail*

"Margaret Spencer is a smart and feisty woman to whom people open up. Original." —*The Saskatoon Star Phoenix*

GWENDOLYN SOUTHIN is the author of four previous Margaret Spencer mysteries. She was born in Essex, England, and launched her writing career after retiring to British Columbia's Sunshine Coast in the 1980s. Her short stories and articles have appeared in *Maturity*, *Pioneer News*, and *Sparks from the Forge*, and she is co-editor of *The Great Canadian Cookbook* with Betty Keller. Gwen was a founding member of the SunCoast Writers' Forge, the Festival of the Written Arts, and the region's writers-in-residence program. She makes her home in Sechelt, BC, where she is at work on more Margaret Spencer adventures. Please visit quintessentialwriters.com/southin.html.